THE THIEF'S BETRAYAL

CASSONDRA BENTON

THE THIEF'S BETRAYAL

The Thief's Betrayal

Copyright ©2019 by Cassondra Benton
All rights reserved.

Published by Rebel Press
Austin, Texas
www.RebelPress.com

No part of this publication may be reproduced, stored in a retrieval system, or transmitted in any form or by any means—electronic, mechanical, photocopy, recording, or any other—without the prior permission of the author.

ISBN: 978-1-64339-939-3

Printed in the United States of America

THE THIEF'S BETRAYAL

Chapter 1

Every part of his body ached with the effort of staying on his horse. Numb fingers grasped reins that felt as though they weighed a dozen pounds each. With the pounding of every hoof against hard-packed ground, his thigh muscles screamed at him, protesting against the task of keeping him upright on the saddle. But Kingsman didn't dare stop. He pushed his mare to run as fast as she could, knowing that he'd have to feed her plenty of carrots to make up for it later.

"Kingsman!"

He slowed down, trying to resist the urge to continue forward. He glanced back at his two most trusted men. Both young, bold, everything he could ask for. They were more than his best men, they were his closest friends. His family.

"What is it? We don't have much time."

"Kingsman," Felix warned, "We understand that you're in a rush, but you need to understand that, whatever you see down there, it's not your fault."

Kingsman took a deep breath.

"You need to promise us." Maddox pushed, his eyes piercing him to the bone.

The mare Kingsman rode stomped the ground. She was as anxious as he was. "Promise what?"

Maddox scowled. "Don't play dumb."

The small smirk on Kingsman's face faltered. He turned his head, preparing himself for what he was about to see. "I can't promise that."

Kicking his heels against the mare's side, he spurred her into a gallop. He could only hope imagining the worst would be enough.

~ * ~

But it wasn't. Not even close. Homes were burned to ash, blood was everywhere. And that wasn't the worst part.

It had been a week since the riot and Kingsman hadn't been able to get an ounce of sleep. Each night he was haunted by the horrors of what he had witnessed. He could still feel the smoke burning in his lungs as it clouded his vision. The screams were ripe in his mind, enough to make him wake in a sweat. He'd glance down at his clothing and expect to see the linen soaked in blood, his own and that of others. To this moment, he could still feel the hands pawing at him, each one as desperate for death as for hope.

Kingsman had come down to help every day since he'd arrived. His hands had blistered from cleaning debris, and the food from the palace kitchen thinned out as he brought more and more loads each day. But there was one thing he could not steel himself against, the one thing that ripped his heart out. The people.

Women and children had been hidden safely indoors when the attack began. The men had not been. Sons, husbands, brothers. All shown no mercy. As Kingsman walked through the remains of an inn, which now served as a shelter, he found himself speechless. Many of the villagers had been beaten bloody, to the point where he couldn't recognize a man under all the dirt and blood. Others had been lucky enough to die.

"Your soul is kind." An older man grasped his hand as Kingsman wiped the dried blood from his face.

Kingsman wrung out the towel and ran the fabric along the man's temple, removing the last trickle of blood. He recognized this man from his monthly visits. He was an honorable man. A man who greeted everyone with a smile as they passed by. Now he sat with a broken nose and fractured hip.

"You grace me with words I don't deserve."

The man shook his head. "It's because of you and your men we are alive. That we have blankets to keep us warm and food to keep our bellies full."

No. It was because of him they were in this situation. Because he hadn't arrived sooner. Because he hadn't pushed hard enough.

Kingsman quietly wrapped the old man in a blanket he had brought down with him that day and excused himself. This place, these people, they were suffocating him. He was given words he didn't deserve. They wrapped around his neck, strangling him. And they would continue to do so until they destroyed him.

The rain pounded against him as he pushed through the door. The bitterness of the cold rushed against his cheeks, granting him a breath of the fresh air he so desperately needed.

He ran a hand through his hair where it stuck to his forehead. He couldn't think straight. It was as if a cloud was hovering in his mind and he just couldn't shake it away. The emblem on his chest weighed heavy. Without taking time to second-guess himself, he reached up and ripped off the emblem. He didn't deserve such a title. A man of his rank should have been able to prevent this.

A rattle broke the silence. Kingsman stood still, listening, waiting. Had someone finally come to kill him? To take revenge for not acting fast enough? Slowly, he unsheathed his sword. Then he heard it again, coming from behind the inn. He slowed his breath as he started to round the corner. He had to at least put up a fight. He wouldn't die without trying.

He had expected a lot of things from his attacker. To be tall, muscular, skilled with a sword even. He'd have a look of anger in his eyes. Of determination. What he didn't expect to see was a frightened child.

Kingsman sheathed his sword and dropped to his knees. He scanned the young girl's eyes as she pushed herself up against a barrel, cowering inside the makeshift shelter she had created for herself. He had seen grown men and women shivering from the rain despite the warm clothes and blankets they had wrapped around them. Yet there she stood in a pair of thin cotton trousers and a shirt that hung loosely on her thin frame. She looked around five or six, although she might have been older and small from hunger and malnutrition.

Kingsman held up both hands. "Where are your parents?"

She gave a shake of her head, her wet, matted hair slapping her face.

His chest clenched. If he had been able to prevent the riot, would she still be living happily beside her parents? Such thoughts made it hard it to breathe. He didn't dare think how many children suffered the same losses she had. "Why don't you go to the shelter?"

"They don't like me," she mumbled. "I've done bad things. But I promise I only steal the food because my stomach hurts so much. I feel like I'll die."

"I see."

Her eyes danced up to him. The fear seemed to have diminished. Had she been treated so badly by other adults that him not yelling at her, not reprimanding her, should have such a profound effect?

Something gave way inside his chest when her pleading eyes met his. Without giving himself the chance to change his mind, he held out his hand. "How about I take care of you? I've never been a father, but if you give me a chance, maybe I can learn."

She hesitated. Then, oh so slowly, she stepped out from the shadow of her shelter. The warmth of her fingers wrapping around his rippled from his hand to his heart. That feeling would keep a man warmer than any blanket ever could.

She shivered under his touch. Her feet were bare and cut from the stones of the street. Her hair was caked with dirt, tattered into tangles upon tangles. Her small figure was much too skinny, nothing but fragile bones. She took a step closer to him. With her other hand she reached out, cupping his cheek.

The touch shot shivers streaking down his spine. She was one of the many who had been traumatized by the riot. Yet he could still see hope smoldering in her eyes. A smile—something he hadn't seen in an entire week—flashed across her face. His throat tightened. He hadn't realized how deeply he had missed the sight of one.

"All right, Mister."

To his surprise, Kingsman was able to return her smile. He let go of her hand and bent down to scoop her up into his arms, holding her trembling body close. "If we're going to be together for a while, I'll need to know your name." He started down the empty street.

"Kira."

"Well, Kira. You can call me Kingsman."

Her eyes sparkled as if she had heard the name of a god. He pushed her bangs out of her face. A drop of rain hit her cheek and he pressed her head to his chest. As the rain poured down on them both, Kingsman unbuckled the jacket of his uniform, tucking her inside it as much as he could. His body heat wouldn't be much, but it would have to do until he got her somewhere safe.

Kira's hand rested softly against his chest, her fingers tracing the pattern of his tunic absently.

His mind raced. He would cook her whatever she liked, buy her whatever dresses she wanted, tell her whatever story came to mind. He would cherish her; he would love her more than anything else in the world.

"Kira, I want you to meet two of my friends."

"Are they nice?" She didn't stop her mindless fumbling of his tunic.

"They are very nice. I think you'll like them."

"If you trust them then I trust them." She beamed another smile up at him.

Kingsman's heart stopped. How could she trust him so easily? How could she still manage to smile, after everything she had been through? Even more amazing, how was she able to make him want to do the same?

"Are you all right, Kingsman?"

Was he all right? His entire life had changed within a blink of an eye. He had only known the girl in his arms for a few moments, yet she had already made a huge impact on him. She had given him hope, a reason to keep going. She had gone from a kid on the streets to his everything, all within a snap of his fingers.

He cleared his throat. "I'm fine. I was just wondering what you'd like for dinner." He tightened his grip on her. "Go on, pick anything you like. I'll make sure that you have it."

Chapter 2

15 years later

THE OLD MAN RAN AS fast as he could. He had to. If he'd screamed for help, she'd kill him on the spot. There was no possible way that he would see the light of the next morning. He threw a glance behind him. Had he lost her? He stumbled into his house, slamming the door and leaning his head against it. Had he left any tracks? His heart raced at the thought of making such a mistake. Though their encounter had been short, he knew she was trained as well as any man and as lethal as a blow from a sword. She was as silent as a mouse, had eyesight like an owl in the night. There was no room for errors.

He caught his breath enough to push away from the door. And froze. The sharp, cold edge of her blade pressed into his throat. He turned, shaking in the very boots he wore. He lifted trembling hands into the air. "Please! Please, I'll give you your money. Just don't kill me."

When she didn't move, he let his gaze drift over her. *Who is she?* A hood and mask covered her face so completely, all he could see were her piercing blue eyes.

She pushed the blade in deeper. "You should have given it to me to begin with." She glanced around the cottage, dimly lit by the dying embers in the fireplace, then her eyes flicked back to him. "Your daughter, how old is she?"

The man swallowed nervously and parted his shaking lips. "She's only five, my lady. She's my granddaughter," he choked out.

The woman looked at him, then turned and walked towards the fireplace.

He breathed a sigh of relief as his hand flew to his throat and came away sticky and red. He tensed again when she knelt down and picked up the doll that had been lying on the brushed-dirt floor. Her touch was soft, almost loving, as she cradled it in her palm.

The man's eyes narrowed. He stiffened when her gaze shifted to the corner of the room. The man's granddaughter slept peacefully on a makeshift bed, waiting for his return. He started to stumble toward her, but the woman held up the knife and he stopped. He stood, wiping his sweaty palms on the front of his coat while watching the woman walk towards his granddaughter.

With a flick of her wrist, the knife was sheathed and put away. The woman crouched down and peered at the child in front of her. She reached out her gloved hand and pushed back a strand of blonde hair that had fallen across the young girl's face.

The man could barely draw in a breath. What was she going to do?

The woman reached out and set the doll down gently next to the girl. Then she stood and held out her hand, palm up. "I can come up with a way to explain why I didn't kill you, but I can't return without what I came for."

The man fumbled in his pocket for the money. "Thank you! Bless your soul, take it all. Just don't hurt my Celeste." He held the bag out. The coins fell heavy in her hand with a clank. She stowed the bag away silently and started for the door.

The man rushed over to his granddaughter. Flinging an arm over her protectively, he glanced back at the woman. "Wait. Your name, what's your name?"

One hand on the knob of the door, she turned to face him. She spoke so softly he could barely make out her words, even in the stillness of night. "My name? My name is Kira."

Chapter 3

Kira walked through the tunnels, the bag of coins clutched in her hand. The torches barely gave off any light, but they all had adjusted so well to working at night that the darkness didn't bother any of them. Their apparel was pitch black to help them blend in. They had to learn each other's ways fast to stop from killing one another on a job.

With a shove, she opened the door and strode inside. The room was full of men. They all sat around a table, some looking angrier than others. All looking at her with desperation written across their faces.

The smell of musk made her nose twitch. Goosebumps had begun to form on her skin and the air was sticky with moisture. She blinked, taking a moment to analyze what she had just walked into. The room was dark from an absence of windows, leaving the flames of the torches to poorly illuminate the men before her. The frustration was thick in the atmosphere and already had begun to work its way over to her. She couldn't let it get the best of her.

"Did you find anything?"

Kira looked over at Astien and her eyes softened. "Outside of another successful job? No." She threw the money on the table and pawed at her hood and mask. She couldn't help but let out a relieved sigh as she drew in a breath of fresh air. She reached for the tie that secured her hair and gave it a tug, her soft golden curls falling. Once she sat down, she allowed herself a moment to relax, until she spotted Russell sitting tensely on other side of the table. Just looking at each other made the two of them angry.

"Maybe if you actually looked, you could find a lead!" He growled as he stood and leaned across the table.

Kira's jaw locked as she stood up and met his intense gaze calmly. From the very beginning they were always at each other's throats, finding some way to piss each other off. But this, this was business. Something Kira wouldn't mess around with. The idea of kicking him under the table sounded like a wonderful idea, but she resisted it. Now wasn't the time to do such things.

"Considering I was the one who first realized that we were being framed, I don't think you have a right to talk. So I suggest you keep your damn mouth shut." Despite her cool tone, her eyes flashed with anger. She wasn't one to allow herself to be tested.

"All right, all right, everyone calm down. We are all frustrated."

Kira wouldn't normally back down when it came to Russell, but sadly, that voice belonged to one man who ranked above them all, Kingsman. The man who had taken her in, the one who raised her and took the place of her father.

As Russell dropped back down onto his seat, her glare following him. Just to feel her fist in his face …

"Kira, I said stop."

Kira waited for a heartbeat before sitting back down. *Another time,* she told herself, *another time.*

"We are all upset over this. The last thing we need to do is lose our heads." Kingsman spoke, his harsh gaze pinpointing each of them in turn.

"Considering we are being targeted and framed as murderers, we have a reason to worry. I mean, I know we are thieves, but we have never killed. Who would do this to us?" Pierceton lifted both hands into the air, palms up.

Kira glanced over at him. He was the youngest in the group, probably the most good-looking of the men. It wasn't too long ago that he and Russell had joined their guild, only a few months. Kira hated him too, but not as much as Russell. Pierceton was too quiet, too inexperienced, and a liar. He had walked in hidden behind a mask of his own kindness and fooled everyone with it. Everyone except for her. She'd grown to love and cherish the men around her; she'd do whatever it took to keep them safe.

Felix shifted in his chair, diagonal from her. "Someone who hates us and who knows who we are."

Pierceton's hands tightened into fists. His chest rose and fell, but when he spoke, his voice was carefully controlled. "That's impossible. Even when we meet our clients we still keep our identities a secret."

Kingsman's palms slammed down on the table and Kira flinched.

"Until we have more information, we will continue on with our jobs. Be on the lookout for anything that may help us. Good night."

Kira stood and returned to her chambers without looking back. She closed the door and began to strip free of her armor. Once it fell to the floor, she stumbled out of it and slipped on her nightgown. The pearl-pink silk and lace seemed too delicate and expensive for her to wear when she first spotted it out in the market, but still, she couldn't resist returning over and over just to look at it. Her secret longing for the piece had not gone unnoticed by the men of the guild. It had been years since they had bought it for her, each one pitching in their coin just so she could have it. Never would she let such a sentimental act be forgotten.

Stretching, she turned to lock her door and froze. A note was stuck to the back of the door with a knife. Kira's eyes darted around. Striding through the room, she yanked open drawers, dropped to her knees to search under the bed, whipped back the curtains, and peered into the bathroom, rummaging through every drawer before she was satisfied the intruder was gone.

Kira yanked the note free of the knife. Should she show it to Kingsman? If it was a joke Russell had played on her, both she and Kingsman would give him living hell for doing such a thing. Kira wrapped her hand around the handle of the knife and let the cold sink into her skin. With a hard tug, the blade came out and rested in her hand. The weapon was light and sharp, good for up-close fighting. Something that Russell was strong in. She would deal with it in the morning. Kira threw both the knife and a note into a drawer and slammed it shut. Out of side, out of mind.

Still, throughout the night, she couldn't help but feel like someone was watching her.

~ * ~

The next morning Kira awoke and found herself unable to think clearly. *I need to go to the practice room.* The room itself wasn't anything to brag about, nor was the hideout in general. The entire space was underground and lined with stone. The practice room consisted of targets for archery, straw dummies for sword play, chests with locks to pick, and a sparring arena. The layout was simple, and burned into her memory due to the countless hours spent training here.

Kira reached behind her back and pulled her bow forward. She took a moment to take in the detailing. It was black, like her leather armor. The detailing was delicate, hand-carved and painted silver. Age had faded the paint over the years, but she never once questioned its strength.

Pull, aim, release.

Kira remembered the countless days Badrick had spent with her here, training her and throwing her to the floor. He would snatch her up from behind, pin her down, and rip her weapons from her hands, demanding that she try and escape.

Pull, aim release.

Kira had wanted to be one of the men and that's what she got. Badrick had been rough on her and left her with more bruises than she could count. His strength had held her back at first, but she began to find it easier and easier to fight against him as the months passed. She'd even developed a childish crush on him for the longest time. But that had also passed as time went by.

Pull, aim, release.

Once Kingsman okayed her training, the rest of the men got in on it. They helped her with lock picking, showed her how to handle a sword, and how to work in the shadows. She was their own protégé and they were proud of it. And of her.

Pull, aim, release.

Everything was fine until Russell and Pierceton came along. Russell walked in believing he was the hotshot and could take over. Pierceton gave off an act of being a sweetheart and often used his youth and looks to help with his jobs. He couldn't even fight relying on his own blade. She should know, considering she had been paired with him on a job once. He almost got himself killed and she needed to step in and save him.

"I think that dummy has had enough torture for today."

A hand landed on her shoulder and Kira jumped. She had been so caught up in her anger that she didn't even realize the arrows were jabbed into the head and stomach of her target.

"Something wrong, kiddo?"

Kira set her bow down and looked back at Maddox. Despite his sweet appearance, he was the reason everyone needed the sturdiest locks on their doors or they'd lose their valuables. Lock picking was his key, and he was capable of moving so silently no one ever heard him coming.

"You know what it is," she mumbled softly.

He gave a laugh and wrapped an arm around her shoulders, walking her over to the chests. "It wouldn't happen to have anything to do with

Pierceton and Russell, now would it?"

When Kira stayed hushed, he gave a small smirk. "How did I know?"

Kira looked up at him. "Please tell me I'm not the only one who sees that they can't be trusted?"

"No, you're not." He patted her on her back.

Kira pulled a pick from her pocket before going to work on the chest. Pierceton and Russell didn't belong. They were a threat that Kingsman was too blind to see. However, just because he was unable to see the menace of these outsiders, didn't mean she wasn't ready to sacrifice herself by fighting without his consent, should the need to ever arrive. "Then why does Kingsman keep them? He needs to throw them out. Everything was perfectly fine with the six of us." She twisted her wrist and found the sweet spot she had been looking for. With a light click, the lid popped open.

"I'm sure Kingsman has his reasons."

"Just as I'm sure to have my reasons when I plow my fist into their faces."

Maddox gave a laugh and, in the personal way he had, smacked her playfully on her back again as she stood up. Her heart warmed at the sound of his reassuring laughter echoing off the walls.

"All in good time, kiddo. All in good time."

Chapter 4

KIRA WALKED TO THE BACK side of the brothel and searched for the young woman she was supposed to meet. The wooden walls were old and stained from leaking water and spilled booze. Kira had received a job earlier that day that required her to go under cover. Being the only girl at the guild, she was the one who was sent on jobs like these. The men expected her to use her female ways to get what she needed and go. Much easier than fighting for what their client had asked for. Kira was sure Kingsman had given her this job to keep her busy. But a brothel?

"Are you Kira?"

She turned and spotted a young girl who seemed much too innocent to work in such a horrid place. Her face was full with plump lips and her frame small and petite. Kira felt she would shatter with a simple touch. "Yes, I am. You must be Isabella."

The girl nodded slightly. "Please follow me."

Kira followed her as they walked through the exit and into the back room of the brothel, making sure to keep her distance. Luckily the night concealed her, despite her lack of armor. Should anyone see her she would die from embarrassment.

Inside she could hear the roaring of the men. Most drunk or well on their way. Kira peered through a crack in the door to the main room and spotted the crowd. Many women walked around, some stumbling, others with marks on their necks, and hair askew. She wouldn't be surprised if a lot of the couples didn't make it to a room. No one seemed to care.

"I know it's scary the first few times. Luckily Ruby has only let me take on the ... non-intimate requests." Isabella held up a set of clothing. "I hope you don't get anything worse than what I get."

Kira licked her lips nervously. "I hope I don't either." *Just how far will I have to take this charade?*

Isabella undid the laces of Kira's dress. The cold against her bare skin made her shiver. But stepping into her *uniform* didn't make it feel any better. Her bosom nearly spilled out over the edge of the corset; the laces were tied too tight and showed her curves too easily, the skirts were thin and slit high. These were merely undergarments, surely.

Kira pinned her hair up and slipped a dark wig on to help hide her blonde hair. The last thing she needed was for someone to recognize her while she was working. Isabella gently grasped her chin and tilted her head back. The bristles of the brush draping across her lips made Kira laugh for the first time that night. In a sense, the treatment was relaxing. Kira felt as though she were becoming a piece of art. A beautiful, unrecognizable piece of art.

When Isabella finished, she handed Kira a mirror. It took Kira a few breaths before she could even recognize herself. Her lips, normally pale pink, had turned a vibrant red, her cheeks as well. The dark charcoal around her eyes made their vibrant blue even more hypnotizing. Any trace of her old self was gone. She gave Isabella a smile of approval and started for the main room.

"Please wear this, in case things get out of hand." Isabella's words were pleading and Kira stopped at the door and looked back at her. The young girl was clearly miserable here. If she wasn't looking over her shoulder, then she was shaking. To think someone so young would be forced into a job like this. Kira's jaw tightened.

"Promise me you'll do whatever you can to escape should anything go wrong." Isabella lifted the item she clutched in her hand.

A dagger. Kira took it from her and strapped it to her thigh, covering it with her skirts so no one would notice. She started to step out into the other room then stopped again. Isabella didn't know Kira could easily kill a man by herself and Kira doubted the young girl even knew how to wield a blade. She couldn't just leave her here alone and afraid.

"Meet me tomorrow behind the bakery at the east end of town during sunset. I won't leave until you know how to use a blade comfortably." She spoke in a soft voice. The gleam in Isabella's eyes—hope—eased her concern. At least the girl would be safer than before.

Kira stepped into the main room and was drowned in chaos. She looked around and began to take in her surroundings. The golden ceilings were high and covered with small details that were sadly ignored. Old tables were scattered about, and a bar had been built into the corner and packed with bottles of rum and wine from top to bottom. She tilted her head back and spotted an obnoxious glass chandelier to finish it all off.

She turned and spotted the staircase. Had it not been for the fact people were managing to walk up and down it, Kira would never have guessed it was safe to use. Now that she knew the layout of the building, she moved through the room, searching for the man she was assigned to steal from. She'd been told to look for a tall, middle-aged man with dark hair, graying at the temples. Some part of her hoped that she wouldn't find him here, but she was out of luck. There he sat in the corner with a tankard in hand, surrounded by women. Kira threw an extra swing into her hips as she walked, barely missing a young couple stumbling up the stairs to a room, their lips sealed together. She couldn't wait to get far from this disgusting place.

You must make him notice you. The men gave you a list of what they like in a woman, so use it to your advantage. This job is huge so you better not let us down.

Kingsman's words echoed in her mind. All she had to do was follow the list the men gave her. Being raised by a group of men, Kira never truly had that feminine figure to look up to. She didn't fully understand how to act "proper," what it felt like to have someone else save her instead of her doing the saving. She'd never had the chance to fall in love or sweep away into the shadows to steal a kiss. Despite Kingsman's attempts to do the best he could do with her education, there were still things she had missed out on.

She wove her way through the crowd, focusing on a man rushing to the door. She planned her steps and stumbled into him. He quickly reached out and caught her before she could fall. Perfect, it only made their encounter look more like an accident.

"Are you all right?"

She nodded and straightened, smoothing out her skirts. Her eyes drifted across the crowded room to Cadwell. She had his attention.

"I am, thank you. I'm still not used to working here."

The man gave a nod. "Aye, it can get stuffy in here. That's why I'm stepping outside. Would you care to join me?"

She so desperately wanted to agree and follow him without question. Anything to get out of the sweat-encrusted room. "I'd love to, but I have something I must do. Please excuse me."

He gave her a small bow, locking eyes with her when he straightened. The look of sympathy was easy to recognize on his face. Kira again fought back the urge to follow him as he turned to leave. Soon. Soon she'd be able to run out of the building and rip these wretched clothes off.

She made her way up the steps, occasionally glancing back to see if her target was preparing to follow, trying not to let her apprehension show on her face. Cadwell excused himself from the women around him. Her chest tightened as his foot hit the first step. She had to keep it together.

Cadwell fell into step beside her as she made her way down the hall.

She chose an empty room and went inside. When she started to close the door, a hand stopped it.

"I came to make sure you were all right, milady."

Kira's stomach churned with disgust. His lies were as terrible as a child's. "Yes, I'm quite all right."

"May I accompany you? I pay well."

She took a deep, calming breath, forcing her lips to curl into a smile.

"Of course." She stepped back to allow him to step inside. Slowly, she shut the door and closed it with a soft click. The noise from downstairs was suddenly muted and the room dangerously dark. She could barely make out the figure who'd settled on the edge of the bed.

"Let's get some light in here so I can see that face of yours."

Kira nodded and walked around the room, lighting every candle she could find. It was hard to resist the urge to cover her breasts and tug her skirts down. When she finished lighting the candles and approached the bed, Cadwell pulled her roughly onto his lap. His arm tightened around her waist and his hand tugged her skirts higher and higher. If he kept going, he'd see her dagger.

"Now where were—"

Kira whirled around and shoved him down onto his back. Shock and something alarmingly close to delight crossed his face as he stared up at her. Kira had always assumed men liked women delicate and easy to control. But it seemed that he took her aggressiveness more as a challenge than a turn-off.

Kira let out a cry as he shoved himself up, grabbed her, and slammed her back against the wall. His lips latched onto her neck and branded her skin. He wasn't even gracious, all he did was slobber all over her. She had to find what she had come for then she could leave.

Kira raked her hands under his shirt and dragged her nails across his skin. His hairy, disgusting skin. His grip on her tightened and she glanced at him. His eyes were shut. *Hurry, Kira.* Her nails caught on something. The pendent!

She carefully played with the chain, trailing it around to the back of his neck. The clasp was cold on her fingertips. Kira fumbled with the clasp and the pendent fell into her hand. Cadwell appeared to be so caught up in the moment he didn't even notice.

"Cadwell."

He growled and peered back at the door. Over his shoulder, Kira spotted a young woman stepping into the room. Her fire-red hair was fashioned on top of her head, out of her face, and nearly matched the color of rouge on her lips. Kira didn't particularly find her appealing or considerate, but at the moment she could have dropped to her knees and thanked her.

"Another man has asked for this lovely lady at once."

"I'm busy, Ruby."

"Well, unless you have more gold, then you've been overruled," the woman snapped.

Kira didn't dare miss a chance to escape. Any man would be better than Cadwell. Of course, she would sneak out before there could be any other men.

"I'll go to him right away." She stumbled out of Cadwell's grip. Behind her, he called out, but she didn't dare look back. All she could do was walk as fast as she could down the hallway, wiping the spit off her neck as she went. When she reached home, she would bathe and scrub until her skin was raw. Anything to get his touch off of her.

As the exit came into view, the clicking of her heels sped up. She needed to leave before Cadwell realized she had stolen the pendant from him. Just a few more steps and—

Someone grabbed her arm and spun her around. Was it Cadwell? Her shoulders relaxed.

"You think you can sneak away after I've already paid for your time?"

Kira glared at the man—the same one she had stumbled into

downstairs—and yanked her arm free. The sympathy she'd seen on his face was gone, his true form shining through. He was just like the rest of them after all.

Anger bubbled deep within the coils of her stomach. She was done with this place. How could any woman live like this, completely at the mercy of the urges of lecherous men, unable to fight and protect herself?

"I'll make sure your gold is refunded."

The man smirked as he grabbed her again. "I don't think so."

Chapter 5

Kira backed up until she hit the edge of the bed, fisting the pendent behind her back. The man locked the door and turned. No way in, no way out.

"I have some questions that you need to answer." He walked towards her. "And don't think I'd be willing to do any of that stuff that's going on in your head. You're flattering yourself."

"I'm sure your mother wouldn't be happy if she heard you talk to a lady that way." Kira moved to the side of the bed and continued to back away. His glare was cold and lethal. Someone Kira knew she had to be careful with.

"You can cut the act," he growled as he backed Kira into the corner. He reached behind her, grabbed her wrist, and slammed her hand against the wall above her head. The pendent slipped from Kira's hand and dropped to the floor between them. Kira gasped. For a moment, time froze. The gold pendant flickered in the moonlight, as if teasing her.

"Stealing from Cadwell, were we?" The man's voice was mocking.

With one quick movement, Kira hiked up her skirt and unsheathed her dagger. The blade swung through the air.

The man leapt back, out of reach.

Kira gritted her teeth. She had to knock him out in order to give herself a chance to escape. She bent down and swept the pendant up, wrapping the chain around her fist before punching. Anything to add extra pain. She managed to land a hit on his face, the chain scratching his cheek and drawing blood.

The man's eyes narrowed to glittering slits as he kneed her, hard, in the side.

Although the hit seemed more of an instinctual reaction than an attempt to inflict damage, Kira bit her lip to hold back a cry of pain. Any other time, her armor would have absorbed some of the blow, but now nothing prevented the boot from connecting with her body through the thin dress she wore.

"Wait, I'm not going to stop you—"

She wouldn't listen to anything that vile man had to say. She had to get out while she had the chance. Kira tried to slip past him and get to the door, but he caught her by the hair. Thankfully, all he grabbed was a fist full of wig. The false hair fell free and she stumbled slightly. The hesitation cost her. Before she could bolt for freedom, the man clasped both her wrists and yanked them above her head, pinning her to the door.

"Thank goodness you're not a brunette. It didn't look good on you."

Every muscle tense, Kira shook her hair from her face.

"Are you here to play games?" she snapped. Normally it would be child's play for her to break free, but his grip felt like iron.

"Maybe I should have handled this a better way." He clutched both her wrists in one hand and rubbed his temple with the other, as if warding off a headache.

Kira rolled her eyes. "Will you let me go before I have to kill you?"

"I don't want to fight, princess, but you need to give up on trying to escape." He pushed his body weight against her, clearly trying to drive home the point. He was young, perhaps in his early twenties. His hair was a few shades darker than her own and his eyes were bright and lively. But he was much stronger than any man she'd needed to wrestle with before. "I want to ask for your help. Something precious has been taken from me."

"And what if I don't help you?"

"Then I guess I'll have to turn you in for theft. After all, I am a witness."

Kira took a slow deep breath in an attempt to calm herself. Blackmailed. Her fists clenched. She could always break out of prison. Besides, if the guild members didn't clear their names soon she would have a bounty on her head anyways. What did she have to lose?

"Fine. What do you want me to do?"

~ * ~

Kira walked down the hall and flung the office door open, so hard it slammed against the wall behind it. Nearby book shelves shuddered from the impact. Kingsman lifted his gaze from a pile of paperwork. Though his face was calm, his fingers tapped on the desk. Had he been worried about her? Kingsman didn't speak. It wasn't often Kira was as angry as she was at the moment, but it wasn't exactly rare either.

"Here's your damn pendent." She threw it at him.

Kingsman reached out and caught it without giving it a glance. "Bad night, I'm guessing?" He set it down on the table.

"Bad night? It was a night from hell!" Kira drove her hands through her hair.

"I can understand having to fight off the advances of an old man isn't exactly pleasing, but don't you think you're overreacting?" He stood and made his way over to her. When he reached her, he wrapped his arms around her and pulled her to him. In spite of the strong father-daughter relationship they shared, both tried to keep it on a business level when it came to their jobs. Neither wanted the rest of the men to accuse Kingsman of playing favorites. He clearly sensed that her level of anger and disgust had far exceeded her limit for the night, however, and was prepared to allow his fatherly instincts to overrule his professional detachment.

The pounding in Kira's chest gradually eased as he held her. His musky scent filled her nose and the comfort of his warmth was tempting to fall into, but she gently pushed away from him instead.

He grasped her upper arms lightly. "What happened?"

Kingsman had always been like a father to her, at times a harsh father, but she knew his worry for her was true. But what was she to say? That she had made a complete and utter fool of herself? That she had found a girl no older than sixteen, afraid and lonely in a brothel full of thirsty men? That she had been slobbered on and blackmailed in the same night?

Kingsman's eyes narrowed as he let her go. "Close the door."

She sighed and did as she was told. After shutting the door, she leaned against it for a moment, her forehead hitting the wood with a soft thud. *I wish this night had never happened.*

"Kira, what really happened tonight?"

Kira didn't turn around. Both hands pressed flat against the wooden door. She could still feel the first man's disgusting touch on her. A chill rippled through her. "There was someone else there." She turned to face him. "He said if I didn't help him that he'd turn me in. My wig got ripped off, so he knows who I am."

Kingsman's jaw tightened. Kira wasn't surprised. In all her exploits, she had never let herself get discovered before. Tonight seemed to be a night of firsts.

"Then do what he needs you to do. Simple as that."

"But what about the guild? I can't afford to waste my time on something so stupid."

"It might lead us to some clues."

Kira bit her lip. She couldn't tell him about the note that had been stuck in the back of her door just yet.

"The Fights are tonight," Kingsman continued, changing the subject. "I'm sure Badrick would let you blow some steam off on him."

She managed a grim smile. "He wouldn't be able to stand tomorrow."

Kingsman opened the door and walked her down the hallway to the practice room. "Never mind then. I would prefer to keep my men in one piece." He followed her into the practice room.

Kira spotted Maddox and Astien going at it in the ring. The Fights was the one time in the year when any member could spar with whomever they wanted. Whether it be for a good match, or to get the anger towards that person out of the way, it was something everyone had to do. No weapons, no tricks, just fists and feet. A way to start clean.

Kira snuck her way to the group of men watching the fight and stopped next to Badrick.

"Maddox is kicking Astien's ass," he whispered to her.

"What does he expect? Maddox might be on the older side, but it doesn't mean he can't put up a good fight."

"But Astien's youth does give him an advantage."

Kira spotted Astien's ginger hair through an opening in the group. Despite his heavy feet, his kicks were as fast as his wits. He and Maddox were complete opposites. One more swift and agile, the other more headstrong. It made for a killer match.

"Who do you think will win, Felix?"

Kira peered at the man on the other side of her, intrigued to hear what he had to say. The jagged scar on the side of his face was clear in the light, starting just above his brow down to his mid-cheek. The one souvenir from the worst night of his life. The entire guild felt bad for him, but he didn't want anyone's pity. He had been blindly in love and had let his guard down. Kira could remember the time when he would smile or even laugh. He was happy and wasn't alone. Then one night he went to propose to the woman and she turned and attempted to kill him. Felix had never been the same after that night. His smile disappeared, the flame of hope in his eyes was blown out, and he kept to himself. Kira never knew what he had done with the ring. It would seem logical to try to return it for the money, considering it wasn't cheap, but something told her he had thrown it into a fire or let it sink to the bottom of a lake. He wanted nothing to do with it.

Badrick shifted next to her. "Maddox is already a step ahead of him, one more hit and—"

"Enough!" Kingsman's voice echoed through the room, declaring the end of the match.

Kira peered through the men and spotted Astien on the floor, dripping in sweat and defeat.

"How did you know?" Kira swung around to gaze at Felix. His hard eyes met hers. He looked at her as if she was stupid to be shocked.

"Have you not learnt anything in the years I've taught you?" he asked.

Kira stayed silent and turned back towards the ring. She did feel a little stupid for asking such a thing. Felix would lead you on, letting you believe that you were ahead of the game, then he'd turn around and know what your next five steps would be. She had always hoped she would be as good as him one day, but had come to the conclusion that no one would ever be.

"Let's go, Kira, a good one-on-one fight like we used to." Badrick smiled as he stepped into the ring and extended his hand to her. Kira hesitated. Badrick could likely see the anger in her eyes from the night, despite her attempt to hide it. He always managed to see past her defenses. Her lips turned upward and she held out her hand, allowing him to pull her up. They both took their stance at opposite ends of the ring. Kira's blood thumped in her ears as adrenaline rushed through her.

Kingsman counted down, and then she launched.

Chapter 6

Kira didn't dare hold back while they both charged at each other. She latched onto Badrick's wrist as she leaned and dodged his punch, leaving him wide open. She lifted her foot and aimed for his chest. Badrick stumbled only slightly before recovering his balance. In a flash, he turned and kicked out his leg, sweeping her feet out from under her. Kira fell to the ground with a thud that echoed across the room. Gritting her teeth, she flung her arms up at the flickering sight of Badrick's fist coming down at her. Apparently he didn't intend to hold back either.

Kira rolled to the left, his fist barely skimming her face. She took a moment too long to recover. His arm locked around her neck and her body lifted from the ground, her back pulled to his chest.

"Come on now, don't tell me this is all you have," he teased.

Blood pounded in her veins. This is what she needed, a challenge, a good strong fight. Something Badrick could be counted on to give her.

"You wish." Kira lunged forward and flung him over her back. The arm around her neck released and she was free. The sound of his impact sent a niggle of guilt through her. Her anger had been building up all night, but she hadn't meant to take it out on Badrick. If she stopped to worry about that, though, he'd have her pinned to the ground. Instead, she seized her opportunity and jumped on top of him.

Badrick looked up at her, a flirtatious grin on his face.

Caught off guard, Kira loosened her grip on him. *What does that look mean?* In the second it took her to wonder, his elbow connected with her face and she cursed herself for falling for something so stupid.

With one quick movement, Badrick flipped her over onto her back. He hovered over her while she glared up at him, completely pinned down from her wrists to her ankles. Kira fought against him but his grip was tight and firm. There was no way for her to win. *No way that he knows about, anyway.* Her training with Felix had not failed her; she was already a step ahead.

"Hey, Badrick." Her voice was low and seductive.

His eyebrows rose.

Kingsman began to count down in the background.

Kira fluttered her eyelashes. "Did I ever tell you how handsome you are?"

A look of pure shock flashed across his face. Now was her time.

With a turn of her wrist, she broke free of his grasp and tossed him onto his back. Clambering onto his abdomen, she threw herself forward, pressing his hands to the floor above his head.

"You tricky thief." Badrick spoke playfully.

Kira held him down until Kingsman declared her the winner. Then she sat back with a victorious smile. Her chest puffed out with pride as Badrick sat up. Her forehead wrinkled at the devilish smile on his face. Just what was up his sleeve?

"Not too bad, Kit." He held out his hand.

Kira slid her fingers into his, her heart fluttering slightly at his use of her old nickname. She remembered when he had first called her that, claiming that, between her stealth and her ability to work in the shadows, she was much like a Kit Fox.

"But never let your guard down, even after your fight." His hand slipped behind her head and tangled in her locks. Pushing himself forward, he leaned in, much closer than Kira had expected. His lips brushed against hers, stealing a kiss. Her spine straightened and her body tensed. She didn't even have a chance to react before he pulled away.

Kira couldn't remember standing up and walking out of the ring. But when she did regain her senses, heat rushed into her cheeks. What would the others think? Though from their focus on the next fight, she doubted they were giving her much thought.

She stole a glance at Badrick and took in his features, his sharp jaw with dark hair and beautiful eyes. She suddenly felt like she was back in her younger days with her childish crush. But a childish crush was the last thing she needed. *Focus, Kira.* As the winner of the last fight, she was expected to take on the next challenger. Russell stood in the middle of the ring looking directly at her. The room went silent. Kira shoved back her embarrassment and jogged toward the ring. Her time to show everyone who was boss was now and she wasn't going to pass it up.

~ * ~

Kira stumbled backward. She touched a finger to her lip and it came away red and sticky. Russell's chest heaved. She had managed a few hits and she'd made sure he'd have some black and blue bruises the next day. If her anger had driven her to be rough with Badrick, it consumed her now. This time she had no qualms about using it.

She took a moment to catch her breath before she ran at him again. This was the fight that the guild had been waiting for. They all knew the tension between her and Russell; it had been deadly to even allow them to be in the ring together. Everyone but Pierceton had trained her and they knew what damage she could do.

Badrick called her name, his voice thick with warning. For a split second she turned in his direction, caught the worry on his face. A second too long. Russell's fist drove into her temple. A loud ringing noise accompanied the pain that jolted through her head. Kira dropped to the floor, her body numb. She tried to move, desperately attempting to regain her feet, but she felt weighted down, as though the hideout itself had collapsed on top of her.

Bodies hovered around her. She heard voices, saw lips moving, but she couldn't make out the words. The ringing continued. Her vision blurred until the men above her became indistinguishable from each other. Then one voice separated itself from the frantic hum of noise.

"You went too far Russell, you know better," Badrick growled as he walked into her view. Russell looked down at her as if she were a piece of trash. Badrick snatched his wrist and held it up, revealing the knife hidden under his sleeve.

"Everyone here is useless. Either you need to step up your game or get out," Russell snarled. Whirling, he swung the knife in Badrick's direction.

Badrick ducked, narrowly avoiding the flashing blade.

Fresh adrenaline coursed through Kira. Summoning every ounce of strength she had left, she struggled to her feet and launched herself at Russell.

"You son of a bitch!" she screamed. Her momentum carried both of them out of the ring and onto the floor. Rage roared inside her like some ferocious beast. She wanted to kill him, truly kill him. He thought he could belittle her, treat her and everyone else like shit, threaten the people she loved and get away it? She would show him how wrong he was.

Kira jumped on top of him and threw punches left and right. Sweat poured from her forehead, trickled down between her shoulder blades. Hands clutched at her, pulling her to her feet. She fought them too, but they held her tight.

Russell managed to sit up.

Leaning toward him, she spoke through clenched teeth. "You can hit me, you can abuse me and hate me. But if you or Pierceton ever hurt any one of these men, I'll kill you both with my bare hands!"

Russell's comment was low but she heard him say it. "Useless orphan."

The hands holding her back suddenly released her. Kira charged at Russell and drove her fist into the side of his head, moving so quickly he never had a chance to block the blow. Kira glared down at him as he collapsed back onto the floor, not moving. His face was bloody and beaten. Blood trickled from his nose, a bruise already forming on his left temple. Strong hands grasped her again before she could go back in and kill him right there on the stone floor.

Fighting for air, she shifted her gaze to Pierceton. The growing hatred in his eyes dared her to push further.

"You want me to do the same thing to you?" Her voice was emotionless now, cold. His eyes widened and he shook his head and took a step back.

Someone tugged at her shoulder and she looked up. Maddox. She paused for a moment, then turned and walk out of the room.

Out in the hallway, Kira leaned against the wall, head thumping and legs shaking. Now that the surge of adrenaline was abating, pain was taking over. Her head throbbed, every part of her body screamed, the hallway spun around her. She focused on the floor and traced the pattern of the stone with her eyes. Anything to keep her conscious. Anything to keep her from breaking down and crying in front of the men.

"Felix, Astien, carry Russell to his room and keep an eye on him. I'll have a nice talk with him once he comes to."

They answered back, but Kira couldn't quite understand what they said. All she knew was that everything began to mute and black spots blinded her vision. Her body felt suddenly weightless and out of her control. Someone called out her name, but she couldn't make out who. It sounded as if they were speaking underwater. Pain washed over her again. The side of her face stung. *That rat got me with his knife.* The floor came toward her. Kira tried to fight with everything she had, but she just couldn't do it.

She gave in, closed her eyes, and her world went black.

Chapter 7

THE SHEETS OF THE BED shifted with a gentle movement of Kira's foot. She started to sit up, but froze at the sound of muffled voices in the hallway. Through the crack of the door she spotted two shadows, both tense and on guard.

"Do you really think she will do that?"

Badrick. She would recognize his voice anywhere.

"Kira was already on edge with Russell. After his little stunt, it's only a matter of time before he pushes her too far. Lord knows what that child will do to him."

Kira's forehead wrinkled. Was that Kingsman?

"It was stupid of us to let him in the ring with her to begin with." Badrick's voice was thick with controlled fury.

What is he so angry about?

"He needed it. What's in the past is in the past. You are to protect her, do you understand me? Now go see if she has come to."

The shadows turned and the door creaked open further.

Kira slammed her eyes shut. The footsteps came closer and a hand settled on her shoulder.

Badrick shook her lightly and called her name.

She opened her eyes as he knelt beside the bed.

"Hey, how you feeling Kit? You had us all worried; you hit the floor pretty hard."

Kira slid her hand up and touched the side of her face. It was sensitive to the touch, possibly would bruise too. A little higher, she traced the scratch of Russell's knife. She was lucky the blade had only skimmed her.

"I'm going to kill him," she spat out.

"You nearly did. You hit him hard; he hasn't even come to yet."

Good. She struggled to sit up. Her head felt numb, which was a vast improvement over the throbbing pain. She looked past Badrick at the mirror on the wall. Her hair was a mess, her wound had been bandaged, and the right side of her face was partly swollen. Hopefully that would go down in the next few days.

"Kira, you and Russell are to be separated at all times."

Kira blinked. She hadn't seen Kingsman slip into the room behind Badrick, but her gaze swung now to his grim face.

"You better be doing that to keep him safe," she mumbled. "Because I'm not afraid to face him again." An awkward silence hung in the room, until she gave a frustrated sigh and threw back the blanket that covered her. She needed to get ready to meet Isabella that night, as well as the pest who was blackmailing her. For him, she would try her best to look as delicate as possible. She had already made the mistake of underestimating his strength. If she could manage to trick him into making the same mistake, she'd have the element of surprise on her side.

Kingsman moved to the side of the bed. "What do you think you are doing?"

"I'm going out."

Badrick frowned. "I don't think so. You are injured, possibly seriously."

Kira swung her legs over the side of the mattress. "I'm fine. Russell isn't going to keep me from my work."

When neither man protested further, she rose and stood on shaky legs. "What time is it?"

"Four hours past noon."

She had plenty of time.

"I have something to attend to tonight, so don't plan any jobs for me." Kira stood and stumbled over to the trunk in the corner of the room. She pulled out one of the few dresses she owned. Clutching it to her, she rummaged through the trunk, looking for weapons that Isabella's small hands could manage.

After grabbing several, she turned to face Kingsman and Badrick, neither of whom looked happy.

"I suggest you keep Pierceton away from me as well."

With that, she strode from the room.

~ * ~

With a quick twist of her wrist, the lock of the brothel window clicked open. After peering over the bottom of the frame to make sure no one was in the room, she hoisted herself up and over the sill. The room was dark and silent, just as it had been the night before when she encountered the man. The sensation of crisp cold outside air ceased as she let the window fall shut. She had only a few moments before the sun set. So she would wait for him to arrive.

Kira sat on a chair hidden in the corner and fumbled with her crimson skirts. Underneath them four daggers were strapped to her thighs, two on each leg. Hidden in her sleeves was a knife that would unsheathe at the flick of her wrist. Another contraption Maddox had created and wanted her to test out. If he wasn't picking locks, he was building something new and exciting for the guild.

The door squeaked open and a figure stepped into the room. Light and noise filled the hall behind him. Kira stayed silent as the man closed the door. She would wait for him to notice her.

With a turn of his head, he spotted her and flashed a crooked smile.

"So you showed up after all. I have to admit I was hoping I could turn you in for the coin on your head."

Kira bit back a snarl while he walked over to the bed and dropped onto it, the last place she would choose to sit. A shudder rippled through her. Despite its neatly-laid sheets, the bed had been torn apart too many times for her taste.

She lifted her chin. "What do you want?"

"Whoa, whoa, no introductions?" His voice was teasing. Kira gritted her teeth. She really didn't have any time to play his games.

"The name is Kira. There, happy?"

"So impatient. I'm Chaol, my lady."

Kira glared at him as he stood and crossed the room to hold out his hand. She didn't take it. What on earth would make him think that she would trust him? Let him touch her?

Her rudeness didn't appear to offend him. His grin widened as he pulled back his hand and stuck it in the pocket of his pants.

Kira rose and brushed past him to go stand by the window. "Now that introductions are done, will you tell me what you need me to do so I can get you off my back?"

When she turned and looked back at him, the playful look in his eyes had disappeared. His mouth hardened into a thin line and his body tensed. Her fingers itched to reach for the daggers strapped to her leg.

"Your guild, it's being framed, is it not?"

"We are thieves. What else would you expect?"

He gave a light chuckle and stepped forward. Kira refused to back down, despite their height difference. Shadows lined his eyes and his dark hair was askew, as if he had been fighting. The aura he gave off was strong, but Kira could sense the weakness within him. She crossed her arms over her chest.

He stepped closer. "Since I got stuck talking to one of your little friends, I've been associated with you. Now I'm being dragged under."

"And just what do you want me to do about it? I clearly have enough to handle already."

"You, my lady, are going to help me clear my name."

"How do I know you aren't guilty of the crime you're accused of?"

"How would you know if I were?"

Kira went to open her mouth but she shut it. There was no way for her to prove his guilt, but he could prove hers. He had won this round. "What do you want me to do?"

Chaol shrugged. "I'm not sure. I didn't think you would follow through."

She rolled her eyes. It was like working with a child.

"When you think of something, let me know." She spun around and strode towards the window. Kira felt his eyes boring into her back as she pushed the window open and peered down. The sun had nearly set. Purples, pinks, and oranges cast a dim glow over the alleyway behind the brothel. She sat on the frame and shot him one last look. "If I ever catch you lying to me, I will slit your throat before you can blink."

"Just what I would expect from a gentle creature like you."

Kira's lips turned up at his sarcasm. "Meet me in the forest at the southern end of town tomorrow night. There's a blacksmith there. If his shop is no longer in your vision, then you've gone too far. Try to actually think of something by then."

Chaol gave her a firm nod and Kira swung her legs over the sill. Grabbing onto the frame with both hands, she lowered herself to the ground. With a click of her shoes, she landed and fixed her skirts once more. Kira gave one last glance up at the open window. Her stomach knotted. Working with Chaol was just one more thing she had to worry about. But at the same time she felt a flutter of hope that she had the chance to make things right.

Chapter 8

THE STREETS SLOWLY CLEARED OUT, making it easier to maneuver through the town. At first, Kira worried she was too late and Isabella had left. But then she found her, standing near woven baskets behind the bakery. Her dark hair had been neatly twisted into a bun and out of her face. Her clothes seemed old and dirty, which Kira was glad to see. Sometimes training could get messy. She'd learned that after wearing one of her favorite dresses when she first started lessons with Badrick. By the time she came out of the practice room, both she and the gown were filthy from constantly being thrown to the ground.

Isabella's face lit up when she saw Kira. "I was worried you had forgotten. I'm so happy you are here."

The smile on her face made Kira regret taking so long with Chaol. "Do you know anything about weapons at all?"

"Ruby taught me the basics. Like how to hold a knife and my stances."

Kira reached under her skirts and unsheathed a dagger. Isabella gaped at it without moving. Kira could understand why the young girl would have such a reaction. Compared to the worn dagger Isabella had given her, this was much more advanced. The blade was much longer, more lethal. Kira always kept her weapons sharp with the edges ready to pierce a body with the simplest of movements.

"When I was first shown this dagger, I had the same reaction." Kira flipped it gracefully and extended it out, handle first." But I quickly learned that if you respect your weapon, then no harm will come to you."

Isabella hesitated, then reached for the weapon and grasped it with tiny, trembling fingers.

While the young girl demonstrated what Ruby had taught her, Kira kept watch for peeping eyes. Should anyone see them, they might call a guard, question why such weapons were in a woman's hands. While women weren't forbidden to carry a blade, it certainly wasn't an everyday sight.

Isabella's technique was surprisingly good and strong. She kept her knees bent and was light on her feet, but she still wasn't strong enough to take a man on by herself. She was young and had yet to develop any real muscles. Her entire body was so fragile that all a man would have to do was pick her up and throw her and she would be done for. But if Kira could manage to teach her how to get out of grips, then she would be a little more at ease, knowing Isabella was slightly less vulnerable than she had been before.

Kira came up behind the girl and held her tight. At first Isabella tried to squirm her way out, but Kira spoke softly in her ear. "Breathe and relax. Look, listen, then strike."

The exact same words Badrick had told Kira. He had done the same routine with her as she was doing now with Isabella. *A man will always be stronger, no matter how much you want to deny it. But if you can use his strength against him, then he is a dead man.*

Isabella dug her heel into Kira's foot, causing just enough pain for her to loosen her grip. Then the young girl slithered her hands up under Kira's arms and pushed out, instantly breaking any grip Kira had on her. Kira gave her a victorious smile, but didn't stop there. She went through all the holds that she could think of. She pinned Isabella to the wall, then to the ground. She captured the girl in a chokehold. She held her hands behind her back and above her head and grabbed a handful of her hair.

Perhaps she was being a little too rough, but she never heard a complaint from Isabella all the way through their lesson.

Finally, Kira released her. "I think that is enough for now. You did very well."

Isabella struggled to catch her breath and gave her an exhausted smile. Her once perfect hair was disheveled and her chest heaved for air. But the pride was there saying *I did it.*

Kira patted her on the back and waited for her to catch her breath. The night suddenly seemed deathly still. Kira's eyes darted back and forth from the trees to the roofs. Dark shadows clustered at the foot of two chimneys caught her eye. Her chest tightened. From the looks of it, there were just the two of them, assuming there weren't more hiding in the forest.

Assassins.

Kira licked her dry lips. They'd been hired, no doubt, to exact revenge for her thievery, or maybe to collect the bounty on her head. Their skills proved they had been well trained. She hadn't heard them scale the buildings to their hiding spots. Although they had forgotten the light of the street lamps behind them would cast their shadows over the roof. *What an amateur move.*

"Isabella, I want to give you this." Kira handed the girl one of her own daggers. "It was one of my first and gave me courage when I doubted myself the most. I hope it does the same for you."

Isabella took the weapon into her hand as if it were fine china. "I will cherish it forever. Thank you so much."

Kira glanced up again. The shadows hadn't moved. At least they weren't attacking while a child was around.

"Good. Now, it's getting late, you should go home. Just promise me you will do whatever it takes to get out of that brothel, okay?"

Isabella nodded. Kira smiled and gave the girl a quick hug. At least she had done something to help her. It felt good to give to the world instead of stealing from it.

"Now run home and don't let anyone see that," she whispered.

Isabella turned and ran, clutching her gift close to her chest.

Once the young girl was gone from her sight, Kira wasted no time flicking out her hidden blades and searching for the assassins. They had moved out of sight, but they were still there. She could sense them. Kira turned and looked through the trees. A slight glimmer caught her eye. She froze for a moment and squinted into the darkness. A blade skimmed past her cheek. She took a moment to glance back at the knife stuck in the wood of the bakery. The style was the same as the one she had found in her room.

Three cloaked figures glided out of the shadows and closed in on her, their steps slow and deliberate. She had prayed that she could at least get a glimpse of them, but masks concealed their faces. Kira backed up as they advanced towards her. She reached the building and pressed her back to the wood. She had taken more men than this on in the past; this would be easy.

She forced herself to wait until they were a few feet from her, then Kira ripped the knife free from the holder strapped to her thigh and threw it at the man in the center. Before he fell, she had already aimed for the one on her right. He was strong, well-built, and dangerously fast. He lunged toward her, caught her fist with ease, and twisted her arm. Kira cried out in pain as he slammed her against the wall. The side of her face smacked the wood and went numb. Another bruise.

A shout from his comrade caused her attacker to lose his focus on her temporarily. Kira took her opening and whirled her elbow around and into his face. She cringed at the sound of his nose cracking, but continued on, grabbing his shoulders and pulling him down into her knee, followed by an elbow to the back of the head.

Kira snapped her head back up and prepared for another fight, but found Chaol standing over her last attacker.

She frowned. "What are you doing here?"

Chaol rolled his shoulder and cracked his neck. "No thank you?"

"I could have handled them myself. Do you forget who I am?"

Her hands slid behind her attacker's head and she unlaced the ties of his mask. The man underneath was a little older than Kingsman, with gray biting at the roots of his raven hair. Crow's feet had settled at the corners of his eyes, as if he glared too much. His face was hard and uneasy. Despite the chills he sent down her back, she had no clue who he was.

Kira searched the men for a note, a clue as to who had sent them, anything, but all she found was a sack of coins. She wanted to scream at the top of her lungs. It seemed that, no matter how hard she tried, she was no closer to finding out who was framing the guild and why. She stood up and flung one of the unconscious men over her shoulder. She threw an icy glare at Chaol. "Are you going to just stand there or will you help me?"

"You might show me a little more respect, considering I can turn you in whenever I please." Chaol picked up another man and followed her into the trees. To Kira, the forest had always seemed more alive at night. The trees appeared taller, the animals seemed louder and more lively. The leaves whispered and the wind moaned. To some it would seem scary, but to her it was an oasis.

"I'm only keeping you alive because you might be of some use to me. That's all you are, a tool." She ducked through the trees and twisted her way through the underbrush until she spotted a small cave dug out of rock, far enough from town that no one should find them. With a hoist, she tossed the man from her shoulder to the ground with a thud. The man didn't move. The impact of her elbow to the back of his head proved a clean kill, no blood in sight. She couldn't say the same for the assassin who had taken the dagger to his chest. Was he dead? Had the royal palace sent them? Or maybe someone the guild had stolen from? Her eyes widened. Could it have been Cadwell? Kira shook her head. No, he had been too drunk to even notice that she had taken his necklace.

Chaol stepped forward and let the body he'd been carrying land carelessly next to the other one.

"Don't you think your words are a little harsh?" His voice was teasing as he looked over at her.

Her gaze flicked to his. "Says the man who blackmails innocent women," she snarled.

He snorted. "You may be many things, but I doubt innocent is one of them."

Her blood boiled at the sight of his mocking smile. Kira turned on her heel and left the cave. She had one more assassin to grab. Chaol could get lost in the forest forever for all she cared.

When she reached the bakery, the body was not where she had left it. Either someone had found him, which was unlikely at this time of night, or he had only been pretending to be dead.

"Where did he go?"

Chaol's voice grated on her like gravel on an open wound. Kira needed to get away before she did something she would regret.

She said nothing as she turned and began to walk back to the guild's hideout. If he followed her, she would lose him on the way. Or maybe she'd finish him off too and toss him into the cave in the forest with the others. She would only be pushed so far, and she had to warn Kingsman and the others. Someone had tried to kill her tonight, and although she had eliminated the assassins he had sent, Kira knew he wouldn't stop until she and the rest of the guild were dead.

Chapter 9

Kira walked down the halls, her heels clicking on the stone. She called out to let everyone know she was home safe, but no one answered back. Her heart fluttered. This was usually the time the guild was most lively. *Something is wrong.*

She ran down the halls, flinging open each door and searching in every corner. No one. She sprinted towards the meeting room, nothing. Same in the training room. With each second that passed, her fear grew. Had the assassins come here and ambushed the guild? They weren't that strong, were they? Fighting an assassin was like fighting a child . . . right?

Blood was splattered on the side of the hallway, bright red and fresh. Kira kicked off her shoes to reduce noise and drew her knife, prepared to find an attacker waiting for her around the corner. Who could have broken in here? Even if someone had managed to find this place, he would still have to get past everyone. It would be suicidal to even step a foot into the hideout.

The blood trailed down the hallway, splattered on the walls and floor as if someone, injured or possibly dying, had stumbled along, trying to get somewhere. Her breath hitched in her throat as she turned the corner. The men were huddled in a circle. She pushed her way through and did a quick head count. Maddox, Kingsman, Bardick, Astien, Felix, Pierceton, they were all there except . . .

Kira stepped forward and pushed her way through the huddle. When she reached the center, what she saw nearly made her fall to her knees. Russell lay on the floor in a pool of his own blood. The side of his face was pressed against the cold, stone floor. His eyes, open and staring at the wall in front of him, contained a look of true terror, as if a demon had been sent down to brutally slaughter him.

Kira covered her mouth with one hand. She'd always known he had it coming. She just never thought this day would come so soon.

~ * ~

Kira huddled in the corner of Kingsman's office, wearing the shadows like a cloak, protecting her from the prying eyes of the men.

"When I heard the scream, I came running." Astien's face was pale "That's how I found him. Dead on the floor."

Kingsman nodded, but he appeared deep in thought. "You saw no one?"

Astien shook his head firmly. "No. If I had, one of us would have caught him, I promise you that."

Kira's body shook. She had hated Russell, yes. She had wanted to kill him. But to actually see him dead on the floor, blood splattered everywhere, was different than her experience of seeing any other lifeless body. The look on his face rippled through her mind and down to her bones. She couldn't form any words, she couldn't even help carry him out of the hideout and bury him. All she could do was hide herself in the dark while the men were being questioned.

"Does anyone else have a clue who might have done this?"

They all looked at each other and shook their heads. Kira's mind flooded with questions and thoughts. Was Russell the one who had left the note in her room? If it wasn't Russell, then who? Was his death somehow connected to the assassins who had attacked her earlier that night? Kira swallowed. Where had that last man disappeared to? The thought of him still out there, watching her, made her shudder.

"Kira, do you have any ideas?"

Kira's head shot up. Her gaze swung to meet Kingsman's. It was unlikely that the murderer could have made it in and out of the hideout without being caught. The only other possibility was that he stood in this very room among them all. But she didn't dare say that. So she shook her head quietly and lowered her gaze to her bare feet.

Kingsman cleared his throat. "Very well, then. We will start guard duty. Maddox, Felix, you'll take the first watch. The rest of you, lock your doors and keep a weapon nearby. There's no telling what else could happen."

The men turned and walked out the door, mumbling amongst themselves. Kira studied each one as they left. Other than Pierceton, each one of them had loved her, raised her, and protected her. To think one of them could have betrayed her and lied to her all these years shattered her heart.

"Hey Kit, you all right?"

Torn from her thoughts, she jumped at the touch of Badrick's hand on her shoulder, but he didn't seem to notice. His eyes were gentle, full of affection as they always were. He had been hard on her, he had sent her walking away with bruises and wounds, but never once did he do so from a lack of care. He was one of the last people she wanted the killer to be.

"You're shaking."

"These dresses aren't made to keep you warm." Kira managed to slither out the lie. She tried to smile, but the strength just wasn't there.

Badrick frowned. He moved around behind her. Cloth rustled, but before she realized what he was doing, warmth enveloped her. Badrick wrapped his cloak around her shoulders. Kira almost smiled, knowing he was not only trying to keep her warm, but to let her know that everything would be all right. The men never wore their cloaks unless they were out on a job. He must have come back and discovered the bloody scene just like she had.

"Come on, I'll walk you to your room."

Normally Kira would protest that she could walk herself, but she suddenly felt the need to be near someone. Badrick kept an arm securely around her shoulders as he led her through the halls. Kira fisted his cloak with both hands, as if it that would keep her safe. But nothing would keep her safe now. If the assassins had killed Russell, they would surely come after her again soon.

When they came to her chamber, Badrick sat quietly on the bed while she locked the door and changed in the adjacent room. She never wanted to wear the dress again. It held too many memories of this terrible night. She carelessly tossed the wad of fabric aside and stepped into her nightgown. She'd burn it tomorrow.

The pale silk hung comfortably from her shoulders.

Kira pulled out the hair that had gotten trapped under the gown. Her mind flashed back to the note in the drawer that still taunted her. After what happened tonight, she needed to tell someone about it. Clearly they were all at risk. She had no right to keep this from the rest of the guild, not after everything they had done for her.

She walked back into the other room. "I found a note."

In the dim moonlight filtering through the window, Badrick's jaw tightened. "What did it say?"

"It said that I was next. I found it a few nights ago, stuck to the back of my bedroom door with a knife. And ... and tonight I was attacked by assassins." Knowing how he would react, she mumbled the words, not meeting his eyes.

Badrick shot up off the bed. "Why didn't you tell us?"

"I assumed it was Russell playing a prank." She drew in a deep breath. "Until I saw what happened to him tonight."

He let out a frustrated sigh, the way he always did when he was mad. He stepped forward and settled his hands on her shoulders. She studied his grim features. His nose, his furrowed brows, the curve of his lips. The same lips that had kissed her only the night before.

"You should have told us, Kira. This isn't just something you can just throw off to the side." His voice had lowered to a soft tone. He was worried for her. That had to rule out the possibility of him killing Russell, right? His eyes searched hers. "I'm telling Kingsman in the morning."

"No, wait. I don't want—"

His grip on her shoulders tightened. "Kira, this isn't a joke. I won't be responsible for keeping this information from the others and having you, or any of them, wind up dead. It's bad enough we are being framed, but now we are being threatened too."

When Kira didn't say anything, he pulled away and strode for the door. He yanked it open and bid her a terse good night. Kira stood in the middle of the room, feeling exposed and naked. For the first time in her life, she was truly *scared*. She was scared of not surviving this threat against them, she was scared of losing everyone, she was scared of being betrayed, she was scared of being alone.

"Badrick."

He froze in the doorway.

Kira crossed the room and grasped his elbow. His muscles were hard beneath her fingers. The strength of him eased her fear. "Please stay with me, just for the night."

For a moment he hesitated. She had never asked him to do anything like that before. Clearly he was battling with himself over the wisdom of it. Would he stay? He knew her better than anyone. Could he see how badly the events of the evening had shaken her?

After a few, agonizing seconds, he exhaled loudly and closed and locked the door again. Taking her by the hand, he led her to the bed and sat down, pulling her down beside him. When he stretched out on the thin mattress, she nestled next to him, her back pressed to his chest. His arms circled her and, for the first time since she had first seen the shadows of the assassins on the roof, the tight knots in her stomach loosened. Perhaps she was foolish to trust Badrick so completely, but she couldn't help herself.

Kira stared at the door of her room. With Maddox and Felix on guard tonight, it was unlikely the killer would strike again. Still, she couldn't shake the feeling that it might burst open at any moment.

Badrick gently raked his fingers through her hair, pushing her bangs out of her face. Suddenly she felt so small. His arms were big and held her close to him. The smell of the seaside radiated off of him. She remembered how he told her that he had lived on the coast when he was younger, often going fishing with his father until he ran off in search of a bigger adventure. Even to this day, the salt from the air, the scent of the water, still clung to him, a bittersweet smell she had come to love.

Despite being in his arms, Kira couldn't find sleep. Russell's horrified eyes haunted her. Nothing would ever wipe the memory from her mind.

Whatever had come after him was something from the depths of hell, and somehow she knew that it was coming for her next.

Chapter 10

KIRA COULDN'T TAKE IT ANYMORE. She was tired of being one of the hunted; she needed to be the huntress. She snuck out each night to search for clues. There had been no signs of intrusion or a weapon left behind or even a footprint anywhere near the hideout. Whoever had killed Russell was no fool. She couldn't avoid it any longer. The only chance she had to find something was to examine Russell's body.

While the men were all out one day, Kira managed to sneak out and meet up with Chaol. If she wanted to go to Russell's grave, she would have to lie. The men wouldn't let her out at night for no reason, especially since Badrick had told Kingsman about the note. She had to have a job.

"I need you to ask me to steal something."

Chaol let out a curt laugh. "Why would you want me to do that?"

"One of the guild members was murdered and I think it has something to do with the assassins from the other night."

"And how would me asking you to steal something help?"

"With the guild under threat, they won't let me out without cause. I barely even made it out today. But if you specifically request me to do a job, they'll have to let me go."

"And what do I get out of it?"

Kira dug her fingernails into her arm. Curse him. Of course he wouldn't do anything for her unless there was something in it for him.

"If we can find the murderer, we might be able to find the people who are framing us. Our names will be cleared, and so will yours." It sounded so simple coming out of her mouth. If only it were that easy. "Come up with something. Some merchant cheated you of money, someone stole your ring, I don't care. Just meet me behind the tavern and bring shovels and a lantern."

Chaol pursed his lips and studied her, weighing the costs against the benefit to himself, no doubt. Kira held his breath until he nodded. Without another word, she spun on her heel and returned home before anyone could discover she had gone out.

Two days later, Kingsman called her into his office. When she walked in, he rose and came around his desk, crossing his arms as he leaned back against it. "A gentleman has approached me, requesting your assistance."

Kira worked to keep an innocent look on her face. "Oh?"

"Apparently his brother stole money from him and he would like you to get it back. He says to meet him at the back of the tavern at midnight tonight."

It took everything she had not to shift under his intense gaze. Kingsman knew her too well. Did he suspect she had set up this situation herself? "All right." She nodded as though this was a routine mission, and turned to head out of the room. She half-expected Kingsman to stop her and question her further, but he let her go.

Just before midnight, Kira threw her cloak on and slipped out of the hideout. Chaol was waiting for her behind the tavern with a shovel in hand and a lantern in other, just like she had said. He didn't ask her where they were going or what they would be doing once they got there. It was almost as though he trusted her not to lead him into trouble. That was the fool's own mistake. She was not a person to be trusted.

Kira had overheard Maddox telling Kingsman that they'd buried

Russell about a mile east of the hideout, so that was where she headed. When she found the mound of dirt, his dagger set as a headstone, Kira lifted the shovel then paused. Regardless of how much she had hated Russell, she was hesitant to disturb his peace. Everyone, no matter how vile they had been in life, deserved to rest in peace. Or, if not, it should be the devil that took care of what was to come for them, as she was sure he would do for her when her time came.

Pushing back the thought, Kira drove the shovel into the ground. It would have taken her the entire night had it not been for Chaol's help. Yes, she was strong, but her slender arms could only work for so long. After thirty minutes, he took the shovel from her without a word and continued to work. By the time he'd uncovered the body, they were both caked in dirt and sweat.

Kira peered into the hole and her breath hitched in her throat. Russell rested against the hard earth, arms crossed and eyes closed. Kira was thankful to see that the fear had been washed from his face. If it hadn't been, she wasn't sure she'd still be standing where she was.

Chaol helped lower her down beside Russell. Taking a deep, steadying breath, Kira patted down the body and searched his pockets, her blistered-covered fingers shaking from pain and fear. Fear that she would find something and fear that she wouldn't. The pockets of his pants were as empty as his damned personality. She reached into his tunic and searched the inside pockets. Still nothing. Her shoulders fell. Chaol reached down and helped her scramble out of the hole. She sat on the edge of it and raked her hands through her hair, not caring how dirty they were. *That's it then. There is no hope.* Whoever was behind all this was stronger and smarter than anyone she had been up against before.

She studied her hands. Dirt was caked beneath her nails and sweat dripped down her back. She would have to slip into the baths and clean up before anyone saw her. The thought of having to sneak back into her own house might have been funny to her, had the circumstances not been so dire.

Chaol stood silently behind her, waiting. Tears pricked the corners of Kira's eyes. She was not a woman prone to crying, but the fear and frustration of the last few days were taking their toll. She felt as if she had been blindfolded and thrown into a strange, locked room and told to find her way out. The task was next to impossible. Clenching her jaw, she stood and began to shovel back the dirt. Chaol moved to her side, shoving back mounds of it with his bare hands.

Finally the mound of dirt appeared roughly as they had found it. Kira grasped Russell's dagger and yanked it from the ground, clutching it so tightly her knuckles gleamed white in the moonlight. He had done something wrong. She knew just from the look of his hands that he had killed the innocent and washed away their blood from his fingers as he had washed away their existence. She was sure he had never hesitated, never gave a second thought to what he was doing. His ears were deaf to their begging and their pleading for mercy. He would do what he set out to do, then turn and move on with the day, as if nothing untoward had occurred. Their souls only added to the number he had taken. He had tried to kill her in the ring, so there was no doubt he was willing to do it. And he would have gone after the others once he had taken care of her, if she hadn't temporarily stopped him. And if someone else hadn't stopped him permanently.

Furious, Kira stabbed the dagger into the mound, over and over. Her hand tingled from the death grip she had on the handle. Her shoulders burned as she pushed it further into the mound as if it would hurt him. One strike, that's all it would have taken to kill him. Right through the heart. She wanted to spit on the very dirt that covered his body. She wanted to bring him back, only to kill him herself. Whatever desire to let him rest in peace was gone. Her energy spent, she tossed the dagger onto the grave and spun away from it.

She brushed past Chaol, but he grabbed her elbow to stop her. "Out of true worry, please listen to my words. Be careful." He let go of her arm and reached for both her hands.

Kira stared up at him. His eyes, usually mocking, had turned gentle. His thumbs rubbed the backs of her hands softly. As if under a spell, she leaned toward him. Realizing suddenly what she was doing, she yanked her hands from his and stepped back. If he thought he could charm her with his looks, or with his words, he was sadly mistaken. "Why are you suddenly worried about me?"

He pressed his lips together tightly. "If you figure that out, let me know, would you?"

Kira whirled away from him. She needed to get back before the men realized she had been out for too long. Another depressing night. All she wanted to do was go home and rest. Most of all, she wanted to get away from this grave.

"There's a place," Chaol blurted out behind her. Kira stopped mid-step and peered back at him. He stared at the ground, as if contemplating whether or not to tell her more.

Kira shifted from one foot to the other, impatient.

After a moment he nodded, as though he'd decided something. "There's a place not too far from here. You can go there and hire people to do dirty work for you."

"You're looking at a girl who does the dirty work."

He shook his head firmly. "No, I mean you can pay them …" He stopped and looked around before moving closer and lowering his voice. "To murder."

Kira's eyes widened. "Where is this place?"

The mocking look was back in his eyes as he stepped closer, close enough she could feel the warmth of his body spreading across her skin.

"Perhaps we can discuss that over dinner?"

She shoved both hands against his chest and spun around to leave. She should have known he just wanted to play games. As long as his name was cleared, that was all that mattered to him. She certainly didn't. He had no murderer coming after him, he didn't have the welfare of an entire guild to worry about, he didn't have a shattered heart.

"Kira, wait." Chaol grabbed her arm and spun her back to face him.

She opened her mouth to tell him what she really thought of him. She didn't care if she hurt his feelings; he needed to hear what an asshole he was.

Before she could speak, words tumbled from him. "I'm sorry. I just can't help myself around you sometimes."

Her mouth snapped closed as she scrutinized him. "Just what does that mean?"

"I think you know very well what that means."

Heat flooded her cheeks. The damn fool. She tugged her arm from his grasp. Without another word, she turned and stomped away from him, not waiting for him to catch up.

Chapter 11

Kira watched Chaol raise his tankard and take a gulp of beer. He had paid for her to bathe at the inn as well as get a warm bowl of stew. Though it was nice, she couldn't forget why she was there in the first place. She had agreed to help him, and to go to dinner with him, now he needed to agree to tell her everything he knew.

"Now about that place," she pushed.

Chaol looked at for a moment at the bustling crowd then nodded. "It's about an hour north by foot, about forty minutes if you take a horse. It's at a trading port so it is pretty easy to blend in with all the foreigners. People don't know if you're a traveler or just strange. Although it's not recommended for a woman like you to go in." He didn't meet her eyes. Instead he focused on the lute player off to one side of the inn.

"Why is that?"

"The women there are just as crude as the men. All they want is money and attention. They don't like attitude, and that, my lady, is exactly what you have."

Kira crossed her arms. She wasn't about to act like polite and sweet as a rose just because someone didn't like her *attitude*.

"The place is called The Grottos. Anyone of bad blood tends to go there to get things done if they don't want their hands to get dirty. Sometimes to even get a few coins themselves. I've got a few friends who visit there. One mentioned a new face climbing up the ranks that fit the description of your little friend. Said he had been traveling around with an accomplice, looking for jobs. Perhaps they weren't happy with their pay in the guild."

Kira's chest tightened. She knew exactly who his accomplice was. That coward of a thief Pierceton. The thought of him still living under the same roof as the guild made her anger spike.

She shook her head. Kingsman made sure customers paid well for the jobs they hired guild members to do. Russell should have been content with what he earned there. There had to be another reason why he was desperate enough to go to The Grottos for a job. If he went to do someone else's killing, whoever had hired him must be the mastermind behind all this. Russell was just a puppet, a clueless puppet.

"You're taking me there," she demanded as she stood up and tossed a coin on the table.

"Did you not just hear me when I said it's not safe for women like you to go in?"

Kira strode for the door. "Since when do I listen to you?"

With an impatient sigh, Chaol followed her out the tavern. "You'll have to listen to me now, because I'm not taking you."

Kira continued to walk down the street with him following behind. Having him take her would have been a lot easier for her, but it wasn't impossible for her to go alone. She had managed to find some of the most secret places in the world, she was sure that she could find The Grottos. But for now she would try a different tactic.

She purposely slowed her pace so he would catch up. "There is nothing I can do to change your mind?"

Chaol moved in front of her and stopped. His face was suddenly stern and serious compared to his normal flirtatious and teasing looks. For the first time since they met, she found him somewhat attractive.

"I know you do a lot of stupid and dangerous things, but this is one I won't let you do. I'm sorry, but no. We will find another way to get information."

"What exactly do you have in mind?"

"I don't know, but we will figure something out. Please promise me you won't go."

The sternness faded. Worry was as clear in his eyes as it was in his voice, almost as if he truly cared for her. Which was a lie. She had to force herself to look past his games and make a promise she would soon break. Not that she cared.

"I promise."

Relief washed over his face. "Thank you." He reached for her hand and lifted it to his lips. His kiss stung her with so much guilt she nearly cringed. To any bystander they must have looked like a young man and his beloved taking a late-night stroll.

If only it were possible for her to have something that precious.

~ * ~

Kira peered around the corner and spotted Badrick and Astien on duty. There was no possible way for her to talk her way past them; she would have to come up with something else. She crouched down and picked up a pebble. It was a rookie move they all learned when they were just barely starting out and, practically speaking, it was stupid. But it usually worked.

She pulled her arm back and flung it as hard as she could into the hall across from her. The sound echoed and she pressed her body as close as she could against the wall. The shadows of Badrick and Astien flickered along the stones as they crept their way down the hall and into the other room. When they were gone, she peeled herself off the wall and slithered towards the exit.

As soon as she was outside, she hid amongst the rocks and held a hand over her chest. Her legs shook from nerves and her ribs hurt from the pounding of her heart. *This plan is never going to work.*

Once she had calmed herself down, she stepped forward and began to head north. She only had a handful of hours before the men would realize she was gone, she had no time to waste.

Kira wrapped her cloak around her and held it tight with one hand to keep the breeze out. She stood in front of the hideout and pondered taking the route through town, but decided it was too risky. The guild members would be out doing their jobs; now wasn't the time to go that way. So she'd keep to the forest.

A leaf crunched. Before she could move, someone touched her arm from behind. Kira spun around and drew back her arm to throw a punch. Whoever her attacker was, he was cloaked in darkness and she couldn't make out his features. With one quick movement, he seized her wrist, stopping her blow. He said something, but Kira couldn't hear the words over the pounding in her ears. *I can't let them kill me.* With a twist of her wrist, she broke free and sprinted for the trees.

Fear flushed through her entire body and she pushed herself to run faster. They had waited for her to come out. They knew her moves. She should have stayed to fight, but she had to lead them away from the hideout. She couldn't risk any of the other men getting hurt.

Someone slammed into her from behind and tackled her to the ground. Her heart dropped. She was a step too slow.

Kira squirmed and reached for her dagger, but before she could grab it, she was flipped over and slammed onto her back. Her pursuer pinned her down, her wrists above her head and her legs held down by his. She squeezed her eyes tightly shut. *What will they would do to me?* Would they tie her up and torture her? Would they burn her alive? Perhaps they would do something more horrible and lock her in a room to slowly starve.

"Kit, it's me!"

Kira took a deep breath and opened her eyes. The clouds had parted. Badrick hovered above her, the moon striking down on him. His shoulders were broad, his lips parted as he breathed hard, hair falling gracefully in front of his face. He looked beautiful.

"What are you doing?" She was thankful to be lying in his shadow so he wouldn't see the blush on her face.

"Do you really think you can sneak past us that easily?" His voice held a teasing smile.

"You can't blame me for trying." It took everything she had to make her tone light, as if they were sharing a joke. Her heart rate was still dangerously high and a slight quiver of fear worked its way through her words, but he didn't seem to notice.

Badrick hauled himself to his feet and held out his hand. Kira took it and, in one swift movement, was up on her feet once again.

"Just where were you going this late at night?"

Kira dusted herself off so she could avoid his gaze. "Nowhere in particular."

"Do your customers believe the kind of bullshit you're feeding me? If so, they must be stupid."

Kira glared at him, but didn't reply.

"I suggest you tell me or I'll go to Kingsman."

"What are you, five?" She spat the words out. Badrick shrugged and waited for her answer. That's what frustrated her so much about him. She hated the fact that he could toy with her. It was as if she were his puppet and he knew the exact strings to pull. It had always been like with him. He would constantly tease her and embarrass her just to see her get flustered. When she was younger, her attraction to him was obvious to the entire guild, no matter how hard she tried to hide it. Every time he would walk in the room her gaze was drawn to him as steel to a magnet; every time he'd talk to her she would stutter. It was one of the secret reasons Kira had asked him to train her. She had hoped that if she began to see him more as an instructor those feelings would dwindle away, and they had. But now she was beginning to question herself again.

"I might have found a clue about Russell's killer." She sighed as she turned and began to walk deeper into the woods.

"Wait, what do you mean?" Badrick fell into step beside her. Kira looked at him out of the corner of her eye before focusing on the trees before her. Shock was clear on his face.

"It's possible Russell was working for someone else."

"Who?"

"That's what I'm hoping to figure out tonight."

"I'm coming with you."

Kira stopped and contemplated him. If The Grottos was as bad as Chaol had led her to believe, there was no way she would let Badrick anywhere near it. The last thing she needed was for him to ruin his reputation with the guild. She shook her head. "No."

She started to walk away, but he grasped her arm to stop her. "Kira, I'm coming with you one way or another. I'm not going to let you go out on your own. Do you forget that we all have a desire to find out who is framing us and put an end to this threat?"

"I can't afford for you to get hurt."

"And I can't afford to lose you," he shot back.

Kira pressed her lips together, the feel of his kiss from days before still lingering. There was no use in trying to talk him out of it; he was as stubborn as a mule. When she said nothing, Badrick offered her a victorious smile and followed her as she turned and trudged along the path through the trees.

Chapter 12

KIRA KNELT BEHIND A ROCK, her gaze locked in front of her. She had managed to find the village Chaol had talked about. All she and Badrick had needed to do was follow a small caravan making their way through the forest. The smell of the ocean was heavy in the air and the humidity began to make her feel sticky. The heat and the moisture combined to make her feel as though she were walking through honey.

Chaol was right about being able to blend in easily here. People from all over the world flowed in and out of the port, some with straight dark hair and olive skin, others with freckled skin and curly orange locks. Many had thick accents that Kira could not understand and some spoke languages that sounded like gibberish to her. Perhaps it would be harder than she thought to get any information from anyone here.

"So, you want to explain more about this place before we head in?" Badrick whispered as he touched the dagger that rested at her hip.

"It's a place where you can hire someone to commit murder for you." She checked around for any listening ears. "I think Russell might have been one of those men and someone sent him to kill me."

"Why you?"

Kira bit her lip. She didn't know that either. "I've been thinking about that. So far my conclusion is that he probably came here often looking for some extra work. God knows he had a bloodthirsty look in his eyes. Someone who knew about the guild and his hatred towards me must have tracked him down. Whoever it was mostly like offered him some hefty coin to kill me, which I'm sure he would have been glad to do."

"So we are here to find that person?"

"That's the plan." Kira eased out from behind the rock and pulled her hair back out of her face. No one had even taken notice of their arrival. Many men shoved past her as if she were invisible, although they did give Badrick space as he followed along behind her. As Chaol had predicted, women in general were clearly not welcome here. Either you were down and dirty like the others or you got out.

Kira stopped and peered up and down the rough dirt main road. No sign of The Grottos. All she saw were shops, ships, taverns, and inns. All crowded together, and tarnished from the salt in the air.

Badrick's hand latched onto her wrist and he tugged it so hard she nearly fell. He led her through the crowd and down into an alleyway. Suddenly he began to run. Kira didn't dare question him as he weaved through the twisted streets and alleys. The town was set up almost like a maze, each turn looking exactly like the last.

"Badrick, where—"

He quickly hushed her before ducking into a lane and stopping. Kira huffed and peered around the corner of the wall, trying to see what had caused Badrick to react in such a way. A young man on the other side of the street stood and looked around before opening a wooden door and slipping inside.

Kira drew in a quick breath. That had to be the place they were looking for.

Badrick tugged her again, this time more gently. "Stay close all right? And try not to get into trouble."

Any other time Kira would have laughed and said that was impossible.

But Badrick wasn't joking. The look in his eyes was serious, deadly serious. Kira felt almost as though she were a child again.

A roar of chatter echoed off the walls as they crossed the street and slipped through the doorway the young man had entered. People of different ethnicities and classes flooded together, some sea sailors, some travelers, others citizens. *So this is The Grottos.* Kira reached for her hood and pulled it over her head before adjusting her mask over her nose. She wasn't the only one covering her face; clearly others wished to remain unknown as well. If Russell had been sent after her, then it was possible that her face was known around here and someone might report back to him that she had been seen.

The two merged into the crowd. Many people surrounded the bar, others sat at tables. Women had somehow managed to make their way down here. Some settled at the bar, others were clearly flirting their way to money or whatever they could manage to steal. A group of young women danced in the center of the main floor. It seemed more like an underground city than a place to find murderers.

"I'll take a tankard of wine."

Kira raised her brows at Badrick as he leaned against the bar and flipped a coin to the bartender. He glanced down at her and she shook her head. They were here to search, not to drink.

The bartender poured the alcohol into a tankard and slid it over to Badrick, gladly taking his coin. Badrick took a sip before putting it down and turning to the man next to him.

"This seems to be the place to go around here." He waved a hand through the air. "Nothing like a good glass of wine after a long week of traveling."

The man looked at him through his good eye, the other one covered by a patch. Kira was thankful for the mask covering her nose. Otherwise she wasn't sure she could handle the stench coming off of him.

"Where ya traveling from?"

"We came from up north. Got tired of the damn cold." Badrick took another swig of his drink, the lies sliding off his tongue easily. "What about you?"

The man gave a hearty laugh. "We travel from all over the world," he answered, his accent thick. "There ain't a place for us to call home. The whole world is our home."

"That it is, that it is." Badrick clinked his mug against the man's.

Kira looked around, assessing her surroundings in case she needed to run. Looked like there was only one way in and one way out.

The man nudged Badrick with his elbow. "Why don't your partner over there relax a little? Make her sit down, have a drink."

Badrick tensed slightly. "The man's right, Kaitlynn. Sit down, make yourself comfortable."

Kira didn't realize he was talking to her until he called out the name again and grasped her arm.

"There aren't any more seats." She shrugged. She didn't know what he was up to but *she* needed to go look for clues. There were plenty of people she could talk to in order to get answers to her questions. Surely someone in here had known Russell.

Kira took a step away from the boring conversation, but Badrick reached out and pulled her into his lap. Heat rushed into her cheeks. Had they not been in public she would have slapped him so hard he would have fallen to the floor.

Badrick's arm slithered around her waist and pulled her to him.

"She doesn't know it yet, but one day I plan to marry this beautiful girl." Badrick planted a kiss on her cheek. Luckily her mask kept his lips from touching her directly.

The man with the patch chuckled. "It's nice to see an innocent woman down here. The ones around her are too brutal sometimes, even for my taste. You're a lucky man."

"That I am. Thank you." Badrick paused and shook his head. "Sorry, your name?"

The man gulped a mouthful of ale and wiped the residue off of his mustache with his sleeve. "Morgan. You?"

"Russell."

A shiver ran through Kira's body.

Morgan eyed Badrick in confusion.

"Is something wrong?" Badrick asked, an innocent look on his face.

Kira repressed the urge to roll her eyes. Deception was second nature to him. Maybe that's why he got as many jobs as he did. If she worked at it, Kira could fool people too. They all could, in fact. It was a skill every thief needed to hone. But just like Maddox specialized in lock picking and Astien was exceptionally fast, Badrick's gift was his quick tongue.

Morgan shook his head and looked absently at the bartender. "No. It's just there was a Russell here not too long ago. I travel a lot, but even I knew his name."

Excitement rippled through her. Russell *had* been here.

"Was? You mean he's gone now?" Badrick's finger drew small circles on her hip.

Kira would have jumped out of his lap, but his other arm tightened around her waist. She smacked his leg with her fist as discreetly as possible, but that didn't seem to faze him. A smirk danced across his lips, which he hid from the man beside him by lifting his mug to take another drink.

Kira gritted her teeth. This was just like him. Anything to pull her strings and get her flustered.

Morgan glanced around the room before lowering his voice and leaning closer to them. "Not a man to trifle with, that one. He'd as soon kill you as look at you."

That sounds about right. Kira shifted on Badrick's lap, straining to catch every word.

Badrick rested a hand on her thigh. "So he was a murderer, then?"

"Well, he didn't exactly carry his orders around with him. But then again, if you work for Silas, that's something to expect."

"So Silas hired him to kill someone?"

"Told him to kill some girl, from what I hear. I guess she was part of some guild. Don't know which one and don't really care."

Would you care if you knew that girl was sitting right in front of you? Kira opened her mouth to lash out at the man, but Badrick spoke up before she could.

"Why in the world would someone want to do that?"

"That's not exactly something Silas posts for people to know. He's very secretive. The only reason I know about this is because of Russell's death. There was another boy involved, but he was the lucky one, apparently. He's still on the job, far as I know. But I say if he doesn't make the hit soon, Silas will have him killed just like that Russell fellow."

Mind whirling, Kira scanned the room. Was this Silas person here, somewhere? If Pierceton was a threat to the other members of the guild, they needed to find Silas and force him to tell them what he knew before it was too late. A familiar face caught her eye. She squinted, taking in as many details as possible. Pierceton. Finally she had a clue as to which way was up. She leaned back against Badrick's chest and crossed her arms.

Morgan leaned even closer to Badrick and whispered, "You just better pray you don't end up like the last Russell."

Kira lowered her voice so only Badrick would hear her next words. "That will depend entirely on how he behaves the rest of this trip."

Chapter 13

Kira and Badrick hustled as quickly as they could. The sun rose, the light shining through the trees. Slowly the forest began to yawn and wake up, the trees groaning and the birds singing their songs. Normally Kira would have gladly sat and watched the day break from the roof of a house, but now they were racing to beat Pierceton back to the hideout.

"Are you sure it was him?" Badrick rasped, his breaths ragged.

Kira pictured the man she'd seen in The Grottos. The youthful features, the strong build, the false kindness in his eyes. There was no doubt that it was him. "I'm positive."

"What was he doing there?"

Kira glanced over at him. "My guess is he's there to find out what to do next now that Russell is dead."

Badrick didn't respond as they closed in on the hideout. They hid amongst the trees and looked around. So far, if their timing was right, no one would notice they had been gone, other than Maddox. And they trusted him enough not to say a word.

They crept their way closer to the entrance. Badrick pulled up the trapdoor set into the ground and waited for Kira to lower herself in first. She scanned the area for anyone who might see them. Once the coast was clear she climbed down the ladder and motioned for Badrick to follow. The door closed silently as he landed on his feet.

"Looks like there's more to this than we thought." Badrick followed her down the hall.

Kira scowled. "I knew I didn't like those two for a reason."

"I think you were determined to dislike them with or without a reason," he joked.

Kira was too exhausted to react. She had barely slept for days, sacrificing rest to stay up and search for clues. Even when she did have the chance to lie down, she couldn't relax. Not with the feeling of someone hovering over her, waiting, planning, poised to kill.

"We need to tell Kingsman." She rubbed her eyes. Now that they weren't running, her body's energy had flooded from her.

Badrick touched her back. "You need to go sleep. I'll tell him."

Kira shook her head. "I'm the main problem behind all this. I need to speak to him."

He exhaled loudly. "Fine. We'll go together as soon as you wake up. Now stop rubbing your eyes. You're going to make it worse." He pulled her hand away from her face. Kira smiled and dropped her arms to her sides. She felt like a little girl again. For once she didn't mind him taking care of her. It made her realize that he still cared for her just like he had when they were younger.

Kira sighed. "All right, but if you go to Kingsman without me, I promise you I won't hesitate to hurt you." She spun on her heel and headed down the hallway, Badrick's laughter accompanying her. The door shut with a soft click behind her as she stepped into her room. Kira made her way to the small window and pulled open the curtains.

When she was younger, the darkness scared her. She had stumbled over to Maddox one night, crying in fear, and he calmly hushed her. He crouched down and hoisted her onto his knee, holding her close. She told him her fear of someone hiding in the dark, her belief that whoever was there was out to hurt her. If anyone had told her then that as she grew older the dark would become her friend and savior Kira would have laughed. The irony was definitely strong.

Maddox's hands were so big that she thought he could crush her if he wanted to. Instead, he reached up and used them to gently wipe her tears away. At the time there were only three men in the guild, Maddox, Kingsman, and Felix, so there was a much more personal connection between them. Even though she was Kingsman's daughter—if by choice and not by blood—they saw her as one of their own. A few years later Astien joined the guild, then, a year after that, Badrick.

Kingsman did not like that she was afraid in her room. Early one morning, he noticed a small gap in a pile of rocks. For days after, he studied them as he returned to the hideout, noting how the sun broke through the opening to shine down on the rocks below. He mentioned the set of rocks to Maddox. It took some time, but as they contemplated the pile, the idea of building a window came to them. It took months for them to construct it safely. Kira gladly switched rooms when it was finished. Every night and every morning she would watch the light slowly pour in, then dissolve.

Drawing in a quivering breath, Kira turned away from the window. She took her time taking her boots off. The feeling of her feet finally being able to relax made her sigh happily. She gave a small wiggle of her toes before stretching out on her bed. For the first time in a long time her mattress welcomed her. No nightmares waited for her on the other side of consciousness. No worries troubled her mind. The soft evening light filtering through the simple piece of glass wedged into her wall calmed her. Kira's eyes fluttered shut, her breath fell into an even rhythm, and she was swept off into the sleep she had been longing for.

Chapter 14

Kira stood in front of Kingsman's desk, clenching her hands in an attempt to settle her nerves. Despite his laughter, Badrick had kept his promise and waited for her to wake up, she was relieved to find. Kingsman listened to their story in silence, a hard look on his face. His brows furrowed together, his mouth tight, his eyes glazed over. Both Kira's and Badrick's breathing hitched as they waited for his response. Apprehension bundled in Kira's stomach as she studied the man who was like a father to her. Would he be angry that they had gone to The Grottos without informing him? Searching for comfort, she snatched Badrick's hand and squeezed.

Normally Kingsman was an easy man to talk to. But this time they weren't bringing him simple information. No, they were accusing one of their own men of treason. Something he would not take lightly.

Kingsman lifted his head. His gaze bore into them. Kira would have stepped backward if Badrick hadn't tightened his grip on her hand. "We received a mission today. A man who attempted to cross the border hired us because the guards harassed him and charged him double at the tolls. He wants us to retrieve his money from the head guard, and to leave him a message while we're at it."

Kingsman stood up and threw a folder towards the edge of his desk. "The job requires two people. Take Pierceton with you, Kira. Learn the way of the palace. You've had missions that required you to break in there before, so you should know the basic layout."

Kira frowned. That was true, she had been in the palace before. Multiple times. But her partner hadn't. "He will fall behind. He doesn't have the skill to keep up with me. Let Badrick come—"

"If he falls behind, that's his fault, isn't it?"

Kira paused for a moment, confused. "If he falls behind, then he will get caught and arrested."

"Again. If he falls behind, that's his fault, isn't it?" A smirk crossed her father's face.

Now she understood. "Just don't expect me to waste my time rescuing him should the situation arise," she answered.

He nodded curtly. "I'll send him to meet you in the front hallway in fifteen minutes."

Grabbing the folder, Kira turned and stalked out of the room.

Badrick followed her. As soon as they stepped out the door, he grabbed her hand and pulled her around the corner where they were both concealed in shadows. His hands cupped her face, forcing her to look up at him. The storm brewing in his eyes told her what he thought of Kingsman's plan.

Kira held up a hand before he could speak. "Listen to me first before you say anything."

Badrick let out a heavy sigh but nodded.

"I'm not going to wait for him. I'll go in, take what I need, and leave."

"But the palace, Kira." Badrick spoke through gritted teeth. "He's sending you into the mouth of the lion. With a man who cannot be trusted."

"I've been doing this for seven years, Badrick. I know what I'm doing. It's not the first time I've been inside there, remember?"

"And do you suppose Pierceton isn't just going to turn around and kill you? He was working with Russell, for Christ's sake!" he hissed.

Kira covered his hands with hers. For the first time in her life she could see that look in his eyes. One filled with fire, burning wild with passion and worry. The look one lover gave another. She had never experienced it herself, but she had seen it and read about it in books. The authors were right. It did send her heart racing and her thoughts spiraling.

"Badrick," she said gently. So soft that it was barely past a whisper. Badrick tensed under her touch. Kira almost smiled. Finally, she was the one pulling *his* strings.

"He won't be able to turn around and hurt me because I plan to be far ahead of him. And if he falls behind and gets caught, then it's his fault, isn't it?" She repeated Kingsman's words as she lowered her hands.

Badrick contemplated her for a few more seconds before letting her go. Kira brushed by him and left without another word. She stalked to the front hallway. No sign of Pierceton. Her patience was on its last legs. If he didn't show up soon, she would throw him to the palace guards herself.

Finally she heard footsteps pounding up the hallway. Kira turned her head and glared at Pierceton as he made his way to her. Judging from his struggle to breathe, he must have run the entire length of the hideout. *Or had he come from somewhere else when he got Kingsman's message?* Kira's eyes narrowed as she contemplated him. He met her eyes, his gaze steady. Kira pushed away from the wall. "Don't expect me to wait for you," she snapped as she tugged her mask from her pocket and yanked it over her head. If he said something to her in reply, she didn't wait to hear it. She pushed through the doorway and into the cold night, focusing on blending into the darkness.

"We'll make our way to the palace on the roofs. We'll raise suspicion if we take the street through town."

Kira pulled up her hood and made her way to a pile of crates behind a store. She hoisted herself up and onto the roof. Not bothering to check that Pierceton was following, she bolted through the night, leaping from roof to roof.

A cool breeze rushed past her. This was why she carried out jobs for the guild. When she was on a mission, she felt free.

Kira made sure to keep her footing as she jumped from one building to the next with ease. The sound of Pierceton following behind her grew fainter. She was too fast and they both knew it.

Finally she came to a stop. Taking cover behind a chimney, she waited for him to catch up before peering out over the palace. Kira glanced at Pierceton from the corner of her eye. He slumped against the chimney, drawing in one ragged breath after another. With a roll of her eyes she focused back on the palace. The greater the importance of the person, the higher the floor he typically occupied. Although the head guard wasn't royalty, he was integral to the system. If he was married, they'd be breaking into a house, but since he lived in the castle, he must be single. His room would most likely be near the king and queen's, for their protection. So if she found their room, she'd find his.

She squinted and studied the windows. One set stood out. The pair was grand and the room beyond them well lit. Down the hall from those windows she could make out another, roughly half their size. That was most likely where the head guard would be.

She shot a glance at Pierceton and lowered her voice. "You ready?"

Pierceton's face grew serious as he locked eyes with her. "Let's go," he whispered back.

Chapter 15

Kira's cloak brushed across the stone walls. They had managed to get past the patrol outside the wall. They were careful to stay high and out of sight, using the darkness of the night to cloak them as they hoisted one another up onto the wall. The ineptitude of the guards was pitiful. Did they never bother to look anywhere besides right in front of them?

But the patrol inside was another story. With guards heavily planted throughout the palace, it was not wise to work on the floor. The only places they would have to hide were corners, pillars, and hallways. The patrol may have some flaws in their training, but they were not amateurish enough to miss seeing two thieves walking in the halls. If she had the choice, she'd avoid them entirely, but life was never that easy. She knew she'd have to deal with them eventually, although she would concentrate on making it inside first. Kira paused and peered up at the window set into the wall in front of them. The light behind the glass ceased and the window went black. Perfect timing.

If she remembered correctly, the patrols often made rounds around the palace with their hounds. She'd have to hurry before they caught her. She looked around silently in a search of a way to make her way up. The walls of the palace were too smooth for her to climb. She bit the inside of her cheek as she contemplated the second floor. All of the rooms on that level had balconies jutting out over the main floor. *Can we use those, somehow?*

A tall oak tree grew near the base of the wall. Kira headed for it and scampered up the trunk, a skill honed from years of climbing the trees that grew around the hideout. She glanced down and caught a glimpse of Pierceton in the dim light of the moon. He was watching her, his jaw hanging open. Kira crawled out onto one thick branch and slowly stood, holding onto another branch to steady herself. The balcony to what she hoped was the room of the king and queen loomed in front of her. She licked her lips and leapt. Like a cat, she landed softly and crouched on the stone floor.

When she waved at Pierceton, he started up, copying her movements. His slight clumsiness did not go unnoticed. If she had to compliment him on one thing, it would be his ability to stay silent. He jumped over the wall and landed in front of her, dropping to the floor as well. Kira waited, making sure that the couple inside was asleep. When she heard no sound or movement for a full minute, she jumped to her feet and hoisted herself up to the next ledge. This one was much smaller than the last. If she was right about the head guard's room being next to the suite of the king and queen, this was the room she was looking for. The ledge was so narrow here that she had to press her body up against the side of the building and hug it, both arms splayed out to the side.

Watching her foot placement, she peered inside the window. There was no sign of movement. At least not from what she could see. Should she let Pierceton go in first? That way, if someone was inside waiting for them, he was the one who would be caught. And she wouldn't hesitate to run and leave him behind if that happened. At the same time, this was still a job. Getting caught wasn't good for business. She would go first.

Her fingers fumbled with the lock before she snapped it off and opened the window with a light push. Kira shook her head in disgust. Why even bother with locks if they were going to be that weak?

She slipped over the ledge and squatted down as she scanned the room.

Empty. She looked back over her shoulder. Pierceton peered through the window, clearly waiting for her next command. When she gestured to him, he climbed into the room and slid onto the floor next to her.

"Search the room. Remember, only take what we came for." Kira started for the door.

Pierceton didn't move. "How do you know this is the head guard's room?"

Kira turned and looked at him. How dumb was this man? "Look at all the weapons around here, the books on his shelf. You wouldn't suppose that a servant would have a series of lessons on sword fighting, now would you?"

Pierceton's face darkened. She'd clearly made him feel as stupid as she believed him to be. Kira rolled her eyes again and headed out of the room. Now that she'd made sure he was busy, her chances of sneaking down the hall would be easier. There was something she had to do before she left.

Kira unlocked the door from the inside and peered out through the crack. Oddly, the corridor was deathly vacant. She opened the door wider and stepped into the hall cautiously, her senses heightening. *Where in the world did that damned guard go?*

Laughter erupted from below her. Common sense told her to go away from it. But she had thrown common sense out the window a while ago. Her descent of the staircase was quick and quiet. Once she made it to the lower floor, she heard footsteps coming down the hall. She ducked behind a potted tree pushed against the wall and crouched amongst the shadows. A servant rushed by, clutching a platter filled with fruits and cheeses. He was too focused to even notice her.

Normally Kira wasn't nervous on a job. But the lack of guards unsettled her. The wall was crawling with them, yet the palace wasn't? Was it that unheard of for someone to sneak past those outside?

Her back pressed to the wall, Kira inched around a corner. As she did, a door in front of her flew open. Startled, Kira scurried back around the corner, peering around it to see who was coming out. A man stepped from a room and gave a laugh before excusing himself. She couldn't make out his facial features very clearly, but she did manage to spot the emblem on his uniform. She had found the guard she was searching for.

Kira laced her way through the shadows as she followed him through the halls. The palace was a huge maze. A few years ago Kingsman had ordered her and Felix to carry out a mission that required sneaking in and stealing some documents. Every day for an entire month Felix made her draw the layout of the structure from the shingles down to the locks. Had it not been for that intense study of this place, she would have been lost.

The guard turned and stepped through a pair of double doors. If Kira remembered correctly the library laid on the other side. She waited for ten breaths before cracking open one of the doors. His back was turned and she slipped silently into the room and hid among the books.

Kira's fingers grazed the leather bindings as she skimmed by. Through the gaps in the towering wooden shelves she kept him in sight. He was somewhat broad, but she suspected strength was hiding under his uniform. She was aware of every one of his movements. If only she could see his face.

Placing one foot in front of the other, she stepped closer to him, moving with deadly silence as Maddox had taught her. Her eyes locked onto the man, measuring his movements the way Felix had trained her to do. She was light on her feet, thanks to Astien. She felt as if she were a tiger preparing to pounce on its prey.

Through the gap of books she stared at the back of her quarry. Nothing but the bookcase separated them. Kira took a deep breath to calm her heart then reached between the books to wrap her arm around his throat. He grabbed her elbow and spun around, obviously hoping to snap her arm. But instead of resisting the move, she spun with him and countered his attack, freeing herself from his grip. One by one he shoved the books off the shelves. Kira raced to the end of the bookcase and into the open, leaping over books sprawled all over the floor.

Muffled words echoed through the hallways outside. *They know I'm here.* She needed to get out while she could. She turned on her heel and charged out the door. Behind her she could hear the clanking sound of the head guard's boots on the floor. Forget the plan; it could always be carried out later. Right now she needed to escape while she had the opportunity.

Kira raked through her memories, trying to recall where the exits were placed. They would all be smothered with guards by now. She cursed under her breath. She should have known better to leave Pierceton alone. He must have been caught. Of course she'd stick to her promise and not worry about wasting her energy on saving him. Oh no, that would be the last thing she'd worry about. However, Pierceton had most likely ratted her out. Now that the palace was sure to be infested with guards on the lookout for her, she had few options and even less time to escape.

She raced down the hall with the head guard on her tail. Luckily, the mask still covered face so her identity remained unknown. Kira flew out one miraculously unguarded exit then turned and sprinted toward the training fields. It wasn't the route out of the palace she would have chosen, but it worked. Haystacks clearly used for archery practice dotted the area and she raced from one to the other, trying to get to the wall without being spotted. The tree she would use to escape the reach of the guard was so close. A few feet from the wall, she leapt, straining to reach the branches that hung down over the stone. Bark scraped across her fingertips as strong arms wrapped around her waist. Her attacker slammed her to the ground, ripping away her last chance to escape.

Chapter 16

The sharp blade of a knife dug into Kira's throat. She glared at the man pinning her down.

Keeping the knife pressed to her neck, he yanked the mask down. A dumbfounded look crossed his face as he stared down at her. "What are you doing here?" he hissed.

Kira's face twisted in a snarl as she bent her leg, attempting to knee him in the stomach. His grip loosened as he dodged her hit. Kira wiggled out of his grasp and jumped to her feet. Before she could run for the wall, he caught her by the arm.

"I said, what are you doing here?" His hold tightened.

"I could ask you the same damn thing, Chaol," she snapped. The sound of boots thudding across the grounds sent her heart racing. Kira turned and a sharp pain jolted through her hip. Chaol let go of her. She tried to limp away, but she couldn't move fast enough. The guards circled her and dragged her off to a cell.

In the cold, stone prison deep in the bowels of the palace, they stripped her of her weapons, confiscated her lock picks, and tossed her behind bars. The feel of the stone floor scraping against her hands made her hiss, but she brushed away the pain and staggered to her feet. The cells were small. Small enough that, even from the back wall, she could reach the bars, if barely. It was a cruel way to give the prisoners false hope that they were close to freedom. A guard locked a cuff attached to the cell wall around one wrist, but Kira refused to take her eyes off Chaol, standing in the doorway. He said nothing. If he thought the ache in his eyes was going to make everything better, he was wrong. She wasn't going to fall for his false sympathy.

When the guards had finished, Chaol nodded and his men came out of the cell, locked it behind them, and dispersed. It wasn't until the sound of their footsteps died away that he faced her, gripping the bars of the cell with both hands.

"Why are you here?" he asked again, this time in a soft voice.

"I think you are the one who should be answering that question," she growled. He ran a hand through his hair. Kira took a step closer, the chains rattling as they reached their maximum length, trying not to let the stench from the cell poison her nose with each breath. The way Chaol fought, his strength, it all made sense now. He wasn't like other men she had fought because he wasn't like other men. A swordsman was one thing, or even a patrol guard, but a head guard? That was not something he should have kept from her.

Chaol exhaled. "I was planning to tell you."

"Really? When was that going to be exactly?" Kira asked, her jaw tight. The eyes that met hers were filled with guilt, and somehow she didn't think his emotions were an act. He slipped his hand through the bars and grazed her cheek with his fingertips.

She jerked away. "I don't need your pity." Her voice was low and dangerous.

"It's not pity." He grimaced sadly.

Kira stayed silent as he dropped his hand. Neither of them said anything until footsteps echoed in the walkway. Chaol stepped back. The sound of struggling bounced off the walls, but Kira didn't need to look over. She already knew who it was.

A guard on either side of him, Pierceton was dragged past her and thrown into the cell next to hers, as roughly as she had been. He growled and scrambled to get out before they locked the shackles around his wrist, only to be shoved against the wall.

"Just give it up, Pierceton." Kira spoke evenly.

She stared blankly at the bars in front of her as the guards slammed Pierceton's cell door closed. He let out a frustrated groan as he dropped down in the corner. Chaol kept his gaze on Kira another moment then spun around and left.

"I was so damn close, Kira. Their dogs caught me at the last minute." Pierceton huffed in frustration. Kira rolled her eyes. If he knew what he was doing, he would have known that they always took their dogs around the perimeter every hour.

She slid down the wall to sit on the floor. There was nothing they could do now except try to think of a way out. Kira scanned the small, dimly-lit space. The only light came from a flickering torch out in the walkway. Weapons hung on the walls, torchlight flickering off the metal, including a sword with the longest blade she had ever witnessed. Just how many souls had they tortured for information with these weapons? Or were they hung there to tease the prisoners? Once again, giving them the false hope that they could somehow get a hold of those weapons and defend themselves, when in reality they had nothing except the clothes on their backs. The walls and floors were smooth. There was nothing to fashion a pick out of, and even if there were, without the use of both hands there was little she could do. *Wait until morning.* Perhaps the light would bring inspiration. Or salvation. Would Kingsman send someone to help them? Or would he consider this situation her own fault, as he had suggested Pierceton's falling behind her would be?

Kira shifted on the floor, trying to find a comfortable position. The cold stone wall pressed into her bruised hip, but she ignored the discomfort.

She wouldn't be able to get out of here if she couldn't think clearly, and for that she needed sleep. She closed her eyes and waited for oblivion to overtake her.

~ * ~

Judging from the thick darkness outside the small window set high up in the cell wall, Kira had only managed an hour or so of sleep before her hip woke her. The fall she'd taken, along with the hard, damp stone, added together to create a stiffness in her joints. She stretched out her legs in an attempt to get feeling back into them.

A muskiness in the air added a layer of thickness to the dirt swirling around. The place was utterly disgusting and she tried to keep her breathing shallow.

The sound of Pierceton shuffling around brought her head up sharply. *What is he doing?* Kira squinted into the darkness and could just make out a rough outline of his body. Pierceton knelt at the front of his cage, hunched over. Silently, she made her way over, until the chain restrained her from going any farther. The sound of a lock being picked rang in her ears. He couldn't possibly—

The lock clicked open and Pierceton stepped outside. How had he managed to get his hands on a lock pick? The guards had searched her from head to toe, inside every pocket and crease of her uniform. It just wasn't possible that he had hidden some kind of tool from them.

Pierceton strode to the wall across from his cell and snatched the sword she'd seen hanging there earlier. He gave a flick of his wrist, parrying the weapon through the air, before turning to face her. The look of kindness was gone. That mask he had been wearing for so long had been ripped away and burned. He walked over to her cell and looked down at her. The same goddamn way Russell used to do.

"You son of a bitch," Kira growled. He smirked and examined the blade in his hand, testing the sharpness with his finger. The bloodthirsty look that haunted her dreams appeared in front of her. He was a perfect reflection of Russell.

"I'm not sure why he wants me to keep you alive all of a sudden." Pierceton's voice held triumph. His eyes flicked from the blade to her face. Shivers ran down her spine. Kira pushed back her shoulders. She couldn't let him see how much his words affected her. The fear in Pierceton's eyes when she fought Russell had been real. If she could make him feel like that again, she would be the one with the power.

"Come into this cell and try to kill me. See what happens." Kira staggered to her feet.

Pierceton chuckled. Maybe he wasn't as stupid as she'd thought. "You're dangerous Kira. I admit it; you could kill me with your bare hands if you wanted." He stepped back from the bars. "That's why I'll leave you in here where you can't do any damage to me or anyone else."

"Coward." She spat the word out as she lunged toward him. The metal shackle around her wrist dug into her skin and she bit her lip to keep from crying out. If only she could smack that grin off his face. But Pierceton was right. There was nothing she could do chained up inside this cell.

"I'm not a coward, Kira. I'm just smart." He tapped the edge of the sword against the metal bar. "No sense wearing myself out fighting you when the king will take care of you soon enough."

Kira hadn't even realized how tightly she clutched the chain hanging from the wall until a stinging pain spread across her palm.

Pierceton's cold laugh echoed off the stone walls. He touched the side of one hand to his temple in salute before whirling around and disappearing into the thick darkness of the hallway.

Kira pounded the wall with her free fist. She was done being played. She was done with dealing with the cowards who were trying to kill her.

The door at the end of the hallway clanged shut behind Pierceton.

Fury rose up in her thick and strong. Maybe there was nothing she could do while she was shut up in here. But he better hope he was right about the king dealing with her before she could escape. Because if she did get out of here alive, his life would be worth less than the dirt that hung in the air of this loathsome place.

Chapter 17

For what seemed like hours, Kira fought with all her might to free herself. Her feet began to sting, her legs grew tired, and the cuff did not loosen. She looked around for anything to make a lock pick out of, but Pierceton had left her nothing. The door to the entrance of the prison cracked open, to her annoyance. If she was making too much noise, they would just have to deal with it. They were lucky she had one arm chained, or she'd reach out and strangle them if they came to shut her up.

When they did come by, it was only to throw her food through a slot in the door. As if she could eat it. Kira didn't move as they stared at her before turning away. When they realized Pierceton's cell was empty, pandemonium broke out. The guards shouted back and forth, raising their voices more each time they responded.

"The king will have my head!"

"You're not the only one who will have his head missing!"

Kira heard them march to her cell.

"*You.*"

When she raised her head, they were glaring at her, most likely trying to intimidate her into providing them with information. It didn't work in the slightest.

"It was you, wasn't it? You helped him escape!"

Kira stayed sitting, her back against the wall, although her aching joints begged her to move. "Now why would I help him and not get myself out? We are thieves. We think of nothing and of no one but ourselves. Do you think I'd waste my breath and let him live over me?"

The guard's palms smacked the bars, the sound echoing through the tiny room. Kira didn't twitch. Did they actually think they could scare her?

"That's a lie; you're clearly covering for him."

"And you're clearly lacking intelligence. How about instead of wasting your time and mine pestering me with these useless questions, you do us both a favor and find and kill that bastard of a thief?"

They had left her alone after that. Kira spent her time trying to get feeling back into her joints. She longed to run, to climb and fight until she could no longer stand. Yet here she was cramped up in this excuse of a cell. She had tried to stand and walk back and forth, but she had only managed to take a few steps before needing to stop and walk the opposite way. The action was driving her crazy rather than easing her pain. So instead she tried to sleep until they decided to come back for her. That wasn't easy either as she faced the dilemma of one arm being chained to the wall. Lying on her back was the only comfortable position, but after awhile, the inability to shift left her muscles aching.

How long would it be before they came to fetch her? Perhaps she could manage to escape once they were about to haul her to her death. Kira furrowed her brows. *What if I can't?* She shook her head. *No. I won't think like that.* Gathering what little hope she had left, she closed her eyes, rested her head against the wall, and waited. Silence. That's all she heard. Yet it inspired her. She'd stay silent. They were bound to interrogate her again, and when the time came silence would be her answer.

Chapter 18

It wasn't long before Kira was pulled out for interrogation. Two guards dragged her from her cell and up to the Council's room. After she had entered, the guards shoved her down onto a seat, both keeping a hand on one of her shoulders. She didn't dare give Chaol a glance as he stood in the corner of the room. Rather, she focused on sticking to her plan. *Silence, give them nothing but silence.*

"As you know, your comrade has somehow managed to escape our custody." The councilman linked his wrinkled hands together above the desk. "You wouldn't happen to know how that happened, now would you?"

It took all Kira had not to correct him. Pierceton was far from a comrade. Truth be told, she wanted him dead more than the palace did.

The councilman cleared his throat.

"If you cooperate with us, this will end much quicker, and result in less pain for you. So let me reword this. Uh, Kira," he paused as he looked down at her file on his desk, "*How* did you help your comrade escape?"

Her silence drove them insane. Just as she had hoped. Silence could be a man's weakness and a man's strongest weapon.

"Will a hefty bag of gold make you open your mouth?"

Silence.

He attempted another approach. "If you refuse to work with us, we will not hesitate to cut your life short."

Still silence.

"Perhaps we shall try something else. Something rarely ever offered. We will let you leave this palace, alive and in once piece, should you give us the answers we are looking for."

If she thought for a moment they spoke the truth she might consider it. But she knew they were incapable of such so she held her tongue. Just seeing them irritated was enough for her.

"You can't stay silent forever," one hissed at her.

Kira kept her cool composure and let a smirk dance across her lips.

The action sent the councilman over his limits and he reached over the table and smacked her across the mouth. Chaol winced then schooled his features so quickly she wondered if he really had. Would he step forward and intervene? The councilman was the one who made lawful decisions when the king was unavailable, including whether or not Chaol would keep his title, so it would be difficult for him to speak out against the man.

Blood dripped down her chin. The councilman leapt to his feet, rounded the table, and hauled her up. Face red, he gripped her tightly and slammed her against the wall. Her head bounced against the stone so hard her ears rang. Anger quickly rose from her stomach. If only she could break free of her cuffs and reach up to—

"Stop." Chaol stepped between them. Kira peered around to the councilman. What would it feel like to give all these men a taste of her skills? Blood stinging cold on her lips fueled her imagination. Just a punch or kick in the jaw would be good enough.

"What are you doing?" Chaol pushed the councilman back a step. "Move out of the way and remember your place. Hitting her will only make her resent you more. You'll never get information from her that way."

"And you think you could get it from her any other way? She's as stubborn as a mule." The councilman spun on his heel and strode back to the table. "I'm done with her for today. You have one chance, Sir Chaol. You have a night to think of a way to get her to talk. If you fail, tomorrow she will die."

Chapter 19

CHAOL PACED HIS ROOM. How long did it take to retrieve one prisoner? Surely it had been nearly a half an hour by now. He glanced out the window. Given that the shadows cast by the trees in the courtyard had barely moved, it had likely only been fifteen minutes or so. A long, dreadful fifteen minutes.

This was his last chance. No, this was *Kira's* last chance. Should she decide not to work with him, there was no doubt she'd be hauled off to be slaughtered. The image sent a shiver through his body. The thought of her bloodied body haunted his mind. Weak, limp, pale. Dead. And she would be dead. The palace would show her no mercy. They'd kill her in the most painful way possible. She'd scream one of those blood-curdling screams that made a man freeze in his tracks. And he'd hear it as he was forced to watch the life drain from her.

"Sir, they are here."

Chaol regained his sense of mind and motioned for them to enter. Kira walked in, never once meeting his gaze. Instead she focused on the windows. The same windows she had snuck through. Was she planning another escape?

"You may leave now."

She cringed at the sound of Chaol's voice. The door closed behind the guards, but she still refused to look at him. Chaol gave a frustrated sigh as he rubbed his temples. He did not want it to come to this. He had hated her in the beginning. Every move she made, the sight of her, drove him crazy him because of the association she had with the guild. But he was stupid enough to help her. Because he'd been stupid enough to let his guard fall. The ultimate irony for a head guard.

"What are you going to do? Interrogate me again?" She spat out the words.

"Actually, yes, I am." Chaol made his way to the table in the center of the room. "Please sit."

Kira's eyes flashed fire as she remained standing. He tried to give her the benefit of the doubt—that she didn't sit because she had been cramped for so long and needed to stretch, not because it was the opposite of what he asked.

Chaol clasped his hands on the table and didn't ask again, unwilling to give her the satisfaction of refusing to obey his order twice. "Your friend. How did he escape?"

"It's more like how did *your* men miss a lock pick?"

Kira shifted her weight. Although she hid it quickly, he caught the wince. She was in pain. Had she hurt herself when he'd hauled her off the wall, or had his guards been overly rough with her? Chaol's jaw tensed at the thought.

He shoved back his chair and stood. "I know you're mad at me." He came around the table and stopped in front of her. "But being angry and not answering me isn't going to help you."

"I've said it once and I'll say it again, you're nothing but a tool to me," she growled.

He hid his own wince, although her words had smacked him across the face as surely as the councilman had slapped her. Just as he'd started to earn her trust he had to throw her into a cell. Iron bars no longer separated them in that moment, although it felt as if they were still there, becoming thicker with each passing second. "You are aware that the punishment for breaking into the palace is a death sentence?"

Kira said nothing.

Chaol gave another sigh and ran his fingers through his hair. He cursed to himself, knowing he was about to do something he would regret. Then again, knowing her was something he regretted so he was getting used to the feeling. "Turn around."

Her eyes narrowed as she studied him. Chaol held up his hand. A key on a ring dangled from his finger.

Kira bit her lip, obviously still not sure she could trust him. Then she turned around.

Chaol slid the key into the hole in the cuffs and twisted it. The shackles around her wrists fell off with a clank. He shoved the key back into his pocket and threw the cuffs into a chest at the foot of his bed. "Hurry up and leave before I change my mind." He jerked his head in the direction of the windows.

Kira stood as if frozen in place, rubbing her wrist where the metal had scraped her raw.

A shiver rattled down Chaol's spine as her intense gaze settled on his face. It wasn't impossible that she could kill him, should she choose to do so. He was defenseless. No sword, no weapon, no drive. Even though he had the strength to over-power her, he doubted he would be able to bring himself to fight her should she attack.

As she walked towards him, Chaol felt as if he was being backed into a corner, even though, through sheer force of will, he was able to hold his ground. "You're taking me to Silas." There was no room for question in her words. Her presence alone was overwhelming. It clutched at his throat, reminding him of who she was and everything she stood for.

Just before she reached him, she spun around and stalked to the window.

Chaol frowned and followed her. When he reached her, he grabbed her by the shoulders, yanking her back around. "You went to The Grottos when I told you not to. You promised me."

Disgust twisted across her face. Kira's arms shot up between his and then out, knocking his hands off of her. "My lie is nothing compared to yours, *Sir* Chaol."

The accusation ripped through him like an arrow. He assumed she could be ruthless with her strikes. He hadn't assumed her words could be just a wounding.

Kira lifted her chin. "Meet me tonight by the bakery. And bring my belongings." She scrambled over the window ledge and crouched on the balcony outside, peering back in at him. "Oh, and if any of my weapons have so much as a scratch on them, you will witness first-hand the damage I can do with them."

Chapter 20

Chaol's leg shook as he leaned against the wall of the bakery, not that he was anxious. His body was tense as Kira's weapons stung against his forearms and against his calf. He couldn't have easily walked out of the castle with her weapons in hand; he'd had to sneak them out. So he was left with no choice but to wear what he could and stuff the rest in his boots. He hadn't realized how deadly her blades were. As he left the gate, Chaol saluted the guards. He made the mistake of flicking his wrist a little too much, and paid the price with a sharp prick to his arm. Thankfully no one heard his indrawn breath, and he'd walked stiffly and awkwardly—while still attempting to move quickly—the rest of the way to her.

He didn't even know if she had made it out alive. The guards wouldn't have hesitated to kill her once she was out on her own. Chaol's official statement read that she had managed to escape her cuffs and knock him unconscious while his back was turned. Of course he'd been reprimanded and a punishment would follow. However, he'd made sure to cover his tracks, even hitting the back of his head with the blunt end of a dagger hard enough to leave a large bump.

Kira was a wanted woman with a hefty bounty over her head. It was no problem at all to concoct the story of her power. He made her sound like a beast, vicious and agile. As if she were another being, something not quite human. And with Chaol's high title, it was easy to persuade his crowd that was he said was true. Which didn't mean his guards wouldn't attempt to strike her down if they saw her. And despite what he'd told them, she was not invincible. He knew her power. Still, like everyone else, she had her weaknesses and limits.

He searched the forest in front of him. Kira was definitely strong and smart. His mind flashed back to the library. He hadn't even realized she was sneaking up on him until her arm was around his neck. He was lucky he had managed to catch her when she tried to escape back over the wall. Her speed was undeniable and her ability to keep her silence under extreme pressure shocked even him. He had underestimated her. And if she was half as skilled as she made herself out to be, he needed to trust she'd be okay. He was definitely not anxious.

The sound of rustling sped up his heart rate. He dropped into an attack position until he recognized her figure emerging from the bushes. She appeared calm and collected. Her mouth was a firm line and her eyes hard as she casually brushed off the leaves stuck to her clothes. Color had returned to her face and the dirt and stench of the cell had been stripped from her. However, it would seem, from the look of contempt she sent him, that the memory of the nights she had spent there hadn't been.

"I'm glad to see you're okay." Chaol felt his worry bleed through his words.

Kira didn't respond. Frustration grew inside him. Any other time he could not have cared less if someone had grown angry with him. They'd talk about it, the person would accept his apology or not, and they would both move on. But not her. She had given him fair warning in the beginning; he was nothing but a tool. But some foolhardy part of him had begun to fall for this woman in front of him. Their eyes met, and something flashed through them before she shut it down. Against his better judgment, he was enticed by her and, for that brief moment, she appeared enticed by him, too. No, he knew it. The emotion was real and raw. And he'd seen those flashes before. They had eaten at him, breaking down whatever bitterness he had towards her. How foolish he was for letting that happen.

"You can get us in to talk to Silas, yes?" She ignored his comment about her well-being and held out her hand, palm up. He couldn't bring himself to believe that she hated him, despite her demeanor. He knew a piece of her heart was falling for him.

"I can as easily as the next person. It's not like I constantly go down there." He gladly removed her weapons and returned them. "Are you sure you even want to do this?"

There was a click as Kira fastened one of the blades to her forearm. She held her arm up. While she inspected the blade, Chaol's chest clenched at the sight of spotted bandages wrapped around her wrist where the shackles had rubbed her skin until it was raw and bloody. She should never have gone to the palace.

"That question was answered a long time ago." Kira silently retracted her blade and strapped on the other before pulling her sleeves over them. Once she had finished equipping herself with the rest of her weapons, she turned and strode away without a backward glance at him. Chaol sighed. They would get nowhere if they continued on like this.

"Kira, stop." He followed her into the forest. To his surprise she listened. This late at night, the commotion of the town was hushed, and if anyone had been about, the cover of trees would keep them out of view. If there was a place and time to talk about their situation, it was here and now.

"There has to be a way to fix this."

"I'm not in the mood for this conversation."

Kira started to turn on her heel, but he snatched her hand, careful not to touch her wounded wrists. "We won't get anywhere acting like this."

"I guess you should have thought of that sooner." She yanked her hand free. Her eyes searched his. It was almost as if she was desperately searching for some sort of answer, an excuse, anything to justify letting her defenses down.

"I did it to protect you," he admitted in a low voice.

Kira took a deep breath, as though to calm herself. "To protect me? Or to protect yourself?"

"Maybe it was to protect myself, in the beginning." Heat crept up his neck. "But I swear that changed. I did start to do it for you."

"What good would it do me?" The uncharacteristic vulnerability in her voice twisted through his gut like a knife.

"I knew you'd be stupid enough to come to the palace to try and get answers I don't have. And I was planning to help you escape. Which I did."

"Why help me? I'm just a thief."

She'd let her guard down enough that Chaol dared to step forward. He didn't stop until he was close enough to feel the heat radiating off her body. Her face was inches from his. He fully expected her to move back, but she held her ground. All it would take was the strength to reach out … "Because I was foolish enough to fall in love with you."

~ * ~

Kira's body went numb. Was this what it was supposed to feel like? She had never had such words bestowed upon her, but she'd heard girls gossiping at the taverns. Some said their breath would be taken away, others said their knees went weak or their heart began to pound. Yet she couldn't feel any of those reactions.

His gaze intense, Chaol reached out and cupped her cheek. Her skin tingled where he touched her, but somehow it wasn't painful. The way Badrick had made her feel when she was younger seemed so different. That had been more powerful, more controlling than the way Chaol made her feel.

"Don't lie to yourself, Kira. You know you are drawn to me too. I've seen it in your eyes. I notice how you react when I get close; I see how hurt you are. You can't feel that unless part of you has fallen the way I have fallen for you. Run away with me, let's forget all this."

His words were sweet like honey, but Kira fought to keep her wits about her. Something had changed about him. The way he talked, the pitch of his voice, made the hairs on the back of her neck stand up. She should be happy, but she couldn't be. Something wasn't right, she wasn't safe here. No one was safe here. "I feel sick," she mumbled, avoiding his gaze. It wasn't a lie. Something in his eyes had made her weak. His fingers left a trail as they slipped from her cheek to her shoulder. The action made her shiver.

He said something in response, but she couldn't hear him. The ground shook, a boom vibrated through the air, and she was thrown to the ground. She struggled to sit up, and squinted to see through the trees, forgetting whatever moment had just passed between the two of them. Smoke stained the clouds and a horrible smell plagued the air. *The hideout.*

Kira glanced at Chaol. He moaned and rolled over. He was alive. She scrambled to her feet and started for home. Kira had never run so fast in her life. Her body trembled but it still somehow managed to function. Her legs ached, her lungs burned. Limbs of bushes and trees clawed at her as she passed, but she was too numb to notice the pain.

Slowly a thick black cloud crawled its way through the forest. The ashes made her gasp for breath, but she didn't slow. Once the trees cleared out she stopped and tried to make out an outline. Her eyes watered and she pawed at them. She didn't have time for this.

Kira blindly stumbled forward. Her foot caught on what she thought was a tree limb and she slammed into the ground. She cursed until she found out what—actually whom— she had tripped over.

"Astien!" She scrambled over to him. "Astien, what happened?"

The redhead coughed and his eyes fluttered open. His pale skin was caked in ash and dirt and blood. The sight of it made the sickness in her stomach swirl again, nearly making her throw up. "Everyone made it out; we knew the attack was coming," he mumbled.

Kira pressed a finger to the pulse point on his neck. Luckily it was still strong and constant. "You'll be all right. Can you walk?" A cloud of smoke brushed by her and she coughed. He nodded and she helped him up. She'd have to get answers out of him later. "Where is everyone?" She kicked at a pile of debris in their path so they could move forward.

"In a cave just west of here; we've been preparing. We've known for a while now."

Kira was just about to open her mouth to respond when a voice calling her name cut her off. Through the trees Chaol made his way closer to them. The sight of him made her pull Astien closer. Though her heart screamed at her to run, she fought against it. Right now Astien needed her.

"I'll explain later," she said as Chaol came up and took the other side of Astien.

Suddenly Astien looked at her. Beneath the dirt, his pale cheeks went white. "Badrick!" he cried. He nearly pushed Kira to the ground as he turned to go back. "Badrick's in there! He went to get you. He thought you were in there."

The tears streaming down the boy's face nearly made her start crying along with him. Their eyes met. She knew as well as he did that Badrick couldn't have survived. But there was a part of her that clung to hope, that would die trying to find him, if that's what it took.

He ripped free of Chaol's grip. Kira's arm wrapped around his waist and she yanked him back. Astien fought against her, but her grip was like iron. She slammed him into a tree, perhaps harder than needed, and pushed against him. "Astien." No response. Kira took his face in her hands, calling out to him softly. He froze, his chest heaving.

"Astien, I'll go get him." She ran a shaky hand through his soft waves. Astien looked down at her, tears pouring down his dirt-stained cheeks. "I promise I'll find him."

He nodded slowly and his body slumped against the tree. Kira gave a nod towards Chaol. Gently, he tugged Astien to him and slid an arm around his thin shoulders.

Chaol will take him to safety. Kira swallowed back a lump in her throat. "Show him the way to the cave. I won't return until I'm back with Badrick."

Kira watched for a moment as the two of them staggered back into the forest. When they were out of sight, she turned on her heel and ran headfirst into the smoke.

Chapter 21

Kira gathered all her strength and pulled the rocks off the trap door one by one. With a final heave, the door was clear. Immediately she flung it open and dropped down inside. Outside the smoke had polluted the air, flames roared, and debris was everywhere. Compared to where she found herself now, that had been heaven.

Inside, Kira could barely see two paces in front of herself, the smoke was so thick. Not only did her eyes water from burning, but her lungs and throat were inflamed with pain that haunted every breath. Her instinct was to stay low, so that's what she did.

Kira racked her brain. Where could Badrick be? Astien said that he had been looking for her. Her head shot up. There were two places he could have gone.

She ran for the training room. As she approached, she could see inside the open door and her heart shattered. Parts of the ceiling were missing, the dummies were now simply wicks for fires, the sparring area was drowned in dirt and smoke. But she couldn't see Badrick.

Everything rumbled around her. Kira stumbled and fell as the training room collapsed before her eyes. She scrambled to her feet and forced herself to run the opposite way and to not look back. If she did, she wasn't sure what she'd do. There wasn't much time left before the whole hideout collapsed.

Kira slammed into her bedroom door and it flew open. Flames leapt toward her and she let out a furious cough. The smoke had begun to settle into her lungs, making her breathing ragged and inconstant. For the first time, she noticed that the bandages on her wrist were singed and her hands were burnt and bleeding. Soot covered her hair and face; the heat smothered her to the point where she thought she might be on fire herself. It wouldn't be much longer before she'd be lying motionless on the floor. At least she would have died trying; she would have died knowing she and Badrick had sacrificed for each other.

Kira called out his name and stepped farther into her bedroom. Her chest clenched. Through the thick haze, she could make out a body on the floor. Debris piled around it hid everything except for the pink fabric he held in his hand. She called out to him again as she shook him violently, but he didn't respond. Flames licked up the walls and across the ceiling. Could she carry him out of here? She'd have to give it her best shot. For him, for her, for everyone.

Kira hauled Badrick out of the debris and flung him onto her back. As quickly as she could, she staggered towards the entrance. Her heart pounded even harder as the rumbling became more frequent. Drawing on the adrenaline coursing through her, Kira snatched the pink fabric from Badrick and used it to tie his arms around her shoulders to free up her hands.

Her foot hit the first step and she began her climb. The weight of Badrick pulling back on her made her body scream in pain, but she pushed on. She was thankful for the countless times he had made her carry the heaviest thing he could find to build up her muscles. And for all the times she'd woken up in the morning, unable to move, covered in bruises and drowning in agony. Those trials added up to help her in this moment. She'd definitely have to thank him once he woke up. If he woke up.

Hard, dry dirt under her hands was the most amazing feeling in the world. The richness of soil and pebbles under her fingernails meant one thing. Life.

The chance to enjoy it was cut short as the roar of the hideout collapsing behind her thundered in her ears. With a last burst of strength, Kira hauled herself and Badrick out into the open and dragged them both as far away as she could. One thing and one thing only was going through her mind. *Keep Badrick safe.*

Kira took her cloak and wrapped it around them both as a shield from the flying debris and smoke. She kept the cloak over her head and let the darkness envelop her, unable to watch the destruction of the only home she had ever known.

Finally the sounds died down. No more rumbling, no more crackling, it was all over. The tears that ran down her face were a mix of smoke and sadness. Her heart sank and her body went limp. All the mementos of her childhood were gone.

She raised Badrick's hands over her head and weakly untied his wrists. Then she froze. The soft silk, the beautiful lace. He had saved her nightgown, the gift she had always cherished. The touch of the fabric against her hand made her recollect herself.

Kira wiped her eyes with the back of her hand then pressed her ear to his chest. A soft thudding against her ear filled her with hope. He was still alive.

Quickly, she threw him onto her back again. Her arms slid under his knees to hold him up and his hands, still clutching the nightgown, hung in front of her. Kira took a deep breath and headed to the spot Astien had told her the men had taken refuge.

Chapter 22

They were coming. Chaol pressed his back to the wall of the cave as Kira and Badrick reached the entrance.

"Back up! Back up!" Kingsman roared as Kira stumbled inside. As gently and as quickly as possible, she laid Badrick down onto a bedroll. Instantly, Maddox showed up and began to work on him. Through the crowd Chaol watched Kira crawl to the corner of the wall and collapse on the cave floor. Never before had he seen her in such a state. Her hands were bloody and cut, her entire body trembled, and her chest heaved with each breath she struggled to take. Even from where he hid in the shadows he could hear the rasp in her breaths and the dryness in her coughs.

Felix came up to her and lifted her up in his arms, barking at Astien to get another bedroll.

She let out a small chuckle. "It's been years since you've held me like this." Gently, Kira raised her hand to Felix's cheek and swiped her thumb across it, catching a tear. The soot and dirt spread across his cheek at the motion, but he didn't appear to notice. He looked at Kira as if she were his own daughter.

Chaol's chest clenched. The feelings these thieves had for each other ran deep. He assumed that Felix, if he was like the other men in the guild, was not one to express a sign of weakness, let alone cry. And from the shocked look on Kingsman's face, he was just as surprised.

"Don't cry, my little thief," Kira whispered to the man holding her. Felix winced at her words. Chaol wondered at the term of endearment, and the reaction it solicited. *A nickname, most likely.*

Astien came to Felix's rescue with the bedroll. He glanced at his friend's tear-stained face then looked away quickly. The scene unraveling before Choal jolted his heart. These people weren't thieves recovering from a battle. They were a family mourning over their wounded members and the loss of their home.

~ * ~

A few hours later, Kira awoke from a restless sleep and rose from her mat. The burns had been treated and were already healing. The dirt and ashes had been washed from her hair and skin. Her throat still burned, but she was told they had sent Chaol out to get tea and honey to help ease the pain, as well as whatever other supplies he could get his hands on. In truth, she had forgotten he was there. Her mind was so focused on everything that had happened, it hadn't crossed her mind that he had witnessed her return.

"What was Badrick doing holding this?" Astien touched the pink silk.

"My nightgown," she explained with a soft smile. "He went back to get it."

"I can't believe I had forgotten about it. I'll take it and put it—"

"No." She stopped him with a hand on his arm before he could tug the gown from Badrick's clenched fist.

Astien's eyebrows rose.

Kira studied him. His face was clean and fresh; he appeared to be back to his normal self, she was happy to see. She dropped her gaze to Badrick. Somehow, he had managed to escape with only a few cuts and very few burns. The most deadly injury was a scrape to the forehead where something, most likely a rock falling from the ceiling, had grazed him.

"Let him keep it." She let go of Astien and stepped away.

Kira felt his eyes on her. Likely he was wondering, as she was, what the relationship was between her and Badrick. The connection between the two of them was strong. It was more than a simple childhood crush, although she wouldn't have been able to put into words what it was, exactly, if pressed. She looked up. Astien's gaze, resting on her face, was intense. Warmth rushed into her cheeks. *Don't do it, Astien. Don't give your heart to me. I'm not worthy of it.* He'd been hurt so badly before; she couldn't bear the thought of causing him more pain.

When their eyes met, his cheeks flushed slightly too, but he looked away quickly and cleared his throat. "You want to see what we've got set up?"

"Will he be all right by himself?" Kira worked to keep her voice even.

"He won't wake up for a bit. We won't be gone long."

Kira hesitated before tearing herself from Badrick's side and following Astien even deeper into the cave. They were in the middle of the forest, so someone finding them was unlikely, but if they did, the thieves had made sure to set up camp far enough back that they wouldn't be seen. Still, the tunnel they were in seemed to continue on for miles. Torches had been wedged into the stone walls to light the pathway, and a few of the boxes they'd used to bring possessions from the hideout were scattered about. Surprisingly, the air wasn't too stuffy or humid. Somewhere above them there must be some kind of opening. She certainly wasn't complaining about having fresh air. She took the chance to take her first deep breath since she had brought Badrick back. Though the stinging air caused pain it was a pain she was happy to feel. It meant she was alive. It meant she had kept Badrick safe.

When Astien had told her that they had been preparing, he wasn't joking. The cave widened to reveal more boxes of supplies. Tents were set up, ready to be used. While she looked around, Astien filled a plate for her with bread and cheese. He handed it to her and nodded at one of the tents. "This one's mine."

Kira gladly took the plate and followed him into the tent. Inside wasn't anything amazing, not that she had expected it would be, but it was roomier than it looked from the outside. It could have easily slept two. From their close relationship, she suspected the empty bedroll was for Badrick once he came to.

Kira made herself comfortable on Badrick's bedroll while Astien sat on his own. Her stomach cried as she eyed the various cheeses and bread. She couldn't remember the last time she'd had a decent meal. Or eaten at all. Her mind couldn't decide what to eat first.

She felt Astien watching her again as she picked up a wedge of cheddar and took a bite.

"Say Kira, there isn't much age difference between us, is there?"

She looked up at him as she popped a piece of bread into her mouth. She waited until she swallowed before answering him.

"You're twenty-one, right? And I'll be the same age near the end of the year, so no, not really." She cocked her head to the side. "Why the sudden interest in my age?"

Astien's fierce eyes met hers. Suddenly, the atmosphere changed dramatically. *This isn't going to be a normal conversation.*

He leaned forward and plucked the bread from her hand, placing it on the tray before removing it from her lap and setting it on the ground. The whole time he kept his eyes locked with hers.

"You're going to have to find a suitable husband soon," he mumbled, moving toward her.

Kira nearly jumped at how close he was. His hand settled on hers, his nose grazing against her own. The action was so unexpected that her cheeks flushed again. She and Astien had always been close, but she had never imagined them to be anything more than friends.

"What are you doing?" She tried to lean back, but she barely moved before the cloth of the tent pressed against her back. He had her cornered.

"You know it's true. So why don't you pick me?" He spoke calmly, not quite touching his lips to hers.

She furrowed her brows together and uncertainty flickered across his face.

Astien swallowed. "I'm strong, I can protect you. I'd give my life for you, Kira. If it's money you're worried about, we both know we will have enough to live off of if we just do a few jobs."

"Astien—"

He grazed his thumb over her lips. "Let me prove to you how much I care for you, Kira."

"Astien, we can't." She pushed a palm against his chest, her voice hardening slightly.

"Why not? No one else is here, they're all out hunting. Is it that guard? To be quite frank, I don't trust him."

Kira scrunched up her nose at the memory of the moment she and Chaol had shared in the forest. She knew Chaol had this ridiculous hope that it had changed everything between the two of them for the good, when in reality it had done the opposite. It proved to her that whatever feelings she had for him were real, but weak.

"No, it's not him." She avoided his gaze.

"Then what's wrong? Are you in love with another man?" His breath whispered across her lips and she shivered.

"No ... Yes ... I don't know."

"Is it Badrick?"

Kira's heart skipped a beat at the mention of his name. "I said, I don't know." She placed her other hand on his chest and shoved harder.

He sank back on his haunches. "How could you not know? I understand why you would fall for him, he's a good man."

"Astien, I—"

They both froze at the sound of footsteps echoing through the cave. Astien looked over at the opening of the tent, giving her the opportunity to slip around him and break away. She left the tent and smoothed down her hair, staticky from contact with the side of the tent. In the entrance way, Kingsman supported Badrick at his side. Kira's heart fluttered. She paused. Were her feelings true? The answer came immediately. She ran to him.

Badrick gave a weak smile as she reached him and threw herself in his arms. They both stumbled back, gently bumping against the wall. Kira melted at the feel of him, one hand stroking her back and the other tangled in her hair. The sound of his heartbeat was strong; the warmth of his touch was overwhelming. It all nearly made her cry as she sighed his name.

He pressed his lips to the top of her head.

"Glad to see you're okay." Astien spoke softly.

Kira stepped out of Badrick's arms and looked back at him. She knew the composure was a ruse. He loved Badrick like a brother. On the inside he had to want to cry as much as she did.

"Glad to see you're all okay too." Badrick offered him a relieved smile, but there was a question in the gaze that rested on her face.

Could he see that her feelings for him had changed? Kira's eyes met his over Astien's shoulder as the two men embraced then Astien helped Badrick make his way over to a chair. As he assisted him to sit down, Astien glanced at her, a small grin on his face. The pieces clicked together.

Astien wasn't in love with her; he wasn't trying to marry her. He knew her better than anyone and understood that she'd been having a hard time sorting her feelings out. He had been trying to help her in the tent. If it hadn't been for him, she'd still be lost in a maze of confusion; because of him she knew what her heart truly wanted.

Chapter 23

CHAOL SCANNED THE KITCHEN TO see if anyone was around. Once he was sure the cook and maids had stepped out for the moment, he began to search the cabinets and drawers. A glass jar of honey glistened in the light when he opened the third pair of cabinet doors. He quickly slipped it into his leather satchel before moving on to find the herbs to make tea. He'd have to sneak his way into the garden.

He drew in a calming breath as he made his way down the halls. The palace was oddly quiet. No, not quiet. It was dead silent. Chaol slowed his steps as the bricks turned to grass. He tilted back his head. The smoke that had hung heavy in the air for hours was slowly dissipating. The entire town had been shaken up. Some were terrified, others confused as to what to think. Rumors were flying that it was the hideout of the thieves' guild that had been targeted which, again, stirred emotions. Many were surprisingly upset at the news. No one had known any of the members well, but they had worked with them. They claimed the guild members had done what they were asked to do and nothing more. They never left with more than they had been hired to take. Others only saw the black side of their work. They were nothing more than thieves, low lives, scum. Those people were happy to think the hideout had been left in ruins.

Chaol tore his eyes from the sky to search through the garden. He wasn't an expert when it came to herbs, but he knew enough to get by.

He took what he recognized and stuffed it into his satchel. Chaol made his way through the garden and followed the side of the wall until he came to the courtyard. There he fixed the strap on his satchel and moved towards the gate.

A few feet outside the compound, he felt a pair of eyes on him. He silently reached for his sword and circled. His gaze went to the trees and he peered through the leaves. Then he saw him.

Pierceton stepped into view. He stood casually, his bow resting on his back, one hand wrapped around the branch above him and the other at his side. The silence between the two of them made Chaol want to bristle.

The look Pierceton gave him was unreadable. There seemed to be a mixture of respect, powerful thirst, and disappointment all mixed together, making his eyes dark and glittering. Chaol took a deep breath and turned his back to him. Although nothing had been said between the two men, the message was clear. He needed to step up his game, and fast.

~ * ~

Kira managed to convince Kingsman to let her take Badrick out on a walk. It hadn't been easy, and the agreement came with a condition, that someone went with them. That way, if they were attacked, they would have a strong pair of fists to back them up. Maddox happily volunteered to accompany them.

Kira was about to step out the mouth of the cave when Chaol walked up. Beside her, Badrick must have sensed her stiffening up because he slid an arm around her and pulled her to his side. Chaol looked her up and down before his gaze flicked over to Badrick.

"I'm glad to see you've recovered." He bowed slightly.

Kira's jaw tightened. Was the kindness in his voice nothing more than an act?

"As we are glad to see you've managed to stay alive." Kingsman came out of the cave to stand beside her. His smile was welcoming, but Kira knew her father too well to fall for it. Hopefully Chaol was smart enough not to push his boundaries.

"I managed to find the supplies you asked for. Please, if you need more, do not hesitate to ask." Chaol passed the satchel to Kingsman, who opened the flap and peered inside.

Apparently pleased with what he found, he nodded and closed it back up securely. "We thank you greatly. This was a huge risk for you to take. We will not let it go to waste."

Chaol gave another small bow, the palace crest on his cloak catching the sun. Kingsman turned and disappeared back into the cave. Chaol and Badrick eyed each other, the tension between them palpable. Kira didn't have time for their alpha-male games. She shook off Badrick's arm and headed into the woods.

"Perhaps Chaol would like to take my place?" Maddox spoke up behind her. Kira stopped. She'd nearly forgotten he'd been there the entire time. Maddox was rarely quiet. Only on a job did he keep his lips sealed. At every meeting, he made his opinions and objectives clear. Now Kira was confused as to what, exactly, his objective was. There was obviously a plan boiling in his mind. The problem was that she couldn't figure it out.

"I'd be honored to. I'll protect you both until my last breath." Chaol rested his hand on the tip of his sword.

A dark look crossed Badrick's face. When he opened his mouth to speak, likely to say something foul, Kira stepped between them.

"I'm sure we'll be fine, but you can come if you wish."

Chaol nodded stiffly.

Badrick stood behind her, but still Kira could feel that every muscle in his body had tightened up. He was often protective, his guard constantly up. It was a natural way for them all to behave when they were outside of the hideout. But the resentment coming off of him was so strong that

Kira could taste it. While they walked, Kira took the lead, the two men trailing behind. Although she managed to walk a straight path, her mind was elsewhere. Where was she to go now? Before she had been taken captive in the palace, her mission had been clear: kill Pierceton and take Silas down. Now it was obvious that Pierceton wasn't going without a fight. The men didn't have to explain it to her. She knew he was the one who had destroyed the hideout. Well, if he thought he could break her that easily, he was wrong.

"Kira, watch out!" Chaol grabbed her arm and yanked her back.

Kira stumbled into him as a bear trap snapped shut inches in front of her foot. How could she have failed to notice it? That was one of the first things they were taught to look for in the woods.

"Damn hunters," Chaol growled.

Badrick strode forward and crouched to examine the trap.

Kira freed herself from Chaol's grasp and moved to stand beside Badrick. The brown coloring, the way it had been placed, it was odd. There wasn't even any bait to attract game.

"This wasn't made for hunting game. This was meant for one of us to step in." Badrick's voice was thick with fury.

"Doesn't that seem a little far-fetched?" Chaol sank down on his haunches on the other side of the trap. "You were ahead of me, how could you have missed it?"

Kira ignored their conversation and studied the trap for herself. The teeth had been sharpened to the point where it would have shattered her ankle, maybe worse.

"What do you mean, how could I have missed it? It was almost completely out of sight. The question is, how could you have seen it?" Badrick straightened up and crossed his arms.

Chaol stood too. "I may not be a thief, but I am the head of the guard. We are put through as rigorous a training process as you are."

Kira bit her lip as she contemplated him. How *could* Chaol, walking behind her, have seen the trap? Perhaps she should give him the benefit of the doubt and believe his words. But believing him wasn't as simple as it used to be, now that she knew he had kept his true identity from her.

While the two men bickered back and forth, her eyes searched the forest. It all looked calm and well. There was no sign of disturbance or harm. The birds still chirped cheerily, which was a good sign.

She spun around to face the men. "Let's go back."

Badrick furrowed his brows. "If Pierceton thinks that he can waltz in here and destroy our home, frame us, and try to kill us, he's got another thing coming. We can't keep sitting here. Now it's getting to the point where we can't even walk outside without—"

Kira gripped his arm. "Let's just go back, Badrick," she repeated calmly.

The tension left his muscles. Did he understand that she didn't want to discuss this in front of Chaol because she didn't trust the head guard? That Badrick had nothing to worry about when it came to her and Chaol?

His eyes met hers and a small smile crossed his lips. It appeared that he had gotten the message.

Kira drew in a deep breath as the three of them turned and headed back to the cave.

Chapter 24

"So you want to explain that little trap you set?" Kira asked as she pushed through the opening of the tent. She had been waiting all day to confront the culprit. It hadn't taken long for Chaol to leave, but it took a while for the others to. She had to wait until sunset when the rest of the men left to go out on a hunt. Normally she would have been ecstatic to go on one; she never missed the chance. But she used the excuse that she was feeling ill and needed some more sleep, asking for Maddox to stay behind with her to keep an eye out.

He stopped rummaging through his bag of herbs, peered up at her, and gave her a lopsided smile. "I don't know what you're talking about." There was a sarcastic tone to his words. He didn't even try to cover it up.

Kira's fists clenched. "That's the crappiest lie I've heard you tell in my entire life. Now, tell me why you set that bear trap." She sat down in front of him.

He cocked his head and raised a brow. "What happened to you not feeling good?"

Kira glared at him. They'd both known that was a lie. It was rare Kira ever fell sick, but when she did she was dangerously sick, so bad that she would be chained to her bed for days.

Maddox took a deep breath and focused back down at the herbs Chaol had given them. The head guard may be a man of the palace, but that did not mean he could be trusted. Anyone outside the guild was suspect and could do them harm. It had happened before and Kira knew Maddox was determined that it wouldn't happen again.

"I was testing the lad," he admitted as he held a piece of mint up to the poor light. After giving it a sniff, he apparently decided it was safe and moved to the next one.

"Who, Chaol?"

His face hardened in concentration as he picked up the next herb. He carefully examined the veins of the leaf, the structure and smell. One mistake and a plant that could kill a man in seconds could be mistaken for something as harmless as a piece of bread.

"I know you've taken a fancy to him, but he is from the palace. They hunt people like us. For him, to go against the palace is a dangerous thing to do. Could cost him his life."

Kira nearly spat at his words. "I have not *taken a fancy to him*," she growled. The sensation of Chaol's fingers grazing her skin, his eyes on her, manifested in her mind. He had claimed to love her, but something wasn't right. Something she just couldn't . . . trust.

"He spotted it, didn't he?" Maddox ignored her protest.

"Lucky for me that he did." She scowled. "Otherwise my ankle would have been shattered."

"He seems to know his herbs rather well too, for a guard." Maddox tossed the bag towards her. "Looked at what he picked."

Kira caught the bag and rummaged through it. At first she spotted simple herbs like mint and rosemary. Then she found others, frostbite and snowberries, which were the best herbs for a healing cream, especially for burns. Not many knew about them and, if they did, they were not easy to get.

"So what are you saying?"

Maddox flashed her another smile, his eyes sparkling with mischief.

"How do you feel about taking Badrick out for a little scavenger hunt?"

For the first time in a while, Kira felt eager to go. Her heart sped up and her body grew restless. It had been a month since her last job. With everything going on, the guild had cut back tremendously on work, afraid to be framed for more than they had done. She was definitely ready to take on a little hunt and she was sure Badrick was too.

"I'd be more than happy to."

Chapter 25

Kira's pulse echoed in her ears; she could feel blood coursing through her veins. The night wind nipped at her cheeks until she was sure they must be a bright rosy red. The mask around her mouth and the hood over her head was comfortable and natural. She felt alive.

Badrick caught up to her and took his place at her side. From the roof they were standing on they could see the palace and its walls. Lights flickered faintly from the torches near the entrance, but the guards wouldn't be able to see them from their perch beyond the reach of the dim glow. Just looking at the palace made it hard for Kira to stand still. The last time she was here, Pierceton had gotten them both thrown behind bars and then left her to rot. But here she stood, proud and strong. Here she stood ready to prove to him and Chaol what she was truly capable of.

Badrick nudged her gently in the side. "Do you remember the layout?"

Kira looked over at him playfully. Unlike her, he preferred not to wear a mask or hood or cloak. Instead he stuck to his simple gear, baring his face to whoever might be lucky enough to catch a glimpse of it.

"What type of question is that?" she teased. "Do you not know me at all?"

He chuckled before giving a courteous bow. "Then, after you my lady."

Kira curtsied in return and took off. She easily led Badrick past the sentries, staying in the shadows. Once they were out of sight of the guards at the front gate, Badrick crouched and cupped his hands together. Kira placed her foot in his hands and he heaved her up. At the top of the wall, she scanned the area on both sides to make sure they had not been caught. Then she reached back down and intertwined hands with his. She gathered her strength, and the next moment he was up next to her.

"Where to first?" he asked in a whisper.

"Let's try his chambers."

He nodded for her to take the lead. Kira took the same route that she had with Pierceton, following it to the window of the head guard's chambers with just as much ease. The only difference now was she knew her back was guarded.

She felt Badrick's eyes on her as she worked, but she focused on the lock. With a final click, the window opened and she gave it a gentle push. Smart man, he had gotten sturdier locks. But it was clear he had underestimated them far too much.

They both climbed over the sill and into the room. Badrick grabbed a rag full of Nightlock from his pouch, a herb that could knock a man out within seconds when inhaled or consumed. The best part, when he woke up, he would forget what had happened. But the bed was empty. The sheets were still made neatly and undisturbed. In fact, the whole room seemed to be in the same condition as it had been the last time she was here.

While Kira searched the room, Badrick disappeared into Chaol's study. So far Chaol seemed to be a good man, a man of the court. But if there was one thing that Kira had learnt, it was that every man has his secrets.

She burrowed through every drawer, chest, nook, and crease she could, but found nothing. She turned to tell Badrick that they should move on to the next area when the door handle began to turn. Badrick stepped out of the study and must have seen it too, as he froze in place. Quickly Kira darted under the bed, the closest hiding place that her petite figure could fit into. While she was underneath, she saw Badrick's feet turn and head back into the study. Her heart pounded with fear. She could only hope he had found a safe place to hide.

The door opened and moonlight poured across the floor. Chaol stepped into the room, his boots in her view. He meandered around to the side of his bed, stripping off his tunic and sword along the way. As he sat, the bed springs creaked loudly in her ear, as if taunting her. One boot came off and fell to the floor with a thud, then the other.

Kira's gaze swept across the room and through the open doorway, looking for any sign of Badrick. Luckily, Chaol didn't show any inclination to go into the study, so, if anything, she was the one she should be worried about.

Chaol's legs disappeared as he swung them up and onto the bed. The frame creaked a few more times as he got comfortable. *Breathe, Kira.* Given his occupation, Chaol was most likely a light sleeper. It wasn't worth the risk to try to escape. She might as well make herself comfortable, too. It seemed that she would be staying the night.

~ * ~

The sound of the door closing woke her. Her head collided with the bed frame above her and she cursed under her breath. She looked around. The boots were gone; there was no more faint snoring. Had Chaol left the room?

Kira took a chance and slowly crawled out from under the bed, just far enough to peer over the mattress. She saw the imprint of a body and the sheets askew but no Chaol. She pulled her mask down and squirmed out, then scrambled to her feet and made her way into the study.

She called out Badrick's name softly and pulled her hood back. She searched everywhere and found no sign of him. Had he left? No he wouldn't leave without her.

Kira walked around to the desk and peered underneath it. There he sat, rolled up in a ball, fast asleep. She gave him a shake and he jolted awake.

"He's gone." She offered him her hand. "We won't be able to escape during the day. They'd spot us too easily. We'll have to find a way to blend in."

Badrick crawled out from under the desk, shaking his head as if to wake himself up. He stretched his arms above him in a stretch. She could have sworn she heard his joints creak from being cooped up for so long.

Kira glanced around the room. "Did you find anything?"

He paused for a moment as if he needed to get his mind working again. Then he reached into his pocket and tugged out a piece of paper.

"Yeah, look at this. It's all the murders within the city from the past few months."

"You mean the ones we've been framed for?"

Badrick nodded. "We're lucky there haven't been any recently, or they'd be pursuing us even more ardently."

Kira searched around until she found a paper and ink. She laid the paper on Chaol's desk and, in her best handwriting, copied it down word for word. That was one thing that Kingsman was determined to teach them all. He said he was not going to let his men roam around without the ability to read and write.

Now to look for more clues. How could they get close to Chaol without him recognizing them?

Badrick strode toward the door. Kira finished scribbling the words before stuffing the paper into her pocket and following him. He carelessly walked out into the hallway. Kira nearly yelled at him. Did he want to get—

"Oh. Pardon me, sir. I didn't see you there, you gave me a fright."

Kira peered out from behind the door and spotted a young servant standing with Badrick. Her smile was bright and kind, her eyes beaming with youth and adoration. Kira could tell had taken an immediate liking to Badrick. *Of course. What young girl wouldn't?*

Badrick returned the girl's smile, apparently aware of her interest. "I'm sorry for causing you to worry. I was actually looking for someone like you." He stepped closer to her, clearly turning on the charm. Kira rolled her eyes. The alluring sound of his voice, the irresistible smile, the bold eyes, and gentle caresses, she had seen him use them all before on other women. He had no shame in flirting with the tavern girls and he certainly had no shame now.

"I-is that so?" The girl stuttered as he stopped inches in front of her. When his hand grazed her hip gently, Kira was sure the girl would topple over. She was young. Her brown hair was thick and lovely, her cheeks were rosy, much like her own. Her hazel eyes followed Badrick's every move. Had Kira not known better, she would have mistaken them for husband and wife. That's how in love the young servant seemed. If only she knew how naïve she was.

"Yes. You see, my dear . . . friend here," he gestured toward the doorway and Kira stepped out into view, ". . . and I have just joined the court. We are the new spies, charged with finding information to give to the king and queen. We are to act as servants here to help assist his and her majesty."

"Oh?" the girl mumbled sweetly as she glanced over at Kira. A cold look flashed across her face then the servant laughed lightly. "Well, you can't go working around in clothes like that. Please, follow me. I believe I have a spare dress you could borrow."

As the young girl walked down the hall ahead of them, Kira met Badrick's eyes. He simply motioned for her to follow the servant. She frowned as she complied. Did he know how dangerous this was for them? If Chaol saw them, what were they to say? *We have no choice.* With a sigh, she turned to follow the servant, on alert for anyone who might recognize her. The trip to the servant's quarters felt as long as the journey from the cave to the palace had been.

The girl was kind enough to loan her a dress that was suitable to work in, though it was a size too small. Kira was much curvier while the girl was younger and in the earlier stages of gaining her womanly figure. The garment was awkward for Kira to move in after the final laces were tied, but it would have to do for now. The girl even went so far as to find something for Badrick to wear.

Kira caught a glimpse of Badrick in the hallway, dressed in servant's garb, as she fashioned her hair into an up-do. Another young girl brushed by him and stepped into the room. She wasn't as young as the one who helped them, closer to Kira's age, or perhaps a year or two younger.

"Anabelle, the queen calls for assistance," the girl blurted out, sounding breathless.

"Oh, I cannot go now! I'm far too busy. Will you take my spot?" Anabelle turned to Kira, her voice pleading.

Kira glanced over at Badrick then nodded. "Of course, I would be more than happy to," she answered softly. Anabelle thanked her multiple times as Kira rose and walked toward the door, trying to get a feel for the dress. Stepping out of the room, she yanked her weapons free. If they were found on her in the presence of the king or queen, she would be sent to her death without question.

Badrick followed her into the hallway and took her things from her. "I'll hide these in the bushes near the wall where we left our armor. We can retrieve them when we leave." His eyes held hers for a moment and he gave her a curt nod, as if reassuring her that she could do this. Then he turned away.

Kira watched him as he strode down the hall and disappeared around a corner. She appreciated his confidence. Her own hopes that they could get the information they needed and leave without being detected were fading. She lifted her chin. She couldn't worry about that now. She needed to focus on the task of seeing to the queen. She kept her back straight and walked as quickly as she could in her restrictive attire, following the path in her mind she had set from her previous visit and her study of the palace. Within a few moments, she stood before double doors of the queen's quarters.

Kira rapped lightly on the door. "Your Grace, I was called for help. May I come in?" The door opened and Kira froze. Chaol, still clutching the handle, was looking back over his shoulder, listening to something the king was saying that Kira couldn't hear over the pounding in her ears.

The queen gestured to her from across the room. "Yes, yes. Do come in."

Keeping her face averted in case Chaol turned back, Kira pushed past the head guard and into the room. Both the queen and king were dressed elegantly and beautifully, yet not to the point of being obnoxious. Kira gave a low curtsy and waited five breaths before she rose. She may not have been raised in a court, but that did not mean she didn't know the ways of one.

Her heart pounded and she discretely rubbed her sweaty palms on her skirts. Chaol stood behind her, still apparently deep in conversation with the king and unaware of who she was. If she was lucky, she could get in and out of the room without him recognizing her.

Although, when it came to the head guard, luck had so far not been on her side.

Chapter 26

"Please take the trays for us and ready a bath for me," the queen requested. She didn't appear to be concerned about the fact that she had never seen Kira before. Obviously she had complete confidence in the guards to keep anyone unsafe out of the palace. A confidence that was rapidly proving to be unwarranted.

Kira was taken aback by her kindness, but did not falter. "Of course, Your Grace." She curtsied again, briefly this time, then began to gather the food from their early meal by the bedside. The silver trays were engraved with beautiful and whimsical designs. The hand-painted cups were formed from flawless porcelain and seemed much too delicate to drink from. She made sure to handle them as gently as she could. The last thing she'd want to do was break one.

"Please do continue, Sir Chaol." The king held his wife lovingly by an arm around her waist.

"Of course, Your Grace. As I was saying, we found another body today at the edge of town."

Kira's ears pricked up. She silently turned and set the tray on the vanity, risking a look into the mirror. In the reflection she could see the back of Chaol as he stood formally before the royal couple. The queen's smile fell from her face. The action removed beauty from her, yet she was still breathtaking. Her hair was long and blonde, much like Kira's, only it still hung loose and thick with curls. She must have recently woken up. Any other time Kira suspected her golden locks would be fashioned into a beautiful hairstyle.

"Who was it this time?" The king held his wife closer.

Chaol paused before answering. "An older man by the name of Delvin. He lived with his wife and daughter, as well as his daughter's fiancé and his granddaughter."

Kira nearly stumbled as she made her way into the opposite room to draw the bath. Not Delvin. No, the last time she saw him he had been begging her not to harm his granddaughter. He had been fair; he had given her his pay. She left him unharmed, expecting him to live a normal life. To go out each day to earn an honest living, knowing his granddaughter would be asleep by the fire when he returned. But now the young girl would be crying. She'd be lying there waiting, waiting, and waiting. She'd never see him walk through that front door again.

"There must be some way to get a lead on who is doing this." The king's jaw was tight.

"I can assure you my men and I are as working as hard and as quickly as we can, Your Grace," Chaol replied.

"We were doing so well. I was hoping that they had stopped," the queen mumbled. The weakness in her voice transferred to Kira as she walked into the bathing room. Her hands shook as she dropped sprigs of lavender into the bath water. She paused for a moment and watched her reflection as the water rippled. Her face had gone pale and her eyes were full of fright. She was so unrecognizable she barely knew herself. Swallowing hard, she went back into the queen's room.

"Is it the thieves?" the queen asked.

Kira opened the wardrobe and surveyed the dresses hanging there. So many hung in front of her, varying in colors from blues to pinks, and in fabrics from silk to satin. Each one was embroidered with perfect detail and lined with the finest lace and jewels.

"My dear, I know they are thieves, but we have no reason to believe that they are murderers. Everyone is innocent until proven guilty," the king reminded her gently.

"Yes, yes. I apologize. I'm just concerned."

Kira caught the queen's eye and held up two gowns. Relief washed over her. The king and queen were not what she was expecting. They were much kinder. She could tell by the looks on their faces that they cared for their people—even those of low station—and did not wish to accuse them unjustly. They did not judge on appearance; they did not let fear control their actions.

The queen waved a hand in Kira's direction. "Please choose for me today. My mind is not able to think clearly." She sighed as she rubbed her forehead. Her husband planted a soft kiss on the top of her head before urging her to step into the bath.

"Thank you, Sir Chaol. Please inform us should anything else come up. And see to it that the man is given a proper funeral."

"Yes, Your Grace."

Kira carried a sunshine-yellow gown into the dressing room. Her eyes flickered again to the mirror. Chaol gave one last bow before turning away. It wasn't until the door closed behind him that she finally let out the breath she had been holding. For now, he had yet to notice her. Hopefully things would go smoothly for Badrick as well.

"Is the bath ready?" the queen asked as she walked into the room.

"Yes, Your Grace." Kira closed the door and hung the gown up on the hook on the back of it to avoid being wrinkled. The queen turned and Kira began to work gently at her laces of her morning gown. Then she helped her highness into the tub. "I used lavender for you bath, Your Grace. It helps relieve stress," she explained as the queen plucked a sprig from the water and held it to her nose.

"And I suppose there is a reason you chose that gown for me to wear as well?"

"Yellow is said to bring happiness." Kira poured a cup of warm water over the queen's locks.

The queen chuckled. "That's very thoughtful, thank you."

Kira smiled. The queen and king seemed to be good people who meant well. For them to not automatically assume these murders were the guild's doing added to Kira's respect towards them. A simple favor of garnishing her bath with lavender or picking a yellow gown was something that could not compare to what they were doing for her and those she cared about most deeply.

After the queen stepped out of the bath, Kira helped her into the yellow dress. Meeting the royal couple had given her hope that they may be given a chance to prove themselves. If she could convince the others to take the risk, perhaps they could work something out with the court.

"Is there anything else I can do for, Your Grace?" she asked as finished tying the laces. The queen walked over to her vanity and turned from side to side, clearly admiring how well she looked. Her face was bright and colorful with beauty and she knew it. Then the queen's eyes landed on her in the mirror. Kira froze. Had she seen through her disguise?

"Are you new, my dear?" she asked as she turned and faced Kira.

Kira gave a small nod. "Today is my first day."

The queen smiled. "It's nice to see a new face once in awhile. I believe I'll send for you more in the days to come. Until then, you are dismissed."

Kira gave a curtsy. She held it for five breaths again before she rose and left the room. Now to find Chaol and track him, and hopefully to garner more information. She needed to know whose side he was on. Only this time she would be careful not to get as close as she had on her last visit.

She closed the door softly. If she played her cards right, she might be able to get the queen on her side. Just how she would do it remained to be unseen. Until she had a better plan, she would focus on Chaol.

Chapter 27

Kira was frustrated. Chaol had done nothing out of the ordinary that day. He trained with his guards, sporting only his trousers and boots, which was hard for her to watch. To see a half-naked man wasn't what bothered her. It was the fact that the half-naked man was Chaol. She had to think of him as an enemy and not as a man who'd had her heart for a split moment. That was turning out to be harder than expected.

She turned and left the courtyard as they practiced, and returned to following him later that day. Even then he did nothing she could consider questionable. He spent an hour in the library, attended dinner, then retired to his chambers at the end of the night. A day wasted.

Not seeing Badrick all that time made Kira eager to meet up with him at the spot where he had hidden their armor. She slipped out of the castle, picked up her skirts, and ran as fast as she could in her borrowed shoes. Once she was sure no one was following her, she snuck out to the wall. There she called out for him in a hushed whisper, only to see him jog toward her.

He looked so handsome in the soft glow of the moonlight that Kira glanced away. "Any news?" she asked.

"You first."

"Well, none on Chaol. I did come up with a plan though." Badrick gave her a questioning look as he cupped his hands together. With ease, she gracefully pulled herself up onto the wall. She turned and watched Badrick throw the armor into a bag—one he had most likely stolen while no one was looking—before slinging it onto his back. Kira leaned over and offered him a hand, attempting to help him scale the wall. When he leapt onto the top of it, his hands circled her waist and he held her close so she wouldn't lose her balance.

"I must say, my lady, I'm liking this new hairstyle." He brushed back the bangs from her face. Kira's skin tingled where his fingers had touched it. She couldn't decipher if he was being honest or merely toying with her feelings again. She took a deep breath to calm her heart. Why did he have to do such things? She lifted her chin. "Now is not the time to dabble in your flirtatious games, Badrick. Whatever my appearance, I'm not some young servant girl to be swept off my feet by your smooth words."

He flashed her a lopsided grin. "Damn, just when the mood was getting romantic."

"You consider breaking out of a palace romantic?"

He chuckled, but she didn't look back at him as she jumped lightly down from the wall. As they snuck their way back to the new hideout, Kira's mind spun. Maddox's observations about the head guard were intriguing. She would have easily questioned Chaol about his alliance when she first met him, but he had blinded her with affection. Now, however, she was beginning to awaken and see the light. If she was going to confront the king and queen about her idea, she'd need some sort of support. She couldn't just step in blindly and expect them to trust her.

The mouth of the cave was dimly lit by the torch Felix held as he stood guard. Something tugged at her to go back to The Grottos. She couldn't explain what it was, but she needed to go.

"What is going on in that head of yours?" Badrick grabbed her arm to stop her and peered down at her.

"I need to go back to The Grottos."

"Now?"

"Yes, now." Her voice was stern and firm. She tugged her arm from his grip and continued walking towards the cave. Felix watched them approach, his brows furrowed. He opened his mouth, likely to pelt them with questions about where they had been.

Kira raised a hand and he closed his mouth. She stepped into the cave and tugged the bag off of Badrick's back. After pulling a cloak from it and tying it around her neck, she strapped her blades back into place. Now she was sure of it. She needed to go and she needed to go alone.

As she strode back to the entrance, Felix stepped in front of her. "Kira, where are you—"

"I'll be back by sunrise." Brushing by him, she stepped out into the open. The eastern sky had lightened. She should have given herself more time, but if she hurried she would be able to make it.

Badrick came up behind her and grasped her elbow. "You're not going to The Grottos by yourself." His grip tightened. "You're still not completely recovered. If they gang up on you, you'll be overcome in the blink of an eye."

"If they can't catch me, they can't hurt me."

Badrick let go of her, hurt flashing in his eyes and his body going rigid. Clearly he didn't appreciate her using his words against him. "If you're not back the second that sun rises, I will come after you."

Is that a threat or a promise? Never before had she seen Badrick so worried about her. It felt . . . nice. Just in case she never saw him again, Kira rose to her toes and kissed his cheek before turning away.

⁓ * ⁓

The Grottos seemed even more crowded than the last time she had visited. She searched the crowd, hoping to find someone she recognized. Annoying laughter roared in her ears and Kira pressed her lips together to keep from yelling at those around her to be quiet. The last thing she needed was to let her smart mouth get her killed.

Kira made her way through the room, careful not to trip over her feet as she pushed through the crowd. In the center of the room, a small group of people stood around a wooden board had been nailed to a post. She stopped to peer at the available jobs listed there. Many had been taken, but there was one that no one apparently dared to touch. Her fingers grazed the paper and she gave it a yank. In the corner of the page, the person advertising the job was identified as Silas. The payment was more than anyone could imagine. Her eyes widened as she read the description of the job: assassinate the king and queen.

Chapter 28

Kira sat with her legs crossed. The room was deadly silent with no sign of life in it. She made sure to keep the hood of the cloak low so it covered as much of her face as possible. She kept her eyes on her skirts. If she played her cards right, they'd believe that she was nothing more than a distressed noble who had just had the worst day of her life.

The sound of the door closing behind her made her raise her head slightly. She felt the presence crush her as the figure stepped closer to her. She had done it. She was alone with Silas.

"So, you are the one who would like to take on my job?" His voice was low and smooth.

Kira stood and gave a small curtsy. "Yes, I am." She spoke with a small accent. She peered past her hood, trying to catch a glimpse of his face, but he stood in the shadows.

He laughed coldly, as if she was pathetic for standing before him. "I do not believe that a young noble woman is capable of doing such a job."

"Do not underestimate a woman with a motive," Kira shot back quickly as he walked over to his desk.

Her words made him stop and turn back to her, head cocked. "Oh? And what is this motive?"

"My husband. I found him sleeping with a servant of the court." Kira spat out the words. "After all the traveling I did to get here, all the love I gave him, he had the nerve to sleep with a … a serving wench!"

He frowned. "Just what does this have to do with the king and queen?"

Kira shot a look at the door, feigning concern that they should be overheard, and lowered her voice. Her palms were getting sweaty, her blood roaring with anxiety. She had to convince Silas she could do this job. It was the perfect opportunity to get back into the castle. "They allowed his infidelity. They did nothing to assist me or to stop his fling. There are many who believe that they are kind, that they love their people. Well, let me tell you one thing, I've been in the country for but a month and I can say without any doubt they are deceiving you all!" The lie slipped off her tongue too easily. Not a word had an ounce of truth to it. "If they think they can deceive me, they are wrong. My foreign ways are not as ignorant as they think."

Silas stood silently, clearly contemplating her words. If he managed to see past her lies, then she would be dead. He would not hesitate to kill her.

Kira's heart pounded. Had she chosen her words too well? Had she been too careful?

"Can you wield a bow and arrow?" he asked.

Despite his inability to see her face, she smirked. "I've hunted plenty of game alongside my father when he and his men go on their monthly hunts. If I can kill an elk, I can kill a king."

"Strong words for a small woman."

"Don't let my size fool you as it did the members of the court. I am not a woman to be taken lightly," she warned.

He paused again before motioning for her to sit. Kira hesitated before complying. Something warned her that an interrogation was about to follow. She took the chair in front of his desk, fixing her skirts as she did. She'd have to think out every word before it left her mouth.

Silas sat down on the other side of the desk. "You say your husband is a man of the court? It so happens I'm quite knowledgeable about the men who wear those titles. None of the ones I have met seem to be ones to do such hateful actions." He poured a glass of wine and set it within her reach. Kira's hand slipped around the curves of the glass and she raised it to her lips.

"The men of the court are the most deceptive of them all," she mumbled under her breath. The lack of effort required to say those words wounded her heart. That had been the only truthful statement she had made during the entire conversation.

"All the court is the most deceptive, my lady," he corrected.

Kira watched the liquid swirl in her glass. "You seem to speak from experience."

"Aye, I do. I've seen it with my own eyes."

The alcohol burned her throat as she took another small sip. She had never been one to drink. Instead she was the one who helped lug the drunken members of the guild home when they decided to go into town for the night. The taste was foreign and bitter. It just didn't taste right.

"Do you not favor wine?" Silas asked as she placed the glass back on the desk.

"My country's alcohol is much sweeter and less bitter."

"Ah, I must apologize, my lady. I will find something more to your taste when you return for your payment." Silas stood and walked around the desk. "Here are your requirements and the details of your task." He held out a piece of paper.

Kira reached out carefully to take it from his hand. He towered high above her, enough for her to have to crane her head back should she dare to look directly at him. She chose against it for fear her hood would slip off. If he was trying to intimidate her, he would have to try something else.

She slipped the paper into the pouch she had brought with her. Silas took her hand and helped her to her feet.

"You have until the end of the month. Until then, have a good night."

Kira followed him to the door. She hesitated when he pulled it open, apprehensive about showing him her back. She trusted him about as far as she could throw him. But she couldn't just stand there forever, so she pushed herself forward through the doorframe. She only turned her back for a few seconds, but it was enough. His hands latched onto her arms and he dragged her back into the room and slammed the door shut.

Kira gasped as her back collided with the wall. Her ears buzzed and her knees buckled. It was as if her entire world had been distorted. She couldn't possibly be this weak from her wounds. It just didn't seem possible.

His hands crushed her shoulders as he shoved her upright. Kira's vision was tainted with black dots. If he kept pressing on her, she'd pass out.

So she did the first thing she could think of. She dug her heel into his toes. Silas bent forward and Kira rammed her knee into his chest. He let go of her and she placed as much space she could between them. Which meant she was farther from the door. She tripped and braced herself on the corner of the desk, barely managing to stay upright. What had he done to her?

"You drugged me," she rasped. She had thought the bitter taste was the natural taste of wine. Oh how wrong she'd been. All the talk of her country and the men of the court had just been to buy time to let the drug settle in. The side effects began to register in her mind. The weakness, the blurriness of vision, the fighting to stay conscious. He had used Nightlock.

"I'm impressed. A typical noble woman wouldn't have caught on so quickly." Silas groaned as he straightened up.

Kira scrambled around the desk as he strode toward her. She needed to keep calm. She could scream, but no one would hear her hoarse voice above the noise in the room outside. She had brought this on herself. She never should have come here alone.

Kira reached for the dagger hidden on her belt and threw blindly. She heard a hiss, but Silas only scowled and moved more quickly towards her. Her vision had degenerated to nothing more than a mass of colors. Silas reached her and grabbed both her arms. He threw her onto her back and pinned her down with no mercy. She squirmed under his grip and raised her knee, then smashed her forehead against his.

His grip loosened. The effects of the drug rippled through her and stole all her strength. Helplessly she began to crawl toward the door. This was it; she was dead.

Her fingers grasped the doorknob just as a dark shadow fell over her. Kira looked up. Seeing Silas's face was deadly all on his own. His face, his features, sent terror coursing through her. She tried to memorize every detail she could, while she could, because the next moment the Nightlock settled in and her world went black.

Chapter 29

Kira opened her eyes with a slight groan. She felt rather ... odd. Almost weightless. She glanced around and found herself in a room that felt vaguely familiar, as if she had been there before. Her mind was still muddled. What was going on?

The door opened and a man walked in. He was tall, with broad shoulders and a cloak that masked his face, much like her own. Her fists tightened as her heart rate sped up. The fabric under her hands didn't belong to her normal attire. Kira looked down. A skirt? How odd, she hardly ever wore skirts.

"So, you are the one who would like to take my job?"

Kira tugged at her ears. His voice sounded groggy, almost distorted. "Yes, I am."

She frowned. Why was she speaking with an accent? She never had spoken with one before. Nothing made sense. Then more foreign words left her lips, telling a story of her husband sleeping with a servant. What was this she spoke of? Why was she telling such a lie? What was this job they kept speaking of?

The next event jolted her. She was about to leave when the man threw her against the wall. Her vision blurred tremendously. Her body felt weak. With each step her vision blackened. Her body shook and she began to imagine someone calling out her name.

The voice penetrated her vision and she jolted upright. Her chest was heaving and her heart raced. It was a dream.

"Kira, hold still!"

She looked up and saw a woman standing there with frustration clear on her face. Kira instantly recognized her.

Fear flowed through her veins and she backed far into the corner of the room. Her hand reached for her dagger and found an empty sheath. Where in the world did it go?

"Kira, stop," the woman repeated.

"Give me one reason why I should trust you after what you did, Sapphire?" Kira snarled.

Sapphire raised her hands in defense. The woman hadn't changed at all. Her hair was still long with that shade of dark crimson, her skin was still tanned with no sign of aging, and her face was still heart-stoppingly beautiful. All the attributes Felix had been drawn to.

"If I was going to kill you, wouldn't I have done it by now? I could have left you to die. Did I? No. In fact, I gave you the last of my antidote. I was hoping to give you back your memories, but you kept squirming. Hopefully I gave it to you in time for you to actually have some recollection of what happened."

Kira studied her. As much as she hated to admit it, Sapphire was a good match for Felix. She was strong, often planned ahead, like he did, and didn't take anything from him. She kept him in line. If only she knew how much she had hurt him.

Sapphire planted both hands on her hips. "Will you put your guard down and trust me?"

"Why would you help me?" Kira growled.

"I came just in time. I heard some noises from down the hall and saw you lying on the floor with Silas over you. He said you wanted to take his job, that he had to make sure that a noble woman was capable of handling such a task."

"And?"

"Well, you surprised him with how well you fought back, that's for sure. Sounds like you impressed him enough to be safe. For now."

Kira tried to ignore the last two words. "You still didn't answer my question."

Sapphire narrowed her eyes. After a moment of silence, she parted her lips. "I've known you for how long? I may seem heartless, but that doesn't mean I don't care for you, and everyone else in the guild."

Kira spat in disgust. She could still envision the night very clearly. Every single detail. She had been young at the time, only fourteen if she remembered correctly. Everyone had been ecstatic for Felix. She had seen with her own eyes how in love he was. There was a special gleam in his, and hope and happiness.

Felix planned to propose to this woman, and everyone hid amongst the trees and shadows to watch. The ring he had chosen sparkled brightly and beautifully, representing all the hard work he had done to get it.

Kira had to admit that on that night Sapphire looked even more beautiful than usual. Her own breath had been taken away; she could hardly imagine how Felix felt. When he proposed, Sapphire had said yes and hugged him. They all cheered as quietly as they could. Kira's heart had leaped for him. He had finally found the one thing that everyone aimed to have, true love. But the happiness her heart leaped for suddenly and dramatically changed to something much darker.

Felix turned around, likely searching out his friends. When he did, Sapphire raised a dagger behind his back. Kira screamed, and darted out of the bushes as fast as she could. Felix spun back around in time to deflect the blow and push Sapphire away. She hesitated, then lashed out with the blade, striking his face. Kira had been the first to tackle her to the ground. She was strong, but she was more naïve than skilled at the time. Sapphire had thrown her off after a few seconds of struggle and disappeared into the trees.

Sapphire may have left Felix with few wounds, but she did not get to see the scarring she had left on him both physically and mentally. For Kira to trust her? That should have been the furthest thing from her expectations.

"Let me past," Kira ordered. "I'm stronger than the last time we fought. I wasn't scared to fight then, and I'm not scared now."

"I don't doubt it." Sapphire smiled slightly. Kira's brows furrowed together. This was not what she needed to be focusing on. She needed to try to grasp hold of the rest of her memories while she had a chance. There was something important. Something to do with Silas.

Surprisingly, Kira stepped past Sapphire without being stopped. She grasped the handle of the door as Sapphire spoke again.

"You're in the south end of town. Just go—"

"I can find my own way," Kira snapped over her shoulder. She waited, but there was only silence from the other woman. Perhaps she was delusional, hoping that she'd hear some sort of explanation or words of regret from Sapphire. People really didn't change, after all.

"He didn't see you. He still doesn't know who you are," she blurted out as Kira opened the door. Kira looked back at her. "I thank you for keeping me safe." She waited. If Sapphire was going to say something, it would have to be now or never. Kira started to pull the door open.

"I didn't do it for no reason, you know," Sapphire blurted.

Kira stopped. She calmly turned and looked at the crimson-haired woman. She'd give her a chance to explain. But only one.

"I did it to protect you."

Kira couldn't stop herself from laughing. "And how exactly was killing Felix supposed to protect me?"

"Not just you. All of the guild." Sapphire frowned and walked closer to her. Kira's laughing dwindled off and her smile fell into a frown. Before it was always her looking up to Sapphire, now it was quite the opposite. "I didn't mean to hurt him." Sapphire lowered her tone as if they were surrounded by people who weren't supposed to hear her words.

"Well, congratulations, because you did anyways."

"You think it didn't kill me? Do you honestly think I didn't love him?"

"I don't know. You tell me. Were you there to see him afterwards? Were you there to see this once strong, happy man close off and harden against the world? Well, I was. I'm sure he would have been happier had you just killed him when you had the chance."

"If you were stuck in the position that I was, I'm sure you'd hesitate too. My mind was racing as I constantly asked myself what would be better, if I let him live and be hunted down? Or would it be better for him if I ended it on the spot?"

Kira's eyes narrowed. "What do you mean, hunted down?"

Sapphire crossed her arms, her nails digging into her flesh. Her emerald eyes were piercing and daring. The same fierce look Kira had seen in them the day she met her.

"I've done my own fair share of work with Silas. I know how he works, Kira. Learn from my mistakes. Don't get involved with him. He's nothing but trouble."

"You said it yourself, Sapphire. Would you rather let the ones you love be hunted like animals? Or would you rather end it?"

Sapphire stiffened. Kira stared at her as if she were a pathetic little rodent. When she offered no response, Kira left her alone in the room. Once the door had closed behind her, Kira pressed her hand against her forehead. What did Sapphire mean? Who had threatened to hunt Felix down? Was it Silas? Who was this man, and why did he want the members of the guild dead? It seemed as if she'd never see the light at the end of the tunnel. Kira dropped her hand. None of that mattered at the moment. The only thing she needed to know was what she had to do to stop him.

Chapter 30

Badrick sat on a rock outside the cave, his leg shaking. The sun had already started peeking over the hills; Kira should have been back already. But he couldn't protect her forever. As much as he hated to admit it, she was a strong, independent woman. It was clear she'd never truly need a man to help her. Perhaps that's what he found so intoxicating about her.

He kept his eyes fixed on the grass beneath him as if he could see the difference as it grew. This was getting ridiculous. He shouldn't be so worried about her. He was a thief, a grown man, and he needed to act like one. He needed to get his head in the game.

He stood up to return inside the cave. He stopped when he saw Kingsman standing in the opening, silhouetted against the flickering flames behind him. A brief wind rippled along his cloak. Badrick stuffed his hands into his pockets and met Kingsman's eyes. Normally Kingsman's expressions were bland and held little emotion. Badrick was good at playing his role, but Kingsman was a master at it.

Tonight, though, his face was soft and his eyes gentle. Kingsman smiled as he walked towards Badrick, the same look on his face Badrick assumed he had when he looked at Kira, trying to comfort her. Was that what this new kindness was? An attempt to comfort?

"She will be quite fine, son." Kingsman clapped a hand on Badrick's shoulder.

"You mean to tell me you aren't nervous?"

"Of course I am." Kingsman's gaze raked over Badrick's face, as though he was carefully considering what to say. "You know how I found her, don't you?"

"Of course. We all do."

Kingsman squeezed his shoulder. "Would you permit me to tell the story to you again?"

Badrick motioned with his hand for him to continue.

"I was just coming back from helping around the city." Kingsman let go of Badrick and rested his booted foot on a large stone. "That night rain poured heavily and the streets flooded so much that it soiled my boots. I had heard a rustling from the side of an inn and, naturally, I checked to see if someone was following me.

"There she was, huddled in between two barrels. She was smart; she'd placed a beam of wood across them to make a small shelter from the rain. Her hair was so filthy I thought she was a brunette and her stomach so small my hands could wrap around her waist completely. I have no idea how she held out for so long."

Badrick kicked at a clump of grass at his feet.

"I took her to the hideout and we nursed her back to health, Maddox, Felix, and I. She said she lost her parents in the riot. Didn't even know if she had any family left to go to."

Badrick's shoulders slumped. He had lost his father and brother to disease. The loss had been a tremendous hit to him and his family. He still had his mother and sister, though, who were still living in their small fishing town. He had only gone through a sliver of the pain Kira had suffered at such a young age. At least he had some sort of clarity, a sense of where he had come from. She didn't. She had nothing except the clothes on her back.

"I didn't tell you to give you an excuse to sulk. I told you to give you confidence."

Badrick chewed on the inside of his cheek. Kingsman was right. Kira was a survivor. If anyone could take on Silas and live to tell about it, it was her.

Still, his heart skipped a beat when he heard her voice. They both turned as Kira ran to them. When she stopped, her hair was a disheveled mess, the hem of her skirts were plastered with mud, and her chest was heaving. In her hand she clutched a paper. While she bent forward, hands on her knees as she attempted to catch her breath, Kingsman took the paper from her fingers and unrolled it. His eyes scanned the page as he read, mumbling the words as he went. Then his voice died out. He crumpled the paper in his fist, his eyes narrowed.

"I think you owe us an explanation."

~ * ~

Tension hung thick in the chamber as the thieves gathered around. Some sat with their arms crossed, others stared at her, foreheads wrinkled, obviously trying to make some sort of sense from the news they'd just heard.

"Kira, I think it's clear that you have some explaining to do." Kingsman threw her contract into the center of the circle. He towered over her, glowering, her boss now, not her father. She'd seen grown men cower before him when he assumed such a position, but she knew better than to respond that way. The first obstacle she needed to overcome was convincing the guild to follow her. If she gave in to Kingman's intimidation now, her quest would be over before it had begun.

Kira pushed back her shoulders and met Kingman's gaze steadily. "Silas is the one Russell was working for before he died. Pierceton is still working for him. I believe it is Silas who is attempting to frame the guild for the recent murders. I need to gain his trust; I need to learn his weaknesses."

Maddox raised a hand, palm up. "So you start off with murdering the king and queen? We are trying to clear our names, not dirty them further."

He'd been sitting on the floor, leaning against the cave wall, but he leaned forward now as if anxious to hear what she had to say.

"That's the thing. I'm not going to dirty our names further." Kira glanced at Badrick and he nodded slightly. She drew in a breath. *Please hear me out.* "I've had the blessing to wait on their highnesses themselves. They are willing to give us a chance. The queen said so herself. They won't pronounce us guilty until they prove it's us who are carrying out the killings."

Felix frowned. "And just how to you propose to get them to listen to you if you show up attempting to murder them?"

"That's just it; I won't be there to murder them, I'll be there to talk to them. Accepting this job will give me the access I need to get in to their quarters. As myself this time, not disguised as a lady's maid. The time for lies and deception is over. We must show them our true selves, convince them that, though we may be thieves, we are also men and women of honor. And, as such, we must no longer slink about in the shadows. We must come out into the light. It's the only way to convince the king and queen, and anyone else who would falsely accuse us, that we are not capable of committing these atrocities." Kira scanned the faces around the circle. She almost had them; she just had to tighten her grip.

Badrick had been standing in front of the wall, arms pressed to his chest. He uncrossed them now and took a step closer to her. "You and I were able to get into the palace before. Why can't we do that again, as ourselves this time? Why involve this Silas at all?" His face twisted as he said the name, his feelings for the man clear.

"That was two of us. Sneaking in the entire guild to meet with the king and queen face to face is a different matter entirely. We need a new plan, and I believe Silas is the key. Showing the royal couple that we had the opportunity to commit a crime and be handsomely paid for it, yet have refused to do so, may be the only way we have to convince them of our innocence."

Astien's eyes were wide in the orange glow of the fire. "You want us all to go in to see the king and queen when we've been accused of murder? They'll hang us on the spot."

"I don't think they will. They seem to me to be open-minded and fair. I believe if we can just talk to them, no weapons and no disguises, just us and our bare faces, there's a good chance we can clear our name and bring down Silas at the same time."

Kingsman's eyes, dark and angry, were locked on hers. Yet Kira held her ground. To know that little girl she'd seen by the fire wouldn't have a grandfather to wait for soured her thoughts. She had finally gotten a lead, especially on Silas. If she could win the royalty over to her side, as well as regain her memory, they could win this war. The souls of all of Silas's victims would finally be able to rest. Kingsman exhaled loudly. "You will plan and lead everything. Don't expect me to help. No one else will be allowed to help you either, not until you have worked out all the details and are ready to carry out your plan. It's about time you've learned what it is like to stand on your own."

Kira cracked a grin. A thrill of pride rippled through her. The time to prove herself was now.

~ * ~

Kira stayed at an inn for the night. With no one there to pressure her, she hoped to have the opportunity to organize her thoughts and come up with a plan. She shut and locked the door to her room in an attempt to block the noise of hungry customers waiting for their dinner, but her tactic failed miserably. Raucous laughter and the clattering of dishes filtered through the walls. She groaned in annoyance and scowled at the door, not that anyone could see her. The noise would most likely carry on into the early hours of the morning and there wasn't a thing she could do about it.

Her hands covered her ears as she peered down at the papers on the wooden table before her. One was a detailed layout of the palace, another was a list of her men and their strong and weak points. Sneaking two people in was easy, a whole guild wasn't going to be quite as simple. Finally, she decided to send Kingsman and Astien through the cellar entrance located at the back of the palace. If they managed to sneak in while the deliveries were being made, they would be able to hold their own until night. Kingsman could play a role better than anyone, and Astien could easily be his apprentice. Next she'd send Maddox and Felix through the western wall. She had seen the two men work together and, despite their differences in strengths, they made a good team. That left Badrick and herself.

Her finger trailed down the eastern wall, where they had entered the palace before, and down the paper. Chaol's men would have figured out their usual entry point by now. Her fingertip ended at the front entrance. The soldiers would never expect them to sneak past right under their noses.

A sudden roar of laughter made Kira jump. Planning this escapade had twisted her stomach into knots. Everyone was relying on her. Should her plan fail, they could be captured or even killed, as Astien had suggested. She had a feeling Chaol wouldn't be so generous the second time around.

A heavy fist pounded on the door. Kira huffed and jumped to her feet to cross the room and stuff her plans into a dresser drawer.

"Just a minute."

Who in the world would be knocking on her door at this hour? Most likely a drunken farmer to ask her join him for a drink. Kira shuddered.

She swung the door open, ready to confront whoever was on the other side. Shock tore through her. For a moment, neither of them spoke. Kira shifted her weight awkwardly from one foot to the other. Suddenly she wished the person standing in front of her *was* just a drunkard.

She couldn't stand the silence any longer. "How did you know I was here?"

Chaol's jaw tightened.

"I saw you walk into town and I followed you."

"Well, you found me."

Chaol frowned. Before she could move, he pushed her back into her room. The door shut with a quick kick of his foot and he had her pinned against the wall in a second. Kira's heart pounded. Images flashed through her mind, the sensations raw and overpowering.

She stood, paralyzed, unable to move or speak or do anything but stare up at him. His eyes were hard, like they had been the first time she had met him. His grip was tight, yet it wasn't painful. He opened his mouth to talk, but she heard nothing except mumbled noises. Kira closed her eyes and groaned. A sudden pain gripped her head in a vice.

She didn't know when she started to cry or what exactly happened afterwards. All she could see was Silas's body standing above her, his hood darkening his face.

If only she could remember. If only she could just remember.

Chapter 31

When she came to, her vision was still blurry. But that was something she could handle, a minor inconvenience compared to the pain she had just endured. Remembering sent shivers down her back, but she straightened her shoulders. She couldn't let fear distract her from her mission.

Chaol sat on a chair beside her bed, his elbows on his knees and his forehead in his palms. She stayed frozen, unsure if he was asleep or not. Then he gave a sigh and sat up. As he ran a hand through his hair, he opened his eyes. Immediately they settled on her. His face softened.

Kira cocked her head. "You seem relieved I'm still alive." Any other time it would have been a joke, this time she genuinely meant it.

He cracked a small smile. "I am." He studied her for a moment. "What happened to you?"

Kira furrowed her brows. What *had* happened to her? "I don't know."

Chaol stood and moved closer to sit on her bed. When he reached his hands out to her ankle she flinched, expecting pain. When she felt nothing but the comfort of his touch she relaxed. Luckily, he hadn't seemed to notice her reaction. The bustling from outside had died down to nothing except the sound of a broom sweeping across the floor. It must be morning already.

She cleared her throat. "Did I make a fool of myself?"

Chaol blinked. "Of course not. But you did scream and cry. You fell to your knees, clutching your head, begging me to make the pain stop. But I couldn't. I couldn't do anything except carry you to the bed and try to get you to relax. I couldn't do a damn thing." He gritted his teeth. "I shouldn't have come at you like that. It was wrong of me. I let my anger get the best of me. I'm sorry."

Kira sat up. To her surprise not a throb of pain lingered. Her fingers trailed along the sheets that were still draped over her knees. What part of his words could she believe?

"Why were you so upset?"

He gave another heavy sigh. Her hand instantly slipped down to the hilt of her knife that was strapped to her thigh, in case he should express his frustration again. Instead he reached for her hands. The feeling of his strong fingers wrapping around hers mimicked warmth and protection. Were her old feelings haunting her again? When Chaol spoke his voice was weak, almost desperate. The look in his eyes was determined and lost at the same time. Kira frowned. What did all this mean?

"Kira, run away with me. I wasn't sure if I meant it before, but I know that I do now." His grip on her hands tightened.

Kira's eyebrows rose. He was the head of the guards; to abandon the court he'd be labeled a traitor, he'd be hung. Kira tried to pull her hands loose, but he hung on.

"Someone is out to kill you. Once they find you they won't hesitate to do so."

She nearly snickered at how obvious his words were. She was sure there were plenty of people wanting to wring her neck. "A … friend of mine, so to speak, asked me a question of great significance recently: Would you rather let the ones you love be hunted like animals? Or would you rather face the threat and end it?"

"But—"

Kira lifted a hand to stop him. "What you say may be true; someone out there might well be after me. But I will not shame the guild or myself by running away." She lifted her chin. "If someone wants to kill me, let them come out of the shadows and try."

~ * ~

Chaol pressed his lips into a thin line, mumbled a few words, then stood and left the room, leaving Kira alone. She stared at the door he'd pulled shut behind him for a moment, before giving herself a shake and rising from the bed. She could worry about Chaol later. At the moment, she needed to focus on where she stood and what was coming next. And to do that, she needed to go home.

After she explained the plan she'd devised to the men, she headed to her makeshift room, away from the other members of the guild. As she'd told the rest of them, they all needed a good night's sleep if they were to succeed in their attempts to infiltrate the palace the next day.

In spite of her admonishment to the others, that night she couldn't sleep an ounce. She tossed and turned endlessly in her bedroll, staring at the walls of her tent. Her blood pumped and her stomach twisted in wonderful knots of nervousness and excitement. They were ready to do this. They had to do this. What other choice did they have?

The next day, at sunset, Kingsman and Astien set off. Before they left Kira made sure not a blade was on them. They needed to gain trust and hiding a weapon was not the way to go about it.

Before she knew it, she found herself reviewing the plan one last time to Felix and Maddox. Then, seemingly in the next moment, she was in the bushes, the entrance to the palace in sight. Just across the path she could make out the faint outline of Badrick, waiting for her. He met her eyes and signaled a thumbs up. He was ready.

She didn't see him slip out of his hiding spot, but by the time she ran up and hit the pressure point of one of the guards stationed at the periphery of the courtyard, his partner was on the ground unconscious. She and Badrick exchanged glances before simultaneously stepping into the open space in front of the palace.

Badrick ran beside her, his steps in sync with Kira's. Whatever movement she made, he mirrored it flawlessly. When they drew close to the entrance, she paused and held her hand up. He stopped and waited for her instructions.

Kira crouched low, keeping the guards in sight. Without her hood and mask she felt naked. Yet there was a thrill to such complete exposure. It was new and daring. She loved it.

Knowing she didn't have to worry about Badrick, she was able to focus on reaching the palace undetected. In minutes, they had reached the guards at the front door, silencing both with a single blow to each of their temples before they could call out. Badrick pulled open the heavy wooden door and held it for Kira as she slipped inside.

Inside the palace, all was dark and quiet. Moving silently, like shadows, Kira and Badrick made their way to the quarters of the king and queen. Kira pressed her ears to the door and listened. What were the king and queen doing on the other side of this door? Were they lying in bed? Maybe in one other's arms as the moon shone through the window and fell across them. Or was her Royal Highness finishing up with another one of her baths in hopes of easing the stress?

Badrick spoke, but not to her. Kira whirled around, ready to fight. Then she let out a sigh of relief. Kingsman, smiling, stood looking at her. The rest of the men had gathered behind him.

"What's our next step, boss?" he asked.

Kira looked back at the door and took a deep breath. Then, with ease, she picked the lock in the handle and stepped inside.

Chapter 32

The king stood in front of the fireplace with his back to the door. His wife sat at her vanity combing the knots from her beautiful locks. Her gaze shifted in the reflective glass in front of her. Instantly, the relaxed look vanished from her face.

"Mikael," she called softly.

The king spun around to answer his wife's call and froze. One by one the men flowed into the room. With each step the king's face hardened further. Soon there was a human barrier in front of the door and the royal couple had no way to escape.

"I'll call for the guards," he threatened.

Badrick, the last one through the door, shut it gently behind him and crossed his massive arms. "I wouldn't do that if I were you."

The queen stood and walked over to stand next to her beloved. Though she wore her dressing gown, she stood just as tall, just as bold as she had before. Kira had to admit it was a beautiful piece. The fine silk and fur trim marked it as something that clearly belonged to royalty. Yet somehow Kira still fancied her own more.

The queen met Kira's gaze steadily. Recognition flickered in her eyes. "What do you want?"

"We want to talk." Kira held her arms out and gave a small spin, showcasing that she had not a weapon on her person. From the looks on their faces, that hadn't changed the opinion of the king and queen towards them at all. Kira slowly reached down to her shoes, never once breaking her gaze with the queen. She pulled them off one at a time, dropping them to the floor with a thunk. The royal couple's eyes followed her hands as she unclasped her cloak, letting it fall to the floor with a whisper. When she had finished, her men did the same thing.

"We can't take any more off unless you want us naked. You are going to have to trust us."

"Why should we trust you?" the queen asked as she narrowed her eyes.

"Simple. We have no weapons. We're defenseless. Even if we did manage to escape, you know our faces. If we were here to hurt you, we wouldn't make it so easy for you to kill us, now would we? You must know this to be true, or you would have had us arrested and hung by now." Kira shifted her weight, making sure that she kept her voice even. "So how about we all sit down and talk?" She held her breath, waiting, until the king nodded, took his wife by the elbow, and guided her over to the chairs in front of the fireplace. Kira shot a look at Kingsman. He was watching her, a look of pride on his face. She nodded, briefly, before following their royal highnesses across the room. When she reached the sitting area, she sank to her knees respectfully and lowered her head before straightening up, ready to begin their conversation.

The other men followed and took seats on the floor. Kingsman stayed near the door and Kira knew he would stop any guards from entering should they attempt to do so.

The king and queen sat upright in their chairs, as regal-looking as if they sat on their thrones. Kira drew in a deep breath. The discussion she was about to lead was the most important one of her life. If she could not convince the royal couple of their innocence, none of the men she loved so dearly would leave the palace alive.

Their lives were in her hands now. She could not fail.

Chapter 33

The carpet pressed into her knees and her legs had gone numb from sitting on them for so long. Kira talked of everything she could think of, from Russell to Silas and her contract. As she spoke, not a word left any of her fellow guild members' lips. Kira caught a hint of shock on the faces of everyone but Kingsman and Badrick. Obviously the others were struggling to comprehend the fact that her plan seemed to be working. She'd heard murmurs the night before from the nearby tents, hints that some of them were making plans to escape from the cells they were sure they'd find themselves in today and take cover in the woods. Kira was disappointed in their lack of faith, although she understood it. Even she was having trouble believing the king and queen would allow them an audience for this long without somehow attempting to summon the guards.

The king shifted on his chair. "How do we know you won't follow through with the job you've agreed to. I'm sure the pay is hefty and you clearly have the skills to do so."

Kira nodded. "That's true, but I've no wish to see harm come to you. You are the only ones who can clear our names. Besides, I can't stop Silas and Pierceton without you."

Her heart pounded in her chest as she spoke. Would the king and queen believe her? She was risking everything by telling them the truth. They could easily refuse to believe her words. She was just a thief, a low life, someone who came from the streets. Why should they trust her? Seeing that the queen had remembered her from the day she posed as her lady's maid, Kira found it necessary told them the story of how she had crept into the castle. If she wanted to earn the couple's trust then she must answer all questions and give as many explanations as possible. She left out Badrick's part, not wanting to implicate him unless absolutely necessary, but he stepped forward.

"I entered the castle with her, Your Highnesses. We meant no harm, only to gather information, but if Kira is to be held accountable for the breach, I should be as well."

Kira kept her features even. Still, her heart filled with happiness from his words. The king studied Badrick in silence for a moment before nodding at Kira. "We can discuss accountability later. Is there anything else you'd like to share with us?"

"Actually, there is. When I was in your chambers that day, I overheard the head guard mention the murder of an older man. He lived with his wife and daughter, as well as her husband and their child."

She paused. The thought of the child sleeping happily by the fire still haunted her mind. It pained her heart and made her stumble across her words. Everyone in the room waited in silence for her to continue. Kira drew in a quivering breath. She couldn't let her emotions ruin the strong composure she had kept all night.

"I had an assignment a few months ago. A man who'd fallen behind on his payments to a tradesman. It was a normal job; I didn't think much of it. The elderly man didn't notice me until he had closed and locked his door, so it was easy to get what I needed. His young granddaughter was asleep by the fireplace." She bit her lip. *No, I must control myself!* "She slept all night long on the hard wooden floor, waiting for him to come back. He feared I'd hurt her. I'd never do such a thing but the look in his eyes as he begged me … it would have jolted your heart if you had seen it. He thanked me as if I were a god. All for not hurting her, when in reality I had done him harm, taking the money he must have needed to take care of his family."

Her voice broke as a tear fell but she swallowed hard and lifted her chin, fighting to hold back more tears as she continued. "Silas had him murdered. To know that she will never be able to greet him again is a heart-shattering thing, even for a thief like me. If he really wanted to thank me, he should have taken his family and run the moment he heard of the murders. Perhaps if I had been quicker to figure out this mess he'd still be alive. He'd still come home to her laughter and the feeling of her arms wrapping around his neck. Do you see? We are thieves, not killers. We understand what it's like not have anyone. We'd never want to bestow that on anyone else."

The room was deadly still. For a long moment, no one moved. Then the queen turned to her husband and squeezed his hand.

The king rose, towering high above Kira. He puffed his chest out and glared down at her.

Kira's chest clenched. It had been stupid for her to bring everyone here. She should have come alone and left the others where they were safe and out of harm's way. She had escaped the cells once, she could do it again. Preferably without dragging the rest with her.

He took a knee and came to her eye level. His wife glided gracefully to his side. Though she was not as tall, her presence was every bit as commanding.

"Go on, Mikael." Her voice was calm.

Kira's eyes met those of the king. Were they going to call the guards? Would they throw them in the dungeon and leave them to rot?

"Kira." His voice was deep and stern. Her stomach lurched. She hadn't done it. She had failed them all. They would live out the rest of their lives, their arms shackled in chains above their heads, eating nothing but questionable muck. She should have known better than to have tried. "We will side with you. But should you do anything to make us second-guess our trust, we will cut all strings completely and every one of you will go to jail. Do you understand?"

Kira's heart leaped. Unable to stop herself, she threw herself at him, mumbling her thanks over and over again. Her childish act made everyone chuckle, breaking the tension. There still were no answers. There still was no clear plan to reveal who Silas was and why he was implicating them in the murders. But now there was hope, and hope was the greatest thing possible.

～ * ～

Tavern music roared. Laughter bounced off the walls and the thick, hot air closed in on her. But the heat was the furthest thing from Kira's mind. She was too busy celebrating. Too busy trying to comprehend what had happened that day.

Maddox stood and tugged her away from the table with such exuberance that she nearly stumbled over the bench in the process. Without missing a beat, she caught her footing and followed behind him. He pulled her into the crowd on the floor and lifted her gracefully in the air as he spun. Kira let out a laugh as her stomach fluttered, which only widened his grin.

"You did it lass, you really did it!" He set her down gently, as though she were a feather. Then he began to lead her around in a jig. There weren't many dances they knew, but everyone recognized the Dance of Lights. It was one of the most well-known dances, often performed at festivals, weddings, parties, balls, and other events. The jig itself involved very quick steps. Once the dancer's feet touched the ground, they immediately flew back up again. It was a dance that required a lot of endurance, something Kira out-matched Maddox in.

After they had danced a minute or two, Astien stood and asked to take his place. Maddox complied, good-naturedly, and took his place back on the bench, holding his hand to his chest and commenting about how he wasn't as young as he used to be.

Kira caught a glimpse of Badrick from across the room. He was watching her. She couldn't read his expression as he lifted his tankard to his lips and took a swig of his ale. When Astien escorted her back to the table, they were both laughing. She felt Badrick's gaze on her and looked over. Something swirled in his eyes that she couldn't quite identify. Was he jealous? Her stomach fluttered at the thought.

"Cheers to Kira!" Kingsman's voice rose over the noise of the chatter. Even the city seemed to celebrate tonight for Kira's accomplishment. Somehow a sense of security had washed over the town and an unusual liveliness gripped its citizens. The people cheered even though they didn't know what for. That was just how happy everyone seemed tonight.

Kira pushed her tankard of ale away and reached for her water. She'd never been much of a drinker, but after what had happened with Silas, she'd never taste the stuff again.

Chapter 34

His head pounded. Badrick pressed one palm against his temple and the other against the wall to steady himself. When was the last time he'd had that much to drink? He couldn't count the number of times he tripped on his way back to the hideout. His senses were a blur, like his thoughts. The pounding intensified and he groaned. The flickering of the flames in the hideout lashed at his eyes. He wanted nothing more than to find a dark corner to sleep off the pain.

A movement in front of him caught his attention. Kira had poked her head out of her tent. It felt as if a hand tightened around his heart. A look of concern crossed her face and she stepped out into the open space and walked toward him. "What's wrong, Badrick?"

Badrick allowed his gaze to sweep up and down the length of her. She appeared much less intimidating out of her armor and dressed only in her thin nightgown. The nightgown he had gone back for. The nightgown he had sacrificed himself for. Had Astien thought to do that? No. Yet she seemed plenty happy dancing with the redhead tonight.

Or what about that sorry excuse of a guard? Had he managed to steal a kiss from her innocent lips? Had he seduced her with his strength and charm? Badrick barely resisted the urge to spit on the ground. Chaol may be strong, but that didn't make him a man. The guard couldn't protect Kira like he could. Badrick knew her weaknesses. He knew her strengths. He knew how she used the dark to her advantage, how she wielded a blade and aimed her bow. He knew her better than that brute ever could. Yet there still seemed to be something about the head guard that caught her eye.

"Astien was right." Badrick's hand continued to cradle the side of his head, trying to ease the growing headache. "This cave is suffocating me. I need to step back outside."

Badrick began to stumble his way through the temporary hideout. That was a lie. *She* was what was suffocating him. He caught the soft padding sound of her bare feet against the cold cave floor and frowned. Why was she following him? If she got too close, if she touched him, he'd explode. He stepped out into the cold night air.

She grabbed his elbow from behind. "Badrick, you're drunk."

He whirled around. "You think I don't know that?"

She lifted her chin. "We need to go back inside before you do something stupid."

"Leave me be, woman!"

She'd been reaching for him again, but his words froze her hand in the air just before she touched him. Her forehead wrinkled in confusion. Then she pulled away completely. Not just physically, but emotionally too.

Please, please just leave.

"Woman?" she growled. "This *woman* has a name. And this *woman* just gave us a chance of winning this damned war."

"Then this *woman* should go celebrate her accomplishments with her guard and red-headed thief."

Her hand lashed out before he could move. His cheek stung. The ringing in his ears was still crisp as he touched the spot. He deserved it. Maybe it was what he needed to pull himself together.

Kira spun around and stalked back into the cave. He found it funny. Just a moment ago he had been begging her to leave, yet here he was frightened by the sight.

Badrick cursed and went after her. He had to jog to catch up with her halfway back to the tents. When he did, he circled her wrist with his fingers to stop her and turn her to face him. He caught her fist as she swung directly for his temple. He knew the goal behind her punch. She had aimed to knock him out cold. The thought of her wanting to do so wrecked his heart more than the action did. She struggled against him, trying to break his grip.

Kira raised her foot for a kick and he tried to take a step back to dodge the blow. The booze slowed his reaction. He grunted and dropped her hand as he took the hit. When he lifted his head to look at her, Kira had already started back toward her tent. *Is this it?* Were all those years of friendship about to be broken because of his stupidity and jealousy? If the other men saw him now they'd laugh in his face. He couldn't let her walk away so easily. Badrick lunged and wrapped his hand around her wrist and his other free arm around her waist, pulling her close. When she opened her mouth as if to yell, he lowered his head and pressed his lips to hers.

The warmth of her lips against his was jolting. For a few more seconds, she fought him, until finally she stilled in his arms. Badrick let go of her wrist and wrapped his other arm around her back, tugging her even closer. Holding her felt so right, so natural, as if they had been created to fit together. Electricity shot through him at the thought of something being so perfect. Badrick groaned and deepened their kiss. How had he ever thought he could push her away?

When he finally raised his head, she met his gaze. "You're drunk," she whispered again. A tear slid down her cheek and he wiped it away gently with his thumb.

"I think you slapping me sobered me up." She knew him better than anyone. Could she hear the apology in his voice?

She must have. Kira rose to her tiptoes and pressed her mouth to his, demanding more. They had shared a kiss or two in the past. But the way their lips met now, the way she looked at him, the way he felt, it was all different than before. In the past he had touched her, teased her, simply to aggravate her. Not now.

He whispered her name as his lips trailed from her forehead to her cheek then back to her lips. For years he had waited for this moment. All those times he had suppressed his desire as he sparred with her, or the times his heart fluttered when she'd look at him a certain way, the feelings he'd shoved down whenever he was around her, all poured out.

After several minutes, she stepped back.

"I should have done that a long time ago," he joked with a small smile.

To his relief, she returned the smile. "Why didn't you?"

His shoulders slumped. "Because I was scared."

Kira glanced up at him. Badrick inhaled sharply. Was that lust he saw in her eyes?

"That crush only went away for a few months, Badrick. Then it came back and hit twice as hard."

"You're good at hiding it."

"I could say the same to you. I guess I learned from the best."

His smile widened. He stood, enjoying her fingers in his hair and her thumb running along his neck. *Let her go now or you'll regret it.* Badrick pulled back his hand. "You should get some rest."

For a moment she looked a little hurt then she nodded. Badrick let out his breath. She understood.

"I'll see you tomorrow." Kira turned away.

"Count on it." He watched her as she walked to her tent and lifted the flap. She hesitated and his chest squeezed. *Don't come back. I don't have the strength to send you away twice.* She turned and glanced at him over her shoulder, as if she had heard his thoughts. Her eyes met his for a moment before she looked away and ducked inside the tent. For a moment he stood, questioning if his consumption of booze had caused him to hallucinate what had just happened. He pushed back his shoulders and went into his own tent. It was best not to question it and simply enjoy the relief his heart felt. He made his way silently over to his bedroll, trying not to wake Astien. *You're a fool, Badrick.* There was nothing but friendship between the redhead and Kira. It was only his jealousy conjuring up something that wasn't there.

Badrick stretched out on his makeshift bed. For the first time in months he was able to relax. Still, as his eyelids grew heavy, he found himself wondering what Kira was doing in her own tent. Impatient with himself, Badrick turned onto his side and forced his eyes shut. Thoughts like those would have to wait until they were in safe waters. From now on they had to be on complete alert. Having the palace on their side was comforting, but that didn't mean that Pierceton would back off.

In fact, now that they were dealing not only with Pierceton, but with the much more dangerous Silas, a man whose true capability was unknown, things were likely to get a whole lot worse.

Chapter 35

He watched the mouth of the cave in the night. He'd be stupid to enter it now, so he'd wait. He had hated her from the beginning, perhaps because she'd seen through his disguise the moment she laid eyes on him. The only difference between them was that she wasn't afraid to voice her opinion. His fingers tingled. He was eager to kill her, every last one of them. If it wasn't for Silas he would have done it already.

He'd had a life before he met Silas. He'd lived in a small farming town a few miles up north where the land was fertile from the rain during the spring seasons. He'd had loving parents who would do anything for their son. That was, until he lost them in a riot. The same riot Kira had lost her parents to. The same one that had left her stranded in the streets to fend for herself at the ripe age of six. His hands tightened into fists. She would understand what drove him to do what he did, wouldn't she?

It was stupid to go against her. He had seen her fight. When she tackled Russell he knew she wasn't afraid to kill when she had to. That's exactly what he needed. He needed her on his side and he had every intention of getting her there.

When rays of light broke over the horizon, he turned and walked away, unnoticed. He'd catch her when she least expected it. Then he'd leave her no choice but to join him.

Chapter 36

Kira sat in a foreign room, one she had not yet entered, on one of the palace's finely-embellished oak chairs, fumbling with her dress. She hated it. She'd insisted that her normal attire was perfectly fine, but Kingsman was stern. *If you are going to walk in the palace, you will act like one of them. You want them on your side? Well, become one of them.* Kira knew what he said was true, but that didn't mean she didn't think this contraption she wore was a waste of money. Kingsman sat diagonally across from her. He too was dressed in formal attire. He sent her a scowl and Kira stopped her fumbling, only to continue to tug at her sleeves under the table.

While they waited, she couldn't stop staring at Felix, who leaned comfortably against the wall. She had yet to whisper a word about her encounter with Sapphire. The whole conversation seemed like a dream. If there was one thing that she learned during her training, it was that some information was better left unsaid.

Kira's eyes drifted over to Maddox, who had taken his place next to Kingsman. Kingsman insisted that he and the two men accompany her, saying that they were more skilled in the speech and manners of the court than she was. Though it was true, Kira wondered just exactly how much they knew and how they knew it. As soon as they stepped into the courtyard, their demeanor changed. They stood straighter, heads high, commanding respect. People stared and whispers were exchanged. While Kira kept her back straight, something told her that they understand the ways of the palace all too well.

The door opened and the men stood, hands hanging at their sides. Kira took a few seconds to follow suit and the guard who had opened the door shot her a look of mild reproof. "The king and queen are ready to speak to you now," he announced.

Kira followed the three men into the adjoining room, where their highnesses sat at the head of a massive wooden table. The three men bowed. Again, Kira was off by a second as she curtsied. For the first time in her life she felt completely out of place.

"You may rise."

Kira hadn't realized how long she had held her submissive position until she felt her legs shake as she straightened up. The couple who sat before her were not the same people she had gone to meet the night before. Their clothes were made of the finest cloth. Across the queen's chest gems sparkled, so much so that Kira was sure they could blind a man. Her lips were ripe with a red stain, her hair fashioned into the finest up-do and adorned with pearls. With her in the room, Kira's dress, though it was the finest she had ever worn, seemed bland. The king was dressed to match the finery of his wife. Gold rings circled his meaty fingers and a beautiful golden shield had been embroidered into the left side of his clothing, just above his heart. *Loyal to the people, loyal to the crown.*

The king gave a nod and the guards left the room. Kira counted seven breaths of stillness. Eyes met as everyone on both sides appeared to evaluate the others. *Be one of them.* She lifted her chin.

Finally the tension broke as the king inclined his head toward the empty seats at the opposite end of table and everyone sat down. Then the discussion began. Questions were shot at her from every angle as she outlined her plan for the royal couple. Kira forced herself to remain calm, to not get irritated. Her tugging at her sleeves ceased and her voice stayed even as she gave a solid answer to every question.

"And just how do you plan to lure him out?" The king's eyes were stern, but not harsh. Kira understood. He needed to know. He was putting his kingdom, his life, and the safety of his queen in her hands. If he did not agree to what she had planned, he could easily throw her back out to the streets to be discarded and forgotten like the dust that collected on his tapestries.

"I will follow through with my contract. At least, I must make Silas believe that I have."

The king rose as his wife frowned. "And why would I let you do that?"

"When I went to visit Silas, he tested me. To him I was nothing more than the role I played. A noble woman grieving over the discovery of her husband in bed with a servant. I passed his test, but that was only the first one. He is bound to follow me, or send someone else to, when I go to follow out his orders. If I fail to make Silas believe that you and the queen are dead, he will send someone else in here to kill you, and then he'll kill all of us." She swept a hand through the air, indicating the other members of the guild.

"The best I can do without actually carrying out the murders is to stage them. Silas's guard will be down once he believes the deed is done, which will buy us enough time to attack when he least expects it. The key will be that he believes the palace is after me for your murders and not him."

Felix planted his palm on the table. "What makes you think he won't kill the king and queen himself if he realizes you have failed to do so?"

She turned to face him.

"Silas hires other people to do his dirty work because he isn't willing to risk making the attempt himself and either be captured or escaping with a bounty on his head. To risk much, one must be willing to lose much." *Meaning one has to have something—or someone—so valuable it is worth risking everything for it.* As Sapphire had said, you either let the ones you loved be hunted down or you end it.

The king sat back down. His fingers ran over the small beard on his chiseled chin. "Why not just go into The Grottos and kill him?"

Kira smoothed the skirt of her dress with both hands. "For one thing, it wouldn't be possible to sneak a group of royal guards into a place full of criminals. And two, there are more men on Silas's side than you realize. The common people both fear and follow him. Such a show of force against a man by the guards, when the palace did not yet have concrete proof he was acting against them, could easily ignite a revolt. And the one leading it would no doubt be Pierceton, who has been carrying out the murders and attempting to set up the guild on Silas's orders. If Silas falls, Pierceton won't hesitate to take his place. If we can lure the two of them to one spot, and gather evidence of their plot to kill the king and queen, any action against them, including killing them, could easily be carried out and even more easily justified."

Kira watched the faces of the royal pair carefully as she spoke. Was she getting through to them at all? She couldn't shake the sinking feeling that her best effort was not going to be enough. She shifted on the hard wooden chair. "Could I see a list of the victims?"

The king called a guard into the room and requested a copy. When the man returned, moments later, he handed her a scroll. She took a deep breath as she took it, her fingers trembling slightly. She had prepared herself to see it with her own eyes. She assumed she would be fine. Yet as she unrolled the paper she felt a part of her heart shatter. All those names. Each one belonging to a person who was as innocent as an angel from the heavens, in comparison to Silas. If she had acted faster, would she have been able to save a soul?

Kingsman he gave her a gentle kick in the leg to jolt her back to reality.

The king brought his palm down sharply on the table and she jumped. "We will consider all you have said."

Kira waited, but he offered nothing more. They had been dismissed. Not a single hint of what the king's and queen's answer would be. *Leave it to the royals to take their time.* Likely knowing she was about to toss protocol aside and demand an immediate response from the king and queen, Kingsman shot her a warning look. Seething with frustration, Kira rose, curtsied as briefly as possible, then followed the men out of the room. Had she done something wrong? She'd worn the dress, walked their walk, talked their talk. What else could she have done?

Anger bubbled in her stomach. Kingsman turned to her and opened her mouth to speak, but Kira brushed by him. She didn't have time to sit around waiting for their royal highnesses to take their sweet time making decisions. She needed someone to act with her, and now.

When she turned the corner, Kira collided against a chest. She looked up, ready to take her fury out on the imbecile who didn't have the sense to stay out of her way. The rebuke died on her lips when she realized who it was she had crashed into. Chaol.

His forehead wrinkled in confusion. Clearly he was trying to make sense of why she was here in the palace. Kira's chest tightened. He wasn't to know of her alliance with the king and queen.

Before he could question her, she turned and fled down the hallway in the opposite direction. Behind her, Kingsman called out her name. Though she never turned back, she knew that the footsteps pounding down the hall after her did not belong to her adopted father, but to someone who was, to her, far more of a threat.

Chapter 37

Kira wanted to go face Silas herself. To kill him, to make him and Pierceton both suffer. When she'd left the palace grounds, she had fled into the forest. Now she ran blindly, shoving branches away from her face and leaping over fallen logs. When she tripped over a root and nearly went headlong into the bushes, she forced herself to slow down. Her chest huffed as her anger boiled. She had to stop herself before she did something she regretted.

The image of a dead man flashed crossed her mind. Then a name, and another and another and another. She couldn't stop herself from thinking about them. Did they have families? Children? Regardless, all had been robbed of their lives and it was wrong. They hadn't done a thing. These were innocent people. As far as she knew, they hadn't committed murders, they had never stolen anything, their hands were clean. Still, they had been killed, all to frame her.

Kira turned to the closest tree and slammed her fist against the bark with all her might. But she didn't stop with just one punch. She put what energy she had left into her hits. Punch after punch, kick after kick. Her legs and feet tingled in pain. The bones in her hands screamed.

After giving her last punch, Kira crumpled against the tree. Tears streamed down her face just as blood trickled down her hands. She must look ridiculous. Thankfully, she was alone with no one to see.

When the tears began to slow, she lifted her head. In her view the remains of the hideout sat among the trees. She began to move towards it, her body numb. Everything was in ashes. The trees around it were singed, the grass lifeless. *We've known for a while now.*

Astien's words echoed through her mind. They had known for a while. They had been planning to leave here. How did they know? And why hadn't they told her? Nothing made sense anymore. What was real and what were the lies? Just who was on her side and who should she kill?

Finally Kira gave up. Movement by movement she lowered herself onto her back. The soot would most likely stain her dress, but at that moment she was glad it would. She wanted her clothes dirty and ruined. Just like she was.

~ * ~

Chaol watched her through the trees. The blood on her hands, the tears on her cheeks, the pain in her eyes. It killed him to watch, but he forced himself to do it anyway. He had planned to catch up to her, grab her by the arms, and force her to talk to him, but that plan quickly changed when he realized how upset she was. He sat down and leaned against a tree, crunching a leaf in the process. He froze. Any other time Kira would have sat up and drawn her weapon. Now, she gave no indication she'd heard the sound. She said nothing. She didn't move. All she appeared to do was watch the clouds pass above her.

Chaol sat there for hours. The sun had begun to set and soon the stars would be out. Kira hadn't moved an inch the entire time. If it hadn't been for the wind that was making her shiver, he would have questioned if she was even alive. Finally he decided he couldn't just leave her out there any longer.

Chaol stood and strolled over to her. He crossed his arms and shook his head as he gazed down at her. Had she been asleep the entire time? At some point, she had given in to the exhaustion. Even a woman as strong as she was needed rest.

"Kira."

He kept his voice soft as he knelt down next to her. He called out again, a little louder. Her eyes remained shut. Tentatively, he rested his fingers on her cheek. She stirred, but didn't wake up. He called out to her one last time. Seeing Kira open her eyes brought him relief.

"You'll catch a cold," he stated simply.

She frowned. "Let me."

"You can't save your guild if you're not at your full potential, now can you?"

She groaned, acknowledging that he was right. Finally she sat up. Chaol's gaze followed her hands as she rubbed her eyes with her palms. Had the blood not have dried, it would have smeared all over her face.

"What do you want, Chaol?"

Her voice was sharp and he repressed a wince. "I want to show you something."

Kira stared up at him. Dark shadows framed her bloodshot eyes. How long had it been since she had gotten a good night's sleep?

When she didn't move, he held his hand out for her to take. She hesitated. Would she ever learn to trust him? After a moment, she placed her hand in his and he pulled her to her feet. "We should go back so you can change first. You'll turn heads walking into town covered in soot."

"Where are you taking me?"

He ignored the question as he let go of her hand. "Did it hurt when I pulled you up?"

She shook her head and the muscles in his shoulders relaxed. "Good. You didn't break any bones. Now let's hurry before it gets too late."

~ * ~

Kira wasn't sure why she followed him. Perhaps it was out of boredom, curiosity even, but either way she had done it. As they approached the main gate of the palace, he stopped and she followed suit, standing silently behind him. Chaol spoke to the two guards, who both stole a glance over his shoulder at her. Did she look as bad as she felt?

"Let me see your hands," he demanded, once they were in the safety of his quarters. When Kira did as he'd asked, shock flashed across his face. Because of her hands or because she'd done what he'd told her?

"My lord, Kira," he gasped. "What did you do? It's worse that I thought." He pulled up the sleeve of her dress and his jaw tightened. "What are these?"

Kira glanced down. Her burns had healed well. In fact, they were nearly gone except for a few. "You were there when I got them."

"I was focused more on the fact that you could barely stand." Though he snapped at her, the care was crystal clear in his voice.

"I couldn't have just left Badrick there, Chaol."

"Of course you couldn't have." He sighed as he let her hands slip from his grasp. Without another word, he reached into a drawer and pulled out what medicine he had. He inclined his head toward the bed. "Sit down."

She paused. Sitting on his bed did not seem like the wisest thing under the circumstances. She contemplated staying where she stood. Unfortunately, her hands were throbbing and she couldn't afford for them to get infected or they would hold her back from the work she needed to do. Lifting her chin, Kira settled on the edge of the mattress.

Chaol pulled a hard wooden chair over from the corner of the room and set it in front of her. He sat down, a frown on his face, his anger shining coldly.

He grabbed one of her hands again and gently cleansed her wounds in silence. Kira winced slightly from the sting, earning a soft apology from him for the pain. But for nothing else. After applying some kind of salve, he reached for the bandage and began to wrap it around the palm of her hand. When he was done, Chaol brought his mouth down close to rip the bandage with his teeth. With a small yank he was able to tear it then tie it so it wouldn't fall off. He did the same with her other hand.

Kira watched him work in the poor lighting of his room. There was something off about him. He moved as gracefully as ever. When he leaned down to tear the bandage, his warm breath had caressed her wrists, sending a shiver up and down her spine. He had paused for a moment each time he'd done it then seemed to push whatever thought he'd been entertaining aside before continuing.

When he finished, she cleared her throat. "Thank you," she mumbled as she took back her hand. He gave a small nod in acknowledgement as he closed the box and locked it with a click. Her cheeks warm, Kira dropped her gaze to her hands and took notice of the fine craftsmanship. Oddly perfect craftsmanship.

Chaol shut the drawer and leaned against his dresser with a sigh. Kira lifted her head at the sound. He stood as he always did, his shoulders broad, his back straight. Only now his fingers rubbed at his eyes before raking through his hair. Finally he looked at her.

Kira studied him. What was he thinking? Clearly he was trying to figure her out. Or maybe trying to figure out how he felt about her, whether he hated her or loved her. Her stomach tightened. Which would she prefer?

His fist hit the wooden surface. Kira didn't flinch. Instead, she watched him as he pushed away from the dresser and began to pace, his fist pressed to his mouth. She wasn't sure what she thought of him anymore either. Seeing how truly worried he was about her suggested that not everything he had told her was a lie. It was just hard to tell what was and what wasn't. Kira repressed a sigh of her own. *Enough.*

"If that was all you wanted to show me, I'll be taking my leave now." She spoke calmly as she stood.

"No!"

Her eyes widened as he stepped forward, his hand out as if to stop her.

"No," he repeated, more quietly, his hand dropping to his side. "It's not the only thing. Follow me."

"What about my dress?"

He looked back at her. "Ah yes. I'd forgotten; I got too far ahead of myself." His lips twitched slightly before his features hardened again. "I'll give you something to change into once we get there. Until then we will take the back way."

Kira nodded and followed him in silence. They weaved their way in and out of the castle, Chaol taking her ways she hadn't known about. She had always suspected were other paths she hadn't had time to learn about, but to go down them in person was another thing.

He led them past the kitchen, across the practice field, and to the stables of the palace. All without getting caught by the guards.

Kira followed him into the stalls and found two mares sitting patiently. Were they waiting for them? Her brows furrowed. The horses were saddled up with bags of supplies hanging down both sides of their rumps. Their reins had been latched on, as if they were ready for a long ride. She glanced at Chaol. His eyes, practically pleading, met hers.

"Kira, we don't have much time." He took her hands in his and gave a squeeze. "Please run away with me. This will be our last chance. We can live happily in another town. I'll work hard to make sure you have whatever it is you need. I'll spoil you, make sure you have a roof over your head and food on the—"

Kira tugged her hands from his. "Chaol, slow down." She stepped back. "What is it you're not telling me?" The horse nudged her shoulder from behind. Kira turned and hushed him quietly as she ran her hand down its snout. Was the animal picking up on the nerves that flopped around in her stomach? She turned back to Chaol. He stood half in shadow. She couldn't decipher the look on his face, but he was beginning to scare her.

"I don't have a good feeling, Kira," he murmured. "I've been trained to be able to push fear aside, but for Pierceton to be able to escape the jail on his own makes the hair on the back of my neck stand up. He wants to kill you. I saw the blood thirst in his eyes in his jail cell; it's clear he has the skill and the mindset to. "

"I can't leave the others here to deal with him."

His hands closed into fists. "Don't you see how much trouble they've put you through? You nearly died saving Badrick, does he appreciate it? No! And Kingsman, he's been lying to you all these years."

Kira's eyes narrowed "Kingsman saved me. I was on the streets alone and about to die. Every single one of them has done so much for me. I think not letting Badrick burn to death was the least I can do."

"Kingsman may have saved your life, but he never cared about you enough to tell you the truth. He was the last head guard, Kira. And Maddox and Felix were his right-hand men. When I saw him, I knew he looked familiar, so I went back and checked the records. His name is there. All of their names are there."

Her whole body froze. She couldn't begin to register how to feel at this news. Heat roared through her as she glared at Chaol. He had gone too far, attacking the men she loved. "All the more reason I should respect them. No doubt the reason they left was to get away from soldiers like you who try to tear people apart instead of protecting them." She spun on her heel and headed for the door of the stable.

"Kira, wait!"

She almost turned back at the sound of desperation in his voice, but she forced herself to keep putting one foot in front of the other. Her heart was being ripped out inch by inch.

"Please!"

She couldn't do it. Couldn't stand being the cause of the pain in his voice. Knowing it was the worst thing she could do, she stopped walking.

"Kira, I love you!"

An arrow pierced her heart. Even after everything he had done to her, guilt and sorrow assaulted her. Exactly what she deserved for trusting someone outside of the guild. She drew in a shaky breath.

"I know you do." She whispered the words without turning around, knowing if she saw his face, his eyes, she wouldn't be able to do what she had to do.

Pushing back her shoulders, she walked away. His footsteps did not follow her.

Chapter 38

Kira took the road on the outskirts of town. Chaol's words echoed in her head as she walked. Her arms wrapped around her stomach and held tight. His warning had jolted her and, worse, the news he brought of Kingsman startled her. Would Kingsman honestly hide something like that from her?

She was so deep in thought that she barely noticed the rustling in the bushes beside her. Her hand didn't reach for the handle of her blade until the intruder suddenly appeared on the road before her.

"Sweet, sweet Kira. Look at yourself. What have you done?"

She growled and went to unsheath her blade, only to find it gone. Curse the rule of having no weapons on her person when she spoke to the king and queen.

"Pesky rules they have, don't they?" He tilted his head towards the palace behind them.

Kira clenched her jaw. "You showing yourself to me is suicide."

Pierceton smirked as his eyes flickered over her. He stuffed his hands into his pockets as if they had known each other for years and had just reunited to catch up. "I actually came to talk. So there's no need for weapons anyway." He waved a hand at her as if she were a child.

"I don't need a weapon to kill you. What makes you think I won't do so to you right now?"

"Because I have answers to all your questions, particularly those regarding a certain head guard." In spite of herself, his words sparked interest and curiosity. From the smug look on his face, he could see that in her eyes. "Chaol, isn't it? Haven't you ever wondered about him? Who he really is? What exactly he does?"

Kira swallowed. "No need to waste your breath telling me; I won't believe a word you say anyway." Her protest was weak and Pierceton chuckled.

"He has allowed us to believe that he became associated with us by mistake, but he didn't exactly tell you who in the guild he knew, now did he? And this nonsense of running away. He was never so keen on it before now, so what exactly made him feel so guilty all of a sudden?"

Kira couldn't let him get to her. That was his goal. He wanted to turn her against Chaol, against the guild.

"I got out of that cell because there was a loose brick with a lock pick behind it. Who do you think told me about that? And what about the guild? How do you think they knew they needed to move the hideout because I was planning to plant a bomb? What happened to not keeping any secrets and trusting one another? Don't you see it, Kira? They are all against you. They are planning to destroy you. From Chaol to Kingsman to Badrick."

Kira gritted her teeth. This was all just games. Pitiful mind games. "Why are you telling me all this?" she snapped.

"It's clear that I can't win if I fight you; that's why I need you on my side."

His calm demeanor drove her insane. He'd planned this encounter. He had practiced his words well because he knew that if he didn't she wouldn't have a problem with ending his life. She scoffed. Surely this was a joke. As if she'd ever side with him. "Give me one good reason why I shouldn't kill you now?"

"You and I, we are similar. You remember that raid, don't you, Kira? You saw the damage; you lived in agony because of it. We both did. We know what it takes to survive and we know the pain of being alone. I had to take on multiple jobs just to get a night's meal and you had to work to find a dry place to sleep. We learned to be strong, but we can be stronger together."

"Over my dead body."

He let out a short laugh and shook his head. "What has Kingsman filled your head with all these years? I was watching when he found you. It infuriated me that someone like you had been chosen to be taken home. To this day I don't understand why I had to continue to work while you were taken in and pampered. I'm trying to see past that now, trying to give you an opportunity to gain your freedom from all this. The lies, the deception. But it seems that you're too blind to take it."

Hands wrapped around her neck. Fear flashed across Pierceton's face, and he whirled around and fled down the road. Kira pawed at the arms of the person choking her. Going on instinct, she drove her heel down on the foot of her attacker. A cry of pain split the air as the grip around her neck loosened. Kira drove her elbow into the stomach of the person behind her, then spun around, grasped the hooded head, and smashed it against her own. Whoever it was dropped to the ground.

"Damn coward." Kira raised her fist, ready to fight, regardless of her wounded hands. Her attacker struggled to sit up, the hood falling from her face as she did. Kira gasped. Sapphire. Her eyes met Kira's.

Something in her gaze cooled Kira's temper. Pursing her lips, she held out a hand and helped Sapphire to her feet. "Trying to kill me?"

"I'm sorry. It was the only way I could think of to help you. When I saw Pierceton, I knew I had to step in. Pierceton is not one to chance blowing his cover, and sticking around for a fight would run that risk. I thought if he were under the impression you were under attack, he would run, which he did."

Kira contemplated the woman. There was something different about her. Perhaps it was the way she stood or the way she carried herself, but it was as if she were a new person entirely. "Why would you want to help me?"

Sapphire brushed dust from her robe with both hands. "The last time we spoke, I saw in you the woman that I've always wanted to be. I'm done making excuses for my actions."

Kira crossed her arms over her chest. "What are you planning to do?"

"Let me talk to Kingsman. I know things that can help the guild win this war you've been fighting."

"And what makes you think I would ever trust you again?" Kira growled. Sapphire hadn't taken a single step towards her as they spoke. Clearly she understood that one wrong move from her would set Kira off, like a bomb.

"I don't expect you to trust me, but I'm hoping you will. Aren't you tired of running, Kira? Tired of playing these ridiculous games? Because I know I am."

Kira's hands fell to her sides. She *was* tired. Of all of it. The secrets, the lies, the deception. She was done. She jerked her head toward the hideout. "Come on."

Sapphire fell into step beside her. *What am I doing?* Kira's mind felt foggy. Why was she taking Sapphire home? Could she really trust her? What would Felix think? Oh by the gods, she didn't want to think of how this would affect him.

Kira took a shaky breath. The decision was made. All she could do now was pray that her choices wouldn't come back to haunt them all.

~ * ~

Kira's chest clenched. She hadn't meant to hurt him.

Felix stood frozen; the dagger in his hand fell to the ground. The clank echoing against the stone made her flinch. She swallowed hard. The others stood just a still as he. The expressions on their faces made it clear they couldn't believe that Sapphire stood in their midst once again. What was racing through their minds? Were they taken aback by her beauty? Sapphire hadn't changed much. She still had that rich-colored hair, those demanding eyes. She was still just as beautiful as the night Felix proposed to her.

"Kira, how dare you bring her back here? I suggest you escort her to town immediately and come back with a logical explanation." Kingsman forced his way in front of her.

Kira pushed back her shoulders. Never before had she spoken against him, let alone given him a foul look. But at that moment, if looks could kill, he would have been slaughtered. "No. I suggest *you* listen to *me* and give me some explanations. How long were you going to hide it from me?" she snarled. The tension in the air thickened.

Kingsman faltered, his anger clearly doused by the fury in Kira's eyes.

"Don't even give me that look like you've done nothing. When were you going to tell me how you knew Pierceton was going to blow up the hideout? When were you going to explain any of this to me?" Her head snapped to Maddox and Felix. "And don't think you two are innocent. In fact all *three* of you have a secret you've been keeping."

Maddox stepped forward and spoke in a soft tone, obviously hoping to calm her down. "Kira, we're sorry—"

"If you were sorry, you wouldn't have kept the truth from me in the first place."

"What truth?"

Kira whirled to face Badrick. He took a step back, as though afraid if he came any closer she'd attack him too. Which she might. She felt as if she were a mountain lion, ready to pounce on the next man who dared step too close.

"Why don't you tell them, Kingsman? No? Felix, how about you?

Maddox?" She flung a hand in their direction. "They were all guards for the palace." She planted her fists on both hips. "You know, with everything we have gone through, I wouldn't have been mad if you'd just told me the truth, if it hadn't been for all these damn secrets. What I want now is some clarity and that's why you *will* let Sapphire talk to you. She might have answers that could help me, help us. Is that too much to ask?"

Never before had Kingsman lowered his gaze to the floor. Not once. Even when he was on the edge of losing a battle or had terrible news to deliver, he always kept his gaze steady, locked on the person in front of him. But now, now it was as if he were a child who had just been scolded.

Kira looked at Badrick again. He was gazing sorrowfully at Maddox and Felix. Kira took his silence as agreement that Sapphire should speak. There had been no reason for them to hide such a secret from the rest of the guild. There were no secrets between them. Or there shouldn't be. Everyone was like an open book. As if each of them could read the others' lives from cover to cover. That's what she had always believed, anyway.

Now she didn't know what—or who—to believe.

Chapter 39

Kingsman sat down and handed Sapphire a plate filled with their typical meal, cheese, and bread, along with a glass of wine. The rest of the guild crowded around. Felix stood in the corner, looking very unsure of how to handle this new development. Kingsman felt for him. Felix hadn't seen Sapphire for nearly ten years. His friend and colleague had hoped to forget her, for her to just to be a washed-away memory. Yet here she was sitting in front of him. The very same woman who had tried to murder him while she stole his heart.

Kingsman followed through with Kira's demand, listening to Sapphire as she explained her story. So many thoughts and emotions swirled through him, he wasn't sure how he could focus on her words, but he willed himself to try. His heart had ached with grief when he heard the pain of betrayal in Kira's voice. The least he could do for her was listen to Sapphire.

"It started years ago. I was young and needed money, and Silas was the highest-paying boss. When I first met him, I knew I had to be careful with how I played my cards. He refused to show his face, something only a man who was involved with things much more dangerous than the average criminal was would do. He started me off with simple theft and sabotage then escalated from there. He never told me much about the clients, but I needed the money and questioning his motives was something that could cost a person their life." She took a deep breath before continuing.

"Pierceton showed up a few months ago. Silas seemed to take a liking to him, but the favoritism never bothered me. I didn't care. I had no desire to put myself in danger or draw attention by questioning the work they were doing, so I just did what I was told, took my money, and waited for the next assignment.

"I never really gave Pierceton a second glance. He didn't seem like much of a threat. In fact, I had no idea what Silas saw in him. To me he seemed like a waste of time and space. It wasn't until Silas started pairing us up for jobs that Pierceton began to let his guard down. He'd let small things slip when he spoke, his schedule was never set, and he was often gone for weeks at a time. All habits I knew Silas would not tolerate unless it was for another job.

"Then rumors started circulating about what Silas was doing, what he was planning. And I got scared. I started searching through Silas's office while he was away. Which, as with Pierceton, seemed to be often. I dug through everything and anything in that room. I read every paper from top to bottom, never skipping a word." Sapphire stopped and sipped from her glass of wine.

Kingsman shot a glance at Felix. He'd moved a little closer so he could take a seat at the table, but he stayed at the end of the bench, as far from Sapphire as possible. If Sapphire noticed him, she didn't give any indication.

She set her wine glass down on the wooden table. "Then one day I saw it, a list of the members from the guild. Kira's name circled." She turned to Kira. "When I found you the night you went to talk to Silas, it was an honest mistake. In fact, you saved me. I thought Silas was gone and was about to break into his office. Had I not heard all the ruckus you were making, I would have come in and he would have caught me red-handed."

Kingsman swallowed a bit of bread. "How did you connect Pierceton with Silas's plans for the guild?"

"I began to spy on him. I'd heard that the hideout had been attacked, but I didn't know who had done it until a week later. I overheard Silas and Pierceton speaking. I couldn't make out everything they said, but Pierceton didn't sound happy.

"For the next few nights I tried to keep a close eye on him and tracked him to you, Kira. He is well aware of your abilities, and I suspect he may be contemplating trying to overthrow Silas. That's likely why he tried to convince you to join him."

Kingsman squared his shoulders. There was silence as everyone took in her words. Kira shifted. Was she waiting for him to respond? Instead Sapphire's voice broke through. "I just want to clear one thing up," she stood up and brushed herself off. "The night I attacked Felix, I was not myself. Silas had used Nightlock on me. I wasn't trying to kill Felix out of my own free will, please believe that. I understand you questioning my loyalty to the guild, but before you send me away, know that I have information about Silas I'm willing to share with you. The man deserves to die."

When no one answered, she cleared her throat, "I'll leave you all to talk things out. I'll be outside."

Again silence fell. Kingsman could feel Kira's eyes on him, but couldn't meet her gaze. Where was he to start? From the beginning? Back from his younger days as a soldier? Perhaps he should wait until Kira had cooled down before he attempted to explain anything to her. Yet he couldn't find the heart to make her, or Badrick and Astien, wait any longer for the truth. Maddox must have felt the same way, because he spoke up before Kingsman could find his tongue.

"When you and I had the conversation after you came back from your job in the brothel, Kira, I knew something had to be terribly wrong for you to feel the way you did about Russell and Pierceton. I had been feeling the same way, only I didn't have any proof so I wasn't ready to say anything.

"After Russell's murder, it was clear one of us had to have been the one who killed him. I suspected it was Pierceton, so I snuck into his room. I found the bomb and immediately warned Kingsman. We began stowing away supplies that very night."

Kira's voice didn't soften an ounce. "Why not tell me?"

"We knew you would have killed Pierceton the moment you found out. But we need him alive to find out who is behind all this mess."

She crossed her arms over her chest. "And the rest?"

Kingsman sighed, his heart sinking deeper and deeper into a sea of guilt. Maddox didn't answer. There was more to that story than he could answer. Kingsman's gaze finally found Kira's. His daughter. His love. His everything. And he had disappointed her.

"I'm not a man of innocence, Kira." He pushed back his plate. "I was similar to you in many ways when I was younger. I grew up in a small hut with my parents. My mother was ill; my father worked from dusk till dawn, earning nothing but a few coins for his labor. I saw how my mother grew thin, how my father's cheek bones began to cave in from lack of nutrients. So I did what I had to do, steal.

"I stole whatever I could get my hands on. Food, clothes, coin. Soon I stumbled into Felix, a boy who was practically his father's slave, and Maddox, the son of a blacksmith. We had skills. We could make our way through a crowd without being seen or heard. We could take whatever we wanted, whenever we wanted, and no one ever caught us doing it. But we got cocky and wanted something more. Something better. So we aimed for the palace."

Kira's shoulders slackened. She uncrossed her arms and waved for him to continue.

Memories of the three of them in their teenage years slipping, invisible, through the night just as he had taught her to do, darted through his mind. They were careless at times, their hearts pounding from the adrenaline and their face gleaming from the wind on their faces.

"We broke in one night. We almost made it out, but a guard decided to make one more lap around the perimeter and caught us. He knew us by reputation, so he gave us an option. Either go to jail or serve our years as guards and no one would know of our crimes."

Astien stepped from the shadows. "So you took the second choice."

Kingsman nodded.

"He promised us we would never go hungry. We were able to return home with more than enough food for our families. How could we let it pass?" Maddox frowned. "But there were sacrifices too."

The pain on Maddox's and Felix's faces reflected the pain Kingsman felt in his heart.

"What happened?" Badrick asked softly as he sat down next to Kira. Her stern look had disappeared.

"Attacks started. People turned on their own townsfolk, afraid of being murdered in the streets. Some killed to get money, others for protection, and some in retaliation for a false accusation. But the palace refused to take the threats seriously. No matter how much we pleaded with them to send our troops out to restore peace. Finally, reports reached our ears that the situation had grown dire. Kingsman made the decision that we could no longer wait for the royals to act. We would take matters into our own hands. We armed ourselves and rode for town, but by the time we got there it was …" Maddox stopped and swallowed. "We were too late."

Even to that day, the sight was vivid in Kingsman's mind. The bodies on the street, the blood staining the cobblestones, the horrid screams and pleas. As clear as if it had happened only a few hours before.

"So many had turned evil, the innocent ones didn't stand a chance. It was a massacre." Kingsman cleared his throat. "Everyone finally snapped. No one knew who to trust and who not to. Who was a killer and who was their friend. I was ashamed that I had let something like that happen. I had grown to love those people during my years of training, and to think

I couldn't protect them from their own kind ... I knew I didn't deserve my title as head guard." He reached for the jug of wine and sloshed some into his glass, hand shaking. He set down the jug and downed the dark red liquid, wiping a drop from his chin before setting down his glass.

"If I had pushed the palace a little harder, a little sooner, I could have saved all those lives. So I stripped off my armor and turned it in for street clothes. I reverted to my old life in hopes of helping others to rebuild theirs."

Felix set down his fork. "And we followed in his steps. We started the guild to try and leave what had happened behind us and focus on what was ahead."

Kira kept her lips sealed, but Kingsman drew hope from the transformation in her. She no longer seemed angry. Instead, he knew she ached, for that was the same look he'd seen on his comrades many years ago. For those who died, for those who had lost everything, for those who suffered. Perhaps hearing his story was what she needed.

Kira stood up abruptly.

"Where are you going?" Astien asked.

Kira looked back at them all, a small smile playing on her lips. "I'm going to visit a friend."

Chapter 40

SILAS CIRCLED HER SLOWLY, AND though his eyes were covered, Kira could feel his gaze drifting up and down her figure. She stood still, her fingers grazing the handle of her dagger in case should she need it.

"A festival, you say?" Silas stopped in front of her. "Why should you make me wait until then? As it is, your deadline is coming up at the end of the week."

"You hate the king and queen as much as I do. Why not humiliate them in public?" she asked, remembering her accent.

Silas paused. "Quite charming, aren't you?" His voice sent shivers down her spine as he circled around again, his fingers dragging along her waist. Then he slowly raised his hand as if to cup her cheek. Kira caught his wrist before he had the chance to touch her.

"Refusing to show your pretty face?"

She could hear the smirk in his voice. "You have your secrets and I have mine."

He tugged his hand from her grip. "You have until the festival." His voice had hardened. "Until then, Sapphire will keep an eye on you. And I will be there at the festival to watch. Should you fail, well, I'd hate to show you what happens to people who do."

His threat was clear. Kira couldn't wait until the night came, and along with it, her chance to end everything once and for all.

Best of all, Silas would never see it coming.

~ * ~

The look of shock on their faces almost amused Kira, although she understood it. First she showed up unannounced, then demanded to see them at once, now she stood in front of them in her typical armor. She was done dressing pretty and talking their language. It was their turn to learn.

"You're going to throw a festival," she demanded bluntly.

The king frowned as he crossed his arms. "Why should we, when you refuse to show respect?"

Kira leaned across the table, far closer than protocol allowed. She needed for him to have nowhere to look but at her.

"Because you won't listen." She planted both palms on the wooden surface. "Which sounds familiar, doesn't it?"

"I suggest you watch your mouth," the queen snipped.

Kira's gaze drifted over to her. She shook her head. "You just don't get it, do you? I was told of a story that happened many years ago, an event similar to something that is happening again now. Very similar, in fact." Kira leaned back in her seat.

"If what I told was right, your people nearly massacred each other. They couldn't tell who was their friend, who was their hunter, or whose prey they were. Apparently three guards begged you, pleaded with you, to listen. But you wouldn't. So they set out to protect the town themselves. Do you know what they found there? Bodies. Dead bodies everywhere. Buildings were on fire, people were screaming, it was true horror."

The king's jaw tightened. "If you think we didn't want to help, you're wrong."

"I never said you didn't want to help," Kira corrected him. "Only that your hesitation in taking action eliminated that possibility." She straightened up. "I know how much you love your people. You want them to be safe. But so do I and so do those three men. They loved them so much that when they realized they had arrived too late to help anyone, they felt they didn't deserve their titles."

Memory clicked in their eyes. Kira nodded. "So you remember them? I'd hope so since you saw them only a few days ago."

A knock sounded on the door. All three of them turned their attention to the entrance as Chaol burst into the room. He was breathing heavily, as if he had just run for his life. His eyes locked on Kira.

The king leapt to his feet. "Speak! What's happened?"

"A riot has started. My men are down there now in hopes of stopping it."

The room went deathly silent. Fear swept across the faces of the royal couple. The one thing they had to be horrified of ever happening again was occurring at that very moment.

The king and queen followed Chaol from the room, Kira right behind them. Without hesitation, they saddled horses and pushed them as hard as they could. As they rode into town, Kira saw was she had feared. Though the damage wasn't like Kingsman had described to her, it was a start. Windows were shattered, some stalls had been broken into pieces, food had spilled out onto the street.

"This is what they tried to warn you about." Kira rode up next to the king and queen, who had wheeled their horses to a stop.

The queen sobbed into her hands as her husband rubbed her back. The king looked at Kira. "Surely this must be Silas's doing. We had no idea he would go to such lengths. We never meant for any of this to happen. We want it to stop."

Yes, this was definitely Silas's doing. It was a warning to her personally. A reminder of how her life would shatter should she fail. Her knuckles whitened as her grip tightened on the reins. She had known that he had power over the people. She had known how he could control a person's mind, but seeing the effects of his games rattled her. *It's my childhood all over again.*

From the corner of her eye, Kira watched a young man help an older man, bleeding from his head, stumble into a house. Though she hated the scene splattered before her, part of her was grateful the king and queen were seeing the horror of it for themselves. "If there's one thing I've learned these past few months, it's that sometimes you have to sacrifice yourself to keep the ones you love safe."

Kira heard the leather of Chaol's saddle squeak as he readjusted. Had her words finally hit him? Did he finally understand the pain and worry she had attempted to convey to him? Did he hear her exhaustion? Her fear of what was to unfold should no one listen to her? Better yet, had the king and queen finally seen her point?

Then she heard the last thing she expected the king to say. "We'll do it. Whatever it is you have in mind, we'll do it."

Chaol rubbed his forehead as he closed his eyes. The dark bags had started to reveal themselves and she realized that, despite the act, he was just as exhausted as she was. He stole a glance at her, frustration clear in his expression. She knew the possible outcome if she were to take the wrong step. It seemed that he too knew just how fragile the situation she was throwing herself into was. Should something go wrong, should the she injure the king more than planned, she would be hauled off to prison with a noose waiting to welcome her. Yet if Silas saw through her plan to deceive him, he would not hesitate to make her suffer until her dying breath. Kira ripped her eyes away from Chaol and continued to take in horror around her. This was a dangerous game she was playing, but it was a game she was willing to take a part in if it meant that her family had the chance to live. Even if it meant sacrificing her own.

~ * ~

The king invited Kira to stay at the palace for the remainder of the week. She was given a room, which she shared with Sapphire. The rest of the guild had also been summoned to the castle and put up in rooms down the hall from her.

When she was first introduced to her room, Kira's breath had been taken away. Though it wasn't as grand as some of the other rooms she'd been in it, it was still mesmerizing. Despite its beauty and warmth, however, she couldn't sleep at night. Her mind continuously drifted to those in the streets. Why should she be blessed with such luxuries when they were suffering?

The morning after her first night, Kira was called down to the practice fields. She gaped at the scene before her. Kingsman stood with a sword at his hip. Beside him were Maddox and Felix, similarly equipped. Her head turned. Out on the field men were paired up and running through their drills. Many had stripped off their tunics. Each one was drenched in sweat from the scorching sun.

An agonized groan stole Kira's attention. Badrick stood over a young soldier. She tried her hardest not to take note of his bare chest. Her stomach churned at the sight of the build all Badrick's gear could hide.

Disappointment was clear on the young soldier's face, but Badrick held his hand out and encouraged the boy to keep going.

"Kira, come here," Kingsman called. She walked over to stand beside him, her eyes grazing over the field before settling back on the man she knew as a father. Everything seemed to have changed about him. He appeared much stronger now. As if being in the castle and wearing a sword at his hip fueled his strength.

"They are good men." He waved a hand over the field. "Chaol has done well."

"Thank you, sir." Chaol walked up to the two of them. "But they still need much work."

Kira grew uneasy as she caught him eyeing her. Her palms grew sweaty as she thought of their last encounter. She stood, her arms crossed and her senses alert. She remembered their night together well. Too well for her own sake. She felt her heart grow cold towards him. It wasn't that she couldn't bring herself to look at him, it was more like she didn't *want* to look at him. She felt as if she had hardened.

Kingsman nodded curtly. "Every man has room for improvement."

"How do you suggest we inspire them to do what it takes to improve?"

"Perhaps if they saw their captain in action."

Kira knew it was coming. She could hear the words forming on his lips before he spoke them.

"Kira, how about a spar with the head of guards?"

She smiled grimly. "If he thinks he can keep up."

Chaol frowned as the men were called in. They circled around him and Kira, clearly curious to see what would happen. Badrick shoved his way to the front, through the crowd.

Kira unhooked her cloak and let it fall to the ground.

Badrick gripped Chaol's arm. "Don't underestimate her, Chaol. It'll be the biggest mistake you've ever made."

As Kira watched, Chaol's eyes flickered to Badrick, then back to Kira. How odd. Was Badrick actually lending a helping hand to the head guard he claimed to hate? Perhaps he knew that sparring with her in such a state was a dangerous thing. Pierceton's words echoed through her mind. *Chaol, isn't it? Haven't you ever wondered about him? Who he really is? What exactly he does?*

In spite of everything that had passed between them, as Kira contemplated Chaol she couldn't help but feel he was a stranger. As if she knew nothing about him.

Because she didn't.

Chaol hesitantly took his stance. She waited for the right moment. Then she saw her opening.

Her first rush nearly overpowered him, but he quickly recovered. Though she wasn't as strong as Chaol, she was fast, and she knew how to use her body weight to her advantage.

"Don't hold back," she growled at him. Heat surged through her. How much had he kept from her? How many lies had he told? Kira clenched her fist and threw a punch. Chaol blocked it and sidestepped out of her path.

I got out of that cell because there was a loose brick with a lock pick behind it.

Pierceton's words echoing through her mind distracted her momentarily. Chaol seized his advantage and threw her to the ground, pinning her down. The feel of his hands on her wrists burned with familiarity. Had someone else held her down the same way? Her mind rushed. The memory was so close, but still so far.

His eyes narrowed as he stared down at her. "What is it, Kira?"

Her heart pounded so hard she couldn't speak. What was it? What had happened to her?

"Kira, what's wr—"

She brought her head up sharply, smashing it against his face. The grip on her wrists loosened and Kira scrambled out from underneath Chaol. Her eyes met Badrick's. He looked concerned, as if he could tell she was fighting with herself. She ran her fingertips over her wrists. She couldn't seem to hold her hand steady. Her mouth seemed to grow dry as the desert and her heart thudded erratically.

Chaol scrambled to his feet. For countless sleepless nights the blurred memory had hovered in her mind. It taunted her, teased her. Whenever she was near Chaol, she felt as if she was a step closer to remembering.

Their fight quickly resumed, but Kira's tactic had changed. She purposefully allowed contact between them. Each touch, when he'd block her punches, or she'd block his, seemed to bring back a shard of her lost thoughts. Excitement rose at the chance of remembering. But fear quickly followed. What would she remember? More importantly, did she have the courage to face what awaited her?

Finally Chaol appeared to grow tired of playing her ridiculous games. He grabbed her hand and tugged her in.

The crowd hushed. Both stood, their fists aimed and ready for the side of each other's head. Yet neither one delivered the final blow. Kira searched Chaol's eyes for some sort of clarity. For that final puzzle piece she needed. Instead, all she got was a mixture of hurt, fear, anger, and lust.

"I'd call that a tie, wouldn't you, Kingsman?" Felix stated calmly.

"Aye, I would."

For a moment, neither of them moved. Then Chaol lowered his fist, and Kira followed suit. She stood silently as the crowd roared.

"That is how you need to fight." Kingsman clapped her on the shoulder. "You must be prepared for the worst to come."

Kira swiped the back of her hand across her forehead. She feared they'd have to be more than prepared for the worst. That they might have to accept it.

~ * ~

Badrick cursed as she grabbed her cloak and strode away. No one seemed to notice. They were all too carried away with the thrill of the fight they just witnessed. His anger began to sizzle as she reached the gates surrounding the practice field and disappeared. He swung his gaze to Chaol. The guard stood there, looking as confused and lost as a child. He lifted his eyes to meet Badrick's. Chaol didn't speak, simply let out a sigh and reached for his own tunic, before nodding at Badrick and heading toward the palace.

Badrick stalked after him. When he reached the man, he grabbed his arm, ripping him around and shoving him up into the side of the palace wall. Chaol's instincts kicked in and he reached for his dagger, but Badrick was too fast. He had something fueling him that Chaol didn't. Rage.

"Look here, *Sir* Chaol." Badrick pushed his forearm against the head guard's throat. "I don't think you quite understand what's going on. That woman you just fought? She is the most dangerous creature you will ever meet, and I, the second."

"What's this? The little thief has feelings for her?" Chaol chuckled. "How cute."

Thick rage pulsed through Badrick. Did the man not realize he could snap his neck before Chaol even realized what was happening?

"What goes on between Kira and me is our business. But let's get one thing straight. Your king and queen seem to trust you. I, on the other hand, trust you as far as I can throw you."

Chaol narrowed his eyes. "I could say the same to you, thief."

Badrick allowed him to shove his arm away and distance himself. Chaol casually pulled his tunic on over his head, as if this was a conversation between friends. Badrick may have a smaller build compared to the guard, but that didn't mean that he couldn't put up a good fight. If the man gave him one reason, Badrick would make sure he'd leave covered in bruises from head to toe. So much that it would hurt to lie down on the softest of feathers.

Chaol tugged his tunic into place. "Perhaps you should stop focusing on being jealous of our relationship, and concentrate more on her well-being. From what I just saw in her eyes, Kira is suffering far more than we know." With that, Chaol spun on his heel and made his way to the door of the palace.

Badrick stood watching him until the guard disappeared inside. Though he hated to admit it, Chaol's words had sparked worry. Had more damage been done to Kira that he had realized?

Chapter 41

Kira sat on her bed, her eyes glued to her wrists where Chaol had grabbed hold of her.

"They won't change just because you keep staring at them."

Kira looked up. Sapphire sat on another bed across the room.

"I keep thinking the answer will just show up if I do," Kira admitted as she leaned back against the wall.

Sapphire let out a laugh. "If only things were that simple."

The corners of Kira's mouth turned up. *If only.*

The blankets rustled as Sapphire stood and blew the lanterns out. All the light swept from the room, leaving the moon their only source. Kira waited for her eyes to adjust so she could make out the outline of her hands in the dark. It just didn't make sense. None of it made sense.

"Sapphire, is it possible to regain your memories after using Nightlock?"

"It is." The bed creaked as Sapphire laid down. "It's not often you hear of it. But it's possible. Mine returned, although countless times I have wished they hadn't."

"How do they come back?"

"With time." Exhaustion was heavy in Sapphire's voice when she replied. "And usually there is something, a word or an action, that triggers them."

Kira stretched out on her side and looked at her. "I've experienced that. Certain ... people seem to bring the memories right to the surface. I feel as though it won't be long, or won't take much more, for them to break through."

Sapphire stayed quiet. Her body was motionless in her bed except for the rise and fall of the sheets as she breathed. She was a beautiful woman. Though Kira had never mentioned it, she had always hoped to look like the redhead when she got older. Sapphire had an exotic aura about her. The cinch at the waist and the curve of her hips and bust. Her cheekbones highlighted and her eyes bright and bold. Part of Kira always wondered what things would have been like had Sapphire chosen a different path. Would her wedding to Felix been simple and charming? Or big and grand? Would they have children by now?

Sapphire would have been more like an older sister than a mother. Perhaps they would have stayed up on nights like these, whispering to each other across the room. Talking of their troubles and giving advice they both longed to hear.

Kira laid down, watching her through the moonlight. Had Sapphire not spoken when she did, Kira would have assumed she had fallen asleep.

"I know what it's like to not remember things you know you should." Sapphire extended her own hand out in front of her. "To have that feeling of almost knowing. You know it's there. It's right there, just out of reaching distance. It sits there. It taunts you, teases you, laughs at you." She closed her hand, pausing in the silence. "It seems the moment you think you have a chance of grabbing it, the memory slips from your fingers."

Kira stayed silent. Her brows furrowed slightly as she thought. Everything that Sapphire had just described to her was true. Every last word of it. Sapphire turned her head and met her gaze. "Silas pulled the same thing with me as he did you. But I was foolish back then. I had turned my back on him; I trusted him too easily. It was child's play for him. All he had to do was hold the rag to my face and I was under. Because of that, I nearly forgot who Felix was. Who all of you were. When I attacked Felix, I didn't even realize what was happening until it was too late. It was because of your scream, of Felix's touch, that I was able to regain what little control I did. Then I saw the pain on your face and the blood on his and I ran. Like a coward."

An odd sensation ran through Kira. One that made her fingers tingle with nervousness.

"Silas didn't used to be so ruthless," Sapphire continued. "For a while I actually respected him. I knew him for years before he assigned me to go after Felix. He had planned it all out perfectly. To get Felix to fall in love with me, then strike when it was the perfect time. I never would have guessed that I would fall in love with him too.

"But Silas showed me no mercy. I refused to carry out the job. I loved Felix too much to do such a thing. The next thing I knew he held the Nightlock to my nose. Each second that passed it was like I was drowning in an abyss. It's scary to think that such a small plant can do so much damage, can make you do things you never would have done otherwise. I've lived with regret ever since that night I turned on Felix. Then when I saw him again for the first time in years, it all hit me like a tidal wave. I realized in that moment just how much I …"

Her words trailed off. She didn't have to finish her sentence; Kira already knew what she would say.

The room seemed to dim. As if it was a reflection of Sapphire's thoughts and emotions. It was odd. Kira often found herself questioning her choices of the last few months. Yet the truth she had been craving was slowly slipping through. Now she began to question if ignorance truly was bliss.

"He still loves you too," she whispered. In the dim light, Sapphire's eyes locked with hers, and Kira finally understood. For years she had clung to the hope that there was a reason for everyone's actions, but the last person she'd expect to confirm that hope was the only person who had been able to.

"I know," Sapphire whispered back. After that there was no more talking. No more thoughts. Instead Kira settled back on her pillow and peered out the window, watching the clouds pass by the moon.

~ * ~

Sapphire stepped into the dining hall, her hair pulled back and her cloak concealing her face. There everyone had gathered for their breakfast, eager to start the day. She took a moment to watch the servants rush to fill drinks and keep the food well stocked on the table. Then she moved forward and took a seat at the first open chair she spotted.

She calmly placed a roll on her plate and looked for something else to her liking. Her conversation with Kira the night before had done something to her. She felt less tense, as if all her secrets had been lifted from her shoulders. Oddly, it felt nice.

"Jam?"

Her train of thought was broken by a voice.

"I'm sorry?"

"I asked if you wanted the jam."

Not wanting anyone to recognize her, she held out her hand without looking at him. "Yes, thank you."

Her hand brushed his and electricity pulsed through her. Sapphire's breath quickened as she glanced up. She met his eyes. Her heart leapt in her chest. "Felix?" she mumbled mindlessly.

He looked as shocked as she felt. "Sapphire?"

The sound of his voice saying her name made her shiver. She had been trying so hard to avoid him. Then one careless act screwed her plan up.

"Why are you dressed like that?" he asked as she took the jam and they both returned to eating, acting as if they were two strangers having a pleasant conversation.

Sapphire gripped her knife to hide the fact that she was shaking. Why was he talking to her? *Why here? Why now?* He needed to hate her. He needed to never want to see her again. "You are welcome here, but I am not. I can't afford for anyone to see me."

"The guild welcomed you for the time being. You are a part of us."

"Don't speak such nonsense," she snapped. She had seen the way he had looked at her when Kira brought her into their hideout. He couldn't believe his eyes. He clearly didn't know what to do, what to say. But she shrank under his gaze. Was that admiration? Love, even? How could he look at her like that, after all these years, after what she did?

Felix took a deep breath, obviously not going to let her words stop him. "Have you talked to Kira? I haven't seen her all morning." He reached for a tart.

"She left me a note saying she was going out for a walk and would be back by noon to discuss plans."

He didn't reply. Sapphire felt as if there was so much more to say, but she couldn't find the words to say it. There was so much she wanted to know. What had happened while she was gone? How were Badrick and Astien doing? How had Kira handled the rest of her teenage years? Did Maddox ever make any new contraptions? The questions were all there, on the tip of her tongue.

"Sapphire I—"

She stood up abruptly. She couldn't do it. She didn't have the courage to face him. Not after everything that had happened. "There are some things I have to attend to. Please excuse me."

Felix didn't go after her as she turned and swept from the room. Though she had been covered from head to toe, surely he could see the wounds on her heart, wounds begging to be healed. Would he ever believe it wasn't really her the night everything happened? Could he ever forgive her?

Even if he could, it might not matter, because she could never forgive herself.

Chapter 42

KIRA STARED AT THE DOOR. She had come to know it well over the last few months. If she pushed past it, a set of stairs awaited her. Then, a few steps after that and she would be in the prison. She could sneak into Pierceton's cell and inspect the walls. Yet she couldn't bring herself to do it. If Pierceton was right, what then?

"Miss Kira, Sir Badrick is calling you to the meeting room."

Kira turned her head and spotted a servant standing nearby, waiting patiently for her.

"Thank you, I'll head up there now."

The servant gave a small bow before disappearing down the hallway, most likely terrified to be in her presence. Though no one was supposed to have uttered a word of the guild's stay in the palace, it was clear that these strangers were no ordinary people with no ordinary skills. After sparring with Chaol on the training grounds, Kira had been treated differently. Often the staff kept their conversations with her short, as if they were afraid of what she could do to them. Even though she didn't have any intention of raising a finger against any of them.

Kira turned and made her way through the hallways. By now she had memorized every detail. Every brick. Every painting. Every turn. Every exit and entrance.

The two guards standing post at the door allowed her in without hesitation. As she entered, she felt as if, for a moment, things were back to normal. The group huddled around the table, planning out their next strike. Except for the presence of the king, the scene was so familiar. But all that was truly familiar was gone now. No longer were they in the hideout, safe underground with nothing but the torches as their source of light. Instead they were high above ground, with sunlight pouring in through the windows. Long gone were the old, beaten table and rickety matching chairs. Now the table they gathered around was polished to its prime and the chairs cushioned with a rich, red velvet.

"Now the meeting will begin," Maddox called out.

Kira took her seat next to Badrick and leaned back comfortably. She did have to admit that part of her didn't mind the new chairs, they were much more comfortable.

At the head of the table, the king surveyed the thieves gathered around it. "We should wait for Sir Chaol to return so—"

Kira cut off his words. "No."

He scowled down at her. A warning she knew she should not take lightly. "And why not?"

"This meeting is to be between the guild and you."

"He is the head of the guards. Does he not have the right to be here?"

Kira's eyes locked on his. She leaned forward, refusing to be intimidated. "With what's going on, there is no longer anyone we can trust. Including your own head guard."

There was silence as the king met her gaze steadily, then he turned and called the meeting to order.

"What are you doing?" Badrick hissed in her ear.

Kira kept her eyes on the king. "Trying to save all of our asses."

She could still fell Badrick's gaze on her, but she didn't look at him. Dreams upon dreams had overwhelmed her the night before. They seemed to be random, but Kira knew better. They were a warning. The room grew dark. Kira glanced at the window. The bright rays of sun had been snuffed out, blocked by a harmless-looking cloud. A reminder that they could not let down their guard, that those who appeared the most innocent could wield the weapon that would destroy them all.

~ * ~

The meeting somehow managed to finish smoothly. Which was a miracle. That night, Kira was to take the layout of the city and draw out where Chaol should plant his guards. Meanwhile, the staff would ready the preparations and decorations.

She had planned to go back to the inn she had stayed at before. She needed alone time, and though it wasn't quiet, there wasn't the stress of everyone looking over her shoulder.

"No need to go." Sapphire clipped her cloak around her neck. "I'm taking my leave."

"Where to?"

"I figured it might be nice to take a walk around the palace after having to stay hidden for so long."

A knock on the door sent Sapphire into the adjoining washroom. Before Kira could call out and ask who it was, Badrick peeked his head into the room, a sheepish look on his face, almost like a child.

"Is it safe to come in?"

"Of course. It's just Badrick, Sapphire."

As Badrick closed the door, Sapphire stepped from her hiding spot, her shoulders relaxing. He eyed her cloak, asking a silent question, but Sapphire didn't offer an explanation. She propped her hood up to protect herself against the cold, exchanged a glance with him, then turned for the door. "I'll be back within the hour."

Kira trusted her word. "Keep a sharp eye."

Sapphire nodded and disappeared. Badrick looked at Kira. "You really think she's safe alone?" he asked as he walked over to her.

Kira turned her attention back down to her plans. Her head pounded. She had been at this for hours. It wouldn't be a simple faking of an assassination. She had to take into account how Silas would react. How many men would he have sent to the area? He'd be at her neck if she missed. If he was as terrible as people made him out to be, and her few encounters with him had convinced her he was, he wouldn't hesitate to kill her, even if it meant taking down any civilians around her.

"I plan to follow her soon," she replied. Badrick leaned in closer. Kira could feel his body heat burning into her. The scent of his leathers drowned her. She took a deep breath to calm herself. She couldn't let herself be distracted by such things. Not until the guild's name was cleared and everyone was safe.

"You're stressing too much, Kit." He spoke softly. "I can see it in your face."

She let out a sigh, dropping the quill onto the table. Hearing her nickname was the last thing she needed. It made her weak in the knees and desire to flood to the surface.

"How did it all come to this, Badrick?" she whispered, pressing her hands to her face. This wasn't how she had planned her life. She only wanted to carry out the duties of the guild, to see all the men find a beautiful woman to marry and settle down with. Why couldn't everyone just let them live life in peace, doing what they loved most? They were thieves. But they weren't monsters.

Badrick's arms wrapped around her from behind. He buried his face into her hair, giving her a kiss. The action had been out of comfort. But Kira wanted there to be so much more to it. How much had the alcohol influenced his words the night they had celebrated her alliance? Were they true emotions he had suppressed all these years, or had they merely arisen in the heat of the moment?

"I won't let anything happen to you. To any of us." He whispered the words, his breath warm against the back of her head. *If only things were that simple.* She took a shaky breath and sat up straighter, which only drew him closer against her. Her eyes burned from pushing back tears. Kira pressed a hand to her stomach. All the fear she'd been experiencing had settled deep in her gut.

She cleared her throat. "You'll be hiding by the stage, with Astien on the other corner should anything go wrong." *Ignore your fear Kira.* "I'll be in this store with my bow and arrow."

Badrick looked down at her plans. He pointed down at the empty space behind the marker that represented her position. "Your back is wide open. Someone could sneak up behind you."

"I need the other men to be with the crowd. If Pierceton or Silas act out, who knows what they are capable of?"

"At least put me there."

Kira shook her head. "I'm not going to let anyone else innocent die, Badrick."

He let go of her and moved to the far side of her desk. When he planted both palms on the wooden surface and leaned in, his lips were pressed into a thin line. "Haven't you realized by now that I'm not going to let you put your life at risk any more than the rest of us?"

Kira averted her gaze. She could feel the anger boiling inside him. If she wasn't careful with her words, all the amends they had made would be shattered.

"I have people I want to protect too, Kira. I know it's hard. Do you honestly think it doesn't rip my heart out when I hear that some bystander has been killed? But I can't just run into battle, prepared to die. Not when I have others who depend on me."

Don't you understand? Even if the name of the guild was cleared, Silas wouldn't stop until she was dead. For some reason, he had targeted her.

Fighting him was something she would have to do alone. She held her breath through a long, heavy silence. Badrick's gaze burned into the top of her head, but she refused to look up. Finally, he pushed himself off the desk with a heavy sigh. "Fine, get yourself killed. We'll be able to go on without you, I can assure you."

Kira finally lifted her head and watched Badrick stalk to the door. His hand gripped the handle and he froze. He sighed, looking back at her over his shoulder.

"You don't have to do this alone, Kit. You never had to do any of this alone. It's you who've made that choice." When she didn't answer, he twisted the door handle. "Be sure to get some rest."

Kira's mind scrambled for something to say. Anything. But before she could open her mouth, the door shut firmly behind him. Her anger exploded. She looked around and grabbed the first item she saw. She picked a book up off the corner of the table and threw it at the door. The sound of the two colliding made her wince. Had she woken the entire castle? Although she listened intently, she heard nothing but the sound of fading footsteps.

Kira sighed as she ran her hand through her hair, her anger gone as quickly as it had come. He was right. She needed to sit back and think everything through. Or perhaps that was the problem. She was thinking far too much. Ink stained the paper as she began to rewrite the plans. She had to be smart, think with her head and not with her heart.

Kira abruptly stood, nearly knocking back the chair in the process. The best thing for her to do was get away from anything involving the festival. For nearly three months now her head had been wrapped around it, along with thoughts of the murders and who might be framing the guild. She needed a break.

Without hesitation, she took the wad of papers and shoved them into a drawer, then locked it and stowed the key in her pocket. Now would be a good time to go find Sapphire.

A cool breeze swept through the room and the fire flickered. Kira wrapped her cloak more tightly around her. Her eyes darted to the fireplace. Where had the breeze come from? The door was closed and her windows shut and locked. Or so she thought. Kira crouched, as though tying her boot. She didn't wear her full complement of weapons when she was in her room, but that did not mean she was unarmed. The dagger she had hidden in her sleeve slipped down into her palm. She had to keep a clear mind. Someone was here. They were watching, waiting, planning. Just like she was.

"That was quite a conversation you two had. It's sad to see that things aren't going well between you and Badrick."

Her head whipped around and she immediately readied herself, tensing her muscles to spring as she gripped the dagger in her hand. Pierceton stood by the window, calm as ever. He smirked as he gave the window a small push. "It's such a shame that the palace doesn't take good care of their locks on the upper floors. You think they'd have learned after the first time you and I broke in."

He must have hidden on the ledge outside, waiting, then taken advantage of her temper tantrum to sneak into the room. As much as Kira wanted to charge at him, she knew she couldn't. She had other lives in her hands now. Many, many more. She couldn't afford to be reckless. *Although, as Badrick assured me, they'd find a way to go on without me.* She lifted her chin. "What is it you want?"

The smile fell from his lips. "You."

She nearly spat on the floor in front of his boots. "As if I'd be willing join you."

His head cocked to the side as if he were confused. "Who ever said you'd do it willingly?"

Kira's eyes widened as he pounced on her. She stumbled and was immediately thrown against the door. Her dagger flew from her hand. When had he learned to move so quickly?

Pierceton appeared amused. "Shocked, are we?"

He drove his fist towards her face. Kira barely had enough time to react, ducking out of the way. His fist smashed against the wooden door. Kira used his momentary incapacitation to drive her foot into his ribs. With a groan, Pierceton tumbled sideways and collided with a bookshelf, sending the books crashing onto the floor. If no one in the castle had heard her before, they surely did now. Would anyone come to her aid? Or would they all, like Badrick, leave her to fight alone, as she'd insisted she must?

Pierceton regained his feet, clutching a long blade in one hand. Kira reached for the knife she had hidden in her boot. She had to be careful with her moves. Silas had clearly been training him. Who knew what tricks he had up his sleeve? If anyone was on their way to help her, she only had to hold him off until they arrived.

"You see Kira, after our last encounter I knew I couldn't make you join us with just a simple conversation." He stood up straight and took a step forward. "He's been watching you. He's learned your strengths, your weaknesses. He even knows about Sapphire, who I believe is out for a stroll all by herself, isn't she?"

Kira's chest tightened. How long had he been waiting outside?

"Don't you dare touch Sapphire." She swung the knife with all her might. Her blade crashed down, colliding with his own. Pierceton's body jerked from the strength of her blow. Kira followed through, bringing her elbow up sharply into his face. Blood flowed from his mouth, but still he advanced. She hooked her foot around and kicked his legs out from underneath him. But he was a step ahead.

Pierceton pulled her down with him. She landed on top of him with a jarring thump. He tossed her onto the floor. Kira's body screamed in pain as she rolled. She struggled to stand, but his foot pushed down on her chest. Her lips parted in pain as he put more and more of his body weight down onto her. It felt as though he'd step right through her.

"Now, for the last time. Will you join us?" He sneered down at her. Kira struggled to breathe as he pushed down harder. She pawed helplessly at his boot, but it was no use. She might as well have been lying under a boulder.

"Did I mention that Silas wouldn't hesitate to kill Sapphire, given the chance?"

Kira couldn't speak. Her lips could barely even form words. She managed a slight nod.

"So you'll join us?"

Sapphire had proven herself to Kira and the guild. She was slowly becoming a part of their family. Kira wouldn't sacrifice Sapphire's life to save her own. *Whatever it takes to keep her safe.* She nodded again.

"That's what I thought."

He pulled back his foot then picked her up by the collar and grabbed the knife from her trembling fingers, tossing it across the room. He shoved her towards the window. "Move."

Kira was barely able to catch herself on the window frame as she doubled over it. Her chest still throbbed with pain. So, so much pain. She turned her head to the right and spotted a small ledge. Though its purpose was for décor, it was wide enough for him to stand on. One foot at a time, she threw herself over. As she jumped from the ledge to the balcony for the room next door, she struggled to stay on her feet. Pierceton landed silently beside her, shoving her harder than the last time.

Finally she scaled the walls and made it out to the forest, where a horse had been tied off. She stiffened as he bound her wrists, pinning her between himself and the beast behind her. When she had been secured, he pulled his cloak back and lifted a vial from his belt.

"Relax. I need you alive for now." He bit down on the cork and tugged it from the vial. His hand closed around her chin and he forced her head back. Kira's eyes slammed shut as he pushed the vial against her mouth. She refused to part her lips. He cursed and brought his knee to her stomach. Kira gasped in pain. He took advantage of the moment and forced the liquid down her throat until it was all gone.

Kira finally managed to rip her head away, but it was too late. The horse whinnied in fright as she pressed back against it an attempt to separate herself from Pierceton. It quickly trotted around the opposite side of the tree. Without its support, she stumbled and fell. He stood over her, frowning, as he waited for her to regain her footing.

"If either of you touch any of them, I will turn against you in that instant and kill you both so quickly you won't have the chance to register that you're on your way to hell," she warned.

He scowled down at her. "I'd expect nothing else from you." With one quick motion, he crouched down and scooped her up, throwing her over his shoulder.

Kira pounded her fists against his back as well as she could with the restraints, but Pierceton's pace didn't slow. When they reached the horse, he tossed her onto the wide back and swung himself up behind her. It wasn't long before she could feel the effects of the poison he'd forced her to take. Her body began to go numb and her limbs tingled. Kira fought to keep her eyelids open as Pierceton clicked his tongue, urging the horse to go faster.

She might have been able to break free of the ropes and snap his neck if it weren't for the drug she'd swallowed. The desire to wrap her hands around his neck was strong. Almost overwhelming. Her thoughts growing hazy, Kira twisted her head enough to catch one last glimpse of the palace. Was one of those rooms with light pouring from the window Badrick's? How long would it take for him to realize she was gone? Would he come after her? She thought of the final words he had flung at her before leaving her room, and pressed her eyes shut again.

After all she'd done to push him away, perhaps he just wouldn't care.

Chapter 43

KIRA BLINKED, TRYING TO FOCUS through the dim glow of the moon and the haze drifting before her eyes so she could see into the trees. She waited for someone, for anything to cause a distraction that might allow her to get away. But there was nothing except for the darkness. The sweet, sweet darkness that called to her. It begged her to join it, to give in to it. But as tempting as it was, she needed to stay awake, to stay on guard.

The poison he had used on her wasn't lethal. At least not in the dosage he had given her. Instead it made her weak. To the point where she didn't even have the strength to sit up straight. Instead she had to lean back against Pierceton, listening to his heartbeat thudding in her ear.

How taunting it was to hear it, the steady rhythm reminding her of all her failures. If only she could pierce through his chest and rip it out.

Her eyes glanced up to the moon wearily. They had to have noticed that she was gone by now. How long had it been? An hour? Two? Or perhaps it had only been a handful of minutes.

She tried to push herself upright. But as soon as she did, the last of her energy drained and she'd collapse again. She cursed in her mind. She had never been one to study potions. In thievery it was rarely used unless absolutely called for. Thieves relied on the dark and their skills to keep them safe. But after this, she'd memorize every single recipe.

"It's no use fighting it. You'll only make it worse."

"What in the world was that damned stuff?" she growled as the horse picked its way casually through the forest.

"I shouldn't tell you, but I suppose you deserve to know."

No, it was something she deserved to use on him.

"It's a poison Silas told me about. Depending on the dose, it will cause someone to become temporarily paralyzed. It'll drain all the energy and strength from you, making your body weak and susceptible to harm. And in some cases, it can cause death."

Kira shivered at his last words. Death by poison was not the way she had planned to go.

She moved her foot and was relieved to still be able to feel it. To convince herself, she moved the other one and sighed in relief. She wasn't paralyzed. At least not yet.

Her eyes grew heavy, to the point that it took every last ounce of strength she had to keep them open. Behind her, Pierceton began to hum a calming lullaby. Its notes sank deep into her ears and down into her system. Her fists tightened as her fight to stay awake intensified. But she just didn't have the strength. Her body began to give in. He was so close to getting what he wanted. And there might not be anything she could do to stop him.

~ * ~

Badrick raced down the hall, his heart pounding. The sun was beginning to rise over the palace, illuminating all its beauty. But he could not stop to admire it.

Staff crowded around the entrance to Kira's room, increasing his trepidation. He didn't hesitate as he pushed through everyone, ordering them to move.

The room was a mess. Books crowded the floor, the curtains hung askew as the wind blew through the open window. Off in the corner

Sapphire stood talking to a guard. Her face was awash with worry and confusion, possibly even guilt. Badrick's eyes grazed over Chaol, who stood in the center of the room. His hair was disheveled, his eyes distraught. Badrick refused to fall for his act. He only cared for Kira because he wanted to use her as a trophy wife. Nothing more.

Badrick shoved right past him, kicking through the books and heading directly for the window. His eyes scanned the fields beyond the walls of the palace. He'd left Kira hours ago; how long had she been missing?

"Everybody out!" Chaol roared, waving his arms. "Don't you have work to do?"

The murmurs hushed immediately. The staff who had crowded around hung their heads in shame and shuffled away. Badrick took a deep breath. As much as he wanted to beat the guard down to his knees, he couldn't. Not here anyways. And not as long as there was any chance he could help Badrick find Kira. Once she was back safely, he could deal with the man once and for all.

"We care for her too."

The lady's maid Kira had covered for when she attended the queen the first time stepped into the room. Badrick searched his memory. What was her name? Annie? No. Anabelle, that was it. The girl carefully adjusted her skirts and kept her eyes focused on the floor, as if too frightened to look Chaol in the face.

"Miss Kira was kind to us that time she came to the servants' quarters. To see her gone rattles us all." She continued fumbling with a piece of hair that had fallen out of her bun. "If there's anything I can do to help, you just let me know."

"Thank you, Anabelle." Badrick stepped forward. "We certainly will. For now, we need to send out a search party. Anyone who wants to go may, the more men the better."

Chaol glared at him. "And who put you in charge?"

Badrick pushed back his shoulders and looked the head guard squarely in the eye. "It seems that we can't trust you to make sure your men are on guard. For god's sake, they weren't even at their post when Kira was taken, or they'd have seen something. If you had been more focused, she wouldn't be gone. It's time I take matters into my own hands." He turned back to Anabelle. "Send word to the guards to gather as many men as they can. We will meet by the front gate and leave within the hour."

She nodded and ran down the hall. The sound of her heels clicking against the stone echoed through the silence. Sapphire and the young guard had stopped their conversation and were watching him and Chaol with wary expressions on their faces, obviously aware of the tension between them. During their stay, Sapphire had shared a room with Kira; if anyone knew about her disappearance, it would be the redhead. When he looked at her, she paused for a few moments before turning her head, staring out the door and taking a deep breath. "We will find her. I won't allow for anything else."

And neither would he.

~ * ~

Kira whimpered as the memory flashed through her head. The way his hands clawed at her, the taste of poisoned wine rich on her tongue, the fear as she reached for the door. He whipped her around, his hood ripped back. But his face was a blur. She squinted, trying to make out what she could, but none of his features would come into focus. All she could remember was his touch.

Cold water splashed over her and her eyes flew open. She gasped, her chest heaving. Another nightmare, another failure to find out just who Silas was.

"I did not mean for you to wake her in such a way, Pierceton."

"You've grown too soft for the brat."

Kira blinked water from her eyes. Pierceton stood in front of her, an empty bucket in hand. From the corner of her eye she caught the outline of another man, but she didn't look over. Pierceton had changed from his armor into a standard tunic and trousers. Perhaps the most vulnerable thing she had ever seen him in.

"Leave us."

At the stranger's command, Pierceton turned on his heel. Kira refused to look up at the person beside him. His voice was harsh, and dare she say, intimidating?

Pierceton strode toward the door, slamming it shut behind him as he disappeared into the hall. A shiver rippled through Kira as water dripped from her hair and down her cheeks. She squirmed in the soaked leather armor she had yet to change out of. The feeling was not pleasant.

The cloaked figure knelt down in front of her. Kira didn't have to look to know who it was. Yet she still allowed her eyes to flicker up. Silas knelt, watching her from the safety of his hood. He lifted the edge of his cloak and brought it slowly toward her. Kira flinched. Her eyes squeezed shut as she struggled to free herself from the shackles that held her hands high above her head.

Silas hesitated, then brushed his cloak along her forehead and down one side of her face. He wiped the other cheek dry. Kira felt his thumb hover over her lips. Her breath turned ragged as she waited.

She could taste the leather of his glove as he traced her lower lip. Though she could not see his eyes, she knew when they met hers. He took a deep breath before swiping away the drops of water that had slid down her neck.

"You were having a nightmare. I asked him to wake you up, not drown you."

A nightmare about you.

"I'm glad to see he didn't go too rough on you. I cannot apologize for the poison, however. You're much too cunning to trust."

Kira's eyes narrowed. Where was all this compassion coming from? This was a man who wanted to kill her, who wanted to make her life—and the lives of so many she cared about—miserable. He should be torturing her, not helping her.

When she said nothing, he stood and let his cloak fall back down to his sides.

"I know who you are, Kira. If you're worried about us killing you, you have nothing to worry about. We only wish to ensure that you follow through with the job I trusted you with."

Kira's chest tightened. He knew her. But how? She had made sure that he wouldn't be able to see through her disguise and Sapphire said he hadn't caught a glimpse at her face. Pierceton must have given her away. *Damn him.*

"We will be gone for a few hours. Don't try anything funny while we are away." She clenched her teeth and yanked on the chains. Silas watched her and his shoulders fell. Was she disappointing him? After a moment, he turned and left the room. Kira fought with the chains until her wrists were raw and tears fell down her cheeks. Silas wouldn't dare attack the palace, would he? Not yet. He and his men wouldn't stand a chance between the guild and the guards. Chaol would lead his heavily-armed security against them and every member of the guild would fight until their last breath.

Chained and helpless, all Kira could do was hope that it wouldn't come to that.

Chapter 44

Badrick peered back over the fields. The colors of the sunset were beautiful, bold, hypnotizing. But he didn't dare allow himself to enjoy it. Not while Kira was gone, not while she was out of his grasp.

"Badrick, we can't do any more searching tonight." Astien spoke softly. Badrick could feel his eyelids begin to droop and rubbed them with two fingers before dropping his hand. "You checked The Grottos?"

"Twice. I went myself both times. Everyone I spoke to told me they hadn't seen either Silas or Pierceton within the last week."

"They could be lying."

"I paid them plenty to open their mouths, and threatened to send the guards after them should they fail to speak the truth."

Badrick's jaw tightened. Had he stayed a little while longer, until Sapphire had returned to the room, Kira would have been fine. No. He had let his emotions get the best of him. He had left her alone in her room. How stupid he had been.

Astien leaned over in his saddle to grip Badrick's shoulder. "We will look again tomorrow. But for now you need to sleep. You're no help to her if you're exhausted."

"I haven't been able to sleep soundly for months," Badrick admitted as he turned his horse and headed back to the palace. None of them had been able to. Yet somehow they had all managed to keep going. So far.

They returned their horses to the stables without a word exchanged. When Badrick came outside, he stood and stared at the palace. Darkness shrouded it, as though the life of the place had been sucked right out of it. There was no liveliness, no confidence, no strength. Kira was gone and she had taken that all with her.

But they wouldn't give up yet. She may have been a thief and she may have been an orphan, but she was this reason this city had something it hadn't felt in a long time. Hope.

~ * ~

The door opened with a creak and Kira lifted her head. She blinked as Silas walked up to her, trying to make out his figure through blurred vision. He yanked on her chin slightly, forcing her to look up at him. For a moment he studied her and then, as if deciding that enough poison still flowed through her system to keep her compliant, unchained her wrists. Kira winced as her numb arms fell to her sides. Her shoulders burned, her neck ached, her back was stiff. She hadn't even realized how much she had been relying on the cuffs to hold her up until that moment.

"Eat."

She looked down at the plate in front of her. Such simple words for such a simple demand. A demand she would not follow.

Silas sighed in frustration. Then he bent down and took a bite of everything on her plate, following them with a drink from the water. Kira eyed him, still suspicious. Still, if there was a chance the food was okay, she'd be stupid not to eat. If she didn't, she would never have the strength to fight her way out of here.

As she ate, Silas sat silently against the opposite wall, his boots barely brushing hers. She took a moment to look at her surroundings. The air was mucky, as if she were underground. The hall they kept her in was lined in stone, decorated with cracks.

She was not in The Grottos.

Fear struck her heart. Even if she did manage to escape, where would she go? From what she remembered, Pierceton had taken her deep into a forest. She could wander through thick trees and brush for days and get nothing for her efforts but more lost. Not that it mattered. She'd rather die at the hands of the forest than at theirs.

Silas must have seen the growing defiance in her eyes, for he cleared his throat. A warning that he knew she was plotting to try and escape.

Kira started to reach for another piece of roll, but he snatched her wrist. Her shoulder screamed in pain and she bit back a whimper. He held her hand to the light, examining every detail. Then he plucked at the bandaging, loosening it until it slid off her palm.

There was silence as he studied her wrists. Kira fought with all her might to not yank her hand away. Now was not the time to antagonize him. Now was the time to try and convince him that he could trust her, that she wouldn't resist him.

He slid off his leather glove off with ease. He hesitated. Then he pushed his bare hand against hers, palm to palm. Her skin tingled as his fingers towered over her slender ones. The nightmare played in her mind, skimming through every moment, every movement. Her heart pounded when it came to the part where he pinned her down, his face raw and exposed. She tilted her head, watching as his fingers laced with hers. This time, she was able to blink away some of the blurriness of the memories. The image of him was getting clearer. Then he pulled his hand back and everything crumbled in retreat.

The door opened again and he tucked his hand safely back inside his glove. Pierceton wasted no time grabbing her arms roughly and closing the shackles around her wrists again.

Kira couldn't understand much at the moment, but one thing had become very clear. Silas's touch was the key to remembering.

Chapter 45

That became the pattern. Three times a day she was visited. Sometimes by Pierceton, others by Silas. Though she began to lose track of the days. Was this her second day? Or her third? There was no way to tell. There were no windows and no source of light other than the torches on the walls.

Each time Silas visited her he'd go through the same routine. Eat a piece from everything on her plate then sit back against the opposite wall in silence. By his fifth visit, Kira realized that he was perfectly aware of her recovered state. Yet he still set her free her for the length of his visit. Each time he combined his hand with hers, pulling away just before she could remember.

By the end of the first day, Kira had decided that she would make her escape at the festival. She'd find Silas in the crowd and turn her arrow on him. Then she'd take Pierceton out with her bare hands. She could only hope that the palace was still in one piece by the time she returned.

Her breath hitched in her throat.

She couldn't let her mind be overrun with fear. She had to be confident. So confident she would be.

~ * ~

Sapphire watched as, piece by piece, the decorations were hauled into place. Excitement washed over the townspeople's face as they volunteered to help. But they were all ignorant of Kira's disappearance. They didn't know that without her there was no chance of bringing these murders to an end.

Ignorance truly was bliss.

After the sunset, there would only be one day left before the festival. That was all. Many vendors had taken advantage of the event; they would have been foolish not to. They all placed their finest costumes out for sale, each one handmade, each different from the last.

And still no sign of Kira.

The team had searched every inch of the forest. They even reached out to the smaller towns on its borders and still nothing. Though the men seemed to have retained their composure, Sapphire knew better than to fall for it. Over the past few days, she had spent more time in the palace halls that she ever expected. And more time with Felix.

That evening she rapped on his door. She pulled her cloak close to her body as she waited in the night. He peered through the crack in the door before pulling it open to let her in.

"Aren't you ever going to get rid of that blasted thing?" he asked as she stepped into the safety of his room.

"No."

Felix sighed and shook his head. "Pull the hood back. If we are going to work together, then show some trust in me at least."

She watched him stride across the room. With a shaky breath, her hands clasped the fabric and pulled it away from her face. Down went her sense of safety, up went her vulnerability.

"We've combed through the entire town, in every building and under every tree. Badrick had hoped Silas hadn't taken her too far, but if she is anywhere near here, why haven't we been able to find them?" His gaze settled on the map tapestry of the entire kingdom. Sapphire's eyes scanned the details. He was right. They had to be hiding her right under their noses. Either that or Silas had taken her so far away they might never find her.

Sapphire shook her head. Thoughts like that weren't helpful. She took a spot next to Felix, her arms wrapped around her stomach to keep it from flipping. Every night since Kira had disappeared, she had shown up at Felix's door. They'd mark the territories they had searched that day, then think of places to try the next. Now, though, their list had become incredibly short. There was nowhere else to go. Except …

She tore her gaze from the tapestry. "There's one spot we haven't checked."

Felix's brow furrowed. "What do you mean? This map would be completely red if we marked everywhere we've been, including the palace."

Sapphire shook her head. Slowly she lifted her hand and pointed to a spot on the tapestry.

"Do you think he'd really take her there?"

She lowered her hand. "We don't have anywhere else to look. It's the only reasonable place left."

His eyes scrutinized her. Something flashed through them as he contemplated her face.

Was he sorry he'd asked her to take off her hood? It had been a mistake. She'd known it, but she'd done it anyway. Now she had to live with the consequences. They both did.

"Sapphire—"

Panic overwhelmed her. She recognized that look in his eyes. It would be too dangerous for her to stay. "We will head out at the first sign of dawn. I should take my leave before anyone sees me." Whirling around, she hurried to the door.

He stopped her after three steps. Sapphire let out a yelp as he grabbed her wrist and turned her back to face him. "Sapphire, look at me," he demanded. When she kept her head turned the other way, he caught her chin, forcing her to look at him. "For the love of god, look at me, Sapphire!"

"I won't." She mumbled the words. She felt so helpless, like a babe.

Her strength was gone and her will faltering.

His eyes searched hers. "We can't keep running from each other like this."

"I'll never stop running."

"Then I'll make you."

She flinched. He wouldn't dare say it; if he did, she wouldn't listen. It would be her downfall. Her weakness. It would be what Silas used to destroy her.

"Sapphire, I love you. I never stopped loving you."

She choked back a sob, refusing to let the tears fall. "I know you do." She fought to yank her wrist away, but his grip was too strong. "Let me go."

"Are you going to make me beg? Can't I hear you say it at least once?"

Desire pounded through her. The words were in her heart, waiting to be said. But she had to control herself. She couldn't cause him pain again. She would die first.

"Do you think this isn't hurting me?" She whispered the words, so quietly he had to lean in to hear them.

"Then why won't you say it, you blasted woman!"

"Because if I do, I'll—"

The door opened, stopping her in the middle of her sentence. Felix abruptly let go of her wrist. Astien stood in the doorway, his fire-red locks disheveled. "I'll come back later if you—"

"No." Sapphire yanked her hood back up over her head. "I'm leaving." Without a glance at Felix, she strode to the door and out into the hallway. Legs weak, she leaned back against the wall, taking in deep breaths to slow the thudding of her heart in her chest.

Astien's words carried out into the hallway. "Should I ask?"

When he spoke, Felix's voice carried weariness. And a warning. "Unless you want to regret it, then no."

Chapter 46

Kira sat, her head resting against her arm for support while she slept. Dreams continuously haunted her mind. Some good, others terrifying. Some nights she had woken up screaming, which brought either Silas or Pierceton down to check on her. But not this night. This time her mind reflected back to when everything was normal. Felix attempting to hide his smile, Maddox bent over his desk as he stayed up late to work on his new-found weapon, Astien with his contagious smile, Badrick constantly giving her a hard time, and Kingsman a proud man. Their eyes wouldn't be strained with exhaustion, their hearts not heavy with worry. Those were some of the most wonderful dreams she had ever had.

Cold metal against Kira's neck woke her. She froze. Silas knelt before her, a glittering blade in his hand.

"I will let you go free for one night." He dug the tip of the knife slightly into her skin. "If you do not return by morning after the festival, I will kill them all. I will be watching you."

He tugged at a chain around his neck and pulled a key out from inside his shirt. Her jaw clenched. It was the key she had used to lock the drawer with her plans in it. Kira scowled. "You are a son of a bitch." She spat the words at him, no longer caring if they made him angry.

"So I've been told." Unfazed, he calmly tucked the key away. As if it were out of sight, out of mind. Kira followed his every movement, from the moment he sheathed his dagger until he tied the blindfold securely over her eyes. He removed the shackles from around her wrists then yanked her arms behind her back. With a jerk, she was pulled to her feet. Silas gave her a rough shove to make her start walking. All the compassion he had shown to her before was gone. Whenever she would trip, he'd keep walking, dragging her until she got her feet back underneath herself. No words were exchanged, not even threats, just silence.

For twenty minutes they continued on like this, Silas tugging her in directions with no pattern that she could discern. He had clearly gone out of his way to taken her down more hallways than necessary, and when the he finally directed her through a doorway and into the warm sunlight, Kira felt as though he had walked her around in circles.

They walked another hour before they finally stopped. Kira's heart pounded. *I'll kill him. End this once and for all.* She would turn and fight him until she took her last breath. Only she was unarmed and outmatched in strength. Yet again she would have to bite her tongue and wait.

But when he let go of her arms, she couldn't stop herself. He gave her a rough shove, nearly making her stumble to the ground. Kira caught herself and ripped the blindfold off. By the time she whirled around to face him, her fists were already up. Only there was no one to fight. He was gone.

Kira's eyes burned from not seeing the sun in days. She pushed the pain aside and turned in a slow circle to scan the area. There was no sign of him. Not in the tree tops, no tracks in the dirt, nothing. It was as if he were a ghost.

Rage filled her. *Where is he?* He had been right behind her. She shook her head. No, he hadn't escaped. She sensed him nearby, watching her, toying with her. She had no time to hunt him now, though. His threat had been clear. She had to be back the morning after the festival or everyone she cared about would die. Kira scrambled up the nearest tree to try and get her bearings.

When she caught sight of the tallest tower of the castle off to the north, she jumped to the ground with a thud. Ignoring the stinging in her feet, she took off running. Praying, hoping, that nothing had happened while she was gone.

~ * ~

The pressure grew inside Badrick until he felt he would explode. For hours they had been sitting around this blasted table, talking, discussing the plans for the following day. The king and queen refused to carry through with the plan unless Kira was there. But they couldn't wait any longer. Already that morning another murder had taken place, this time a young child. There was no more time to wait for Kira. No matter how much Badrick wanted to.

"I will carry the job out myself."

The queen frowned at him, ruining the beauty of her face. "We did not make the deal with you."

Badrick shoved back his chair and stood, slamming his hands on the table. Beside him, Kingsman snapped a warning, but he paid no heed. "Kira is gone. We've searched everywhere and then gone back and searched again. Even as we speak there is a search party triple-checking every inch of land. We need to carry through with our plans. These people don't deserve to suffer any longer."

The king opened his mouth to respond. Badrick readied himself to argue against whatever the king lashed at him.

"My king!"

They all turned their heads as a young guard rushed into the room unannounced. Behind him, two guards lunged for him, prepared to haul him away and punish him for his breach of protocol and security. His next words saved him.

"They've found her. She's alive."

Chapter 47

BADRICK PUSHED HIMSELF TO WALK as fast as he could without running. Even that didn't seem fast enough. Over his time in the guild he had learned the halls of the palace to the point that he could walk down them blindfolded. Now his thoughts were so frenzied, it seemed as though he had been thrown into a maze.

He rushed to the entrance gate. The guard said they had found Kira a mile outside of town, near their old hideout. They had immediately scoped out the ruins, but if Silas had been there, he had fled, leaving no trace.

Badrick prepared himself for the worst. Silas could have beaten her until she was covered in blood and wounds. He could have threatened to kill her, holding a knife to her throat until she talked. They said she was in good condition. But the definition of 'good condition' was subjective. Unless she was utterly unharmed and untouched, she wasn't in good condition, as far as Badrick was concerned.

Then he saw her.

Kira stood with a blanket wrapped around her shoulders, handmaids and the palace's medic crowding around her. She appeared to be trying to reassure them that she was well, but when she mentioned she was a little hungry, they dashed off to the kitchen. Despite what she had been through—whatever that was—she let out a small laugh. The sound was like music to Badrick. Then she looked up and froze.

Badrick couldn't hold himself back any more. He ran as fast as his feet could carry him. The blanket fell from Kira's shoulders as she started forward to meet him. Kira collided with him, nearly sending him tumbling. But Badrick didn't mind a bit. Her arms around his neck, her body pressed to his, was the most wonderful feeling he'd ever known.

His hand held the back of her head while the other wrapped around her waist. He buried his face in her hair and inhaled her scent, thanking the guardians that they had returned her to him.

The minutes passed by quickly. Five turned to ten in the blink of an eye. He could have honestly spent the entire day like that, Kira in his arms as he mumbled her name over and over again. As if she'd disappear if he stopped saying it.

When the maids returned, they insisted on taking her away to wash her up and get her into fresh clothes. Reluctantly, he let her go, but his eyes stayed locked on hers as they dragged her away with them. Badrick finally let out his breath. Whatever Silas had done, she had held her ground.

~ * ~

The women took Kira to her chambers where a warm bath waited for her. They left her alone, but she could hear the commotion outside. Maids mumbling of her return to the guards, who, in turn, ran to tell the next pair of ears. Word traveled quickly in the palace, as she well knew.

Aware that this would be her only time alone, Kira began to think. Her mind replayed Silas's words. He'd be watching her. He could be in the same room as her and she would never know it. The thought gave her chills. He'd go to the festival in disguise. Finding him would be harder than she imagined, but she would do it. She had to do it.

She sank deeper into the water, until it lapped against her chin. Her hair flowed around her gracefully. To see Badrick was a blessing, a reminder of why she had been fighting for so long. The way he held her—as though he hadn't seen her in years—made her heart ache. What was she to do? Now that Silas knew who she was, Kira was left with no alternative. Either she refused to kill the king and queen, sacrificing everyone she loved, or she followed through with it, leaving the throne empty and chaos reigning. Self-hatred swarmed over her. She should have been more careful with the key. Now that Silas had their plans, well, that changed everything. Was it even possible to come up with an alternative? Not likely, with the festival starting the following morning.

A soft rapping on the door interrupted her whirling thoughts. Sapphire's voice came from the other side of the door. "Kira, it's me."

Kira hesitated then drew in a deep breath. "Come in." She peered up at Sapphire as she stepped into the room. The young red-head had donned a violet dress that showcased her figure in all the right places, something that Kira had never thought to see her in.

"My leathers stank," she explained as she closed the doors behind her. "I didn't have a choice. You won't either." Sapphire held up the dress she had slung over her arm.

Kira grinned. "Making me suffer with you?"

"You should see the dress the men picked out for you to wear to the festival. It's quite beautiful."

Kira stiffened as Sapphire walked past her to hang the dress up. Suddenly Kira wasn't in the mood to joke anymore. If she didn't play her part right, they would all be in grave danger.

Sapphire stayed silent as she smoothed the skirts out. Then she turned and lifted a lock of Kira's hair out of the water.

"You're terrible at washing your hair." She gave a click of her tongue before reaching for the soap beside the tub.

Kira offered her a half-hearted smile. "Someone's turned into a proper lady."

Sapphire massaged the soap into Kira's hair. "I'm far from it. But there isn't anything wrong with pampering yourself once in a while."

"I suppose not."

After that, no words were said. Sapphire kept her lips sealed as she washed Kira's hair, keeping her touch soft and gentle. Though there was no more conversation between the two women, Kira felt as if she had spoken a thousand words, as though she had clearly explained her situation to Sapphire. Even though she couldn't explain it to herself, Sapphire seemed to fully grasp how Kira was feeling.

For those few wonderful moments Kira allowed herself to close her eyes. All her worries were washed away. There was nothing wrong. There were no fears, no threat of danger or death. Nothing but the calming touch of Sapphire's fingers as they worked their way through her hair.

Chapter 48

After her bath, Kira wandered down to the kitchen where her supper was waiting. Soon after she took her first bite, Astien flew through the door, calling out to her. As his arms wrapped around her, Kira's fork fell to the floor. Though she didn't mind, the chef grumbled about having to get another for her.

Moments later the others toppled in. Every one of them plied her with questions on top of questions, wanting to know what had happened to her. Never before had she seen Kingsman so disarrayed. He checked every visible piece of skin, then went back and checked it again. She was sure that even as they talked his eyes still wandered, in case he should find a wound he had missed the first time.

"I bet it was terrifying," Astien commented as she cut off a bite-sized piece from the fish on her plate. Kira paused. Terrifying? Was that the word to describe it? No. Silas had treated her with compassion. It hadn't been terrifying at all. But she couldn't tell them that; they'd think she had been brainwashed.

With all the commotion, Kira wasn't able to finish her meal, but she didn't mind. Their questions and comments kept her from fixating on what was to come. She did manage to eat at least half of what was on her plate before she sent it away, only making the chef grumble more over the wasted food.

Finally she stood, "I promise everyone I'm all right. Not a single scratch on me."

"We were all worried sick about you. We searched every day and spent the nights planning where to look the next day," Maddox explained.

Kira's heart warmed at his words. "And I thank you for that." She could only hope that it wouldn't hurt them all too much should she not survive the festival. They'd have to move on. She didn't want them to mourn; she wanted them to go on living their lives. Not that she would go easily. Kira pushed back her shoulders. If she died, she would die fighting.

They had moved her chambers to one that could be better guarded. The room was much more beautiful, exotic even. But she felt restricted in it, as though she couldn't breathe. Outside her door, two guards were posted. She moved to the window and peered down only to find another three. There was no balcony to hide on, no nearby trees to climb in. The room itself was a prison.

Kira turned and found a dress lying on her bed. Sapphire was right, the gown was beautiful. No, flawless. She picked up the garment and held it in front of her as she peered into the mirror. The deep red velvet was soft against her touch. Softer than any feather. The black fur trimming would stand out against her pale skin, showing her collarbone and bare shoulders. If only she could enjoy wearing such a treasure.

Noises outside her door stole Kira's attention. She laid the dress back down on the bed, scooped up the knife she had hidden under her pillow, and made her way over to the door, keeping her footsteps light. Her heart pounded. Silas couldn't have come for her already, could he?

Sweat gathered on her palms with each step. Once she made it to the door, Kira pressed her ear against it. Now that she was closer, she could make out that the noises she heard were two people arguing.

"I said leave her be!"

Kira's brows furrowed. *Badrick?*

"I need to discuss something with her away from prying ears. Now get lost."

Her lips quickly fell into a frown. *Chaol.* Just thinking his name made her mouth sour. Her chamber door suddenly swung open. Kira mustered a smile. "Sir Chaol, good to see you again. Hopefully our match didn't leave you too sore."

He flinched, as though her words had slapped him across the face. He quickly straightened his clothing, "My lady, I need to speak with you. Alone."

"Surely whatever you have to say to me can be said in front of Badrick."

Chaol cursed under his breath. "Very well." He stalked toward her. Before she could move, he wrapped an arm around her waist and pulled her to him, his lips covering hers.

Kira's heart stopped and her body froze. Chaol's lips moved hungrily against hers. Clearly, he didn't care that Badrick was watching. Her traitorous body responded, longing to give in to his kiss. Wanting to wash away every wrong he had ever done. Every wrong she herself had done. To let him cherish her with the kisses and touches he longed to bestow upon her. At the same time his kiss withered her heart. This was not the man she longed to taste.

Her hands pushed against his chest, but he caught her hand. Her irritation grew. It was one thing to kiss her; it was another to do it without her permission, in spite of her protests. And in front of Badrick.

Then as quickly as the kiss began, it ended. Chaol's arm slipped from her waist and his lips were ripped from hers. Kira stumbled, nearly falling before she caught herself on the door frame. Her chest heaved and her head throbbed. And suddenly all the pieces began to fall into place.

Kira snapped back to reality. In front of her, Badrick slammed Chaol into the wall with such force she was sure that the bricks would crack. The world slowed as he drew back his fist, but Chaol did nothing to block the blow. The hall went silent. So silent that Kira could hear the sound of blood dripping onto the floor.

Chaol raised his head, showing a cracked lip. His eyes locked onto hers. His once kind and captivating eyes were now as hard as stone.

Badrick voice was low. "Get out of here. And stay away from Kira. You've done enough to her."

Kira brought her sleeve to her mouth, wiping away whatever trace of Chaol left on her.

Chaol pushed himself away from the wall. "Don't worry, I'll go." He shot a look at Kira. "I just had to know for sure." He offered her a mocking bow. Then, without another word, he turned on his heel and left.

Kira watched Chaol disappear into the dark. Her eyes narrowed. "Where are the two guards? Had they seen you, they would have thrown you into a cell for attacking their head guard."

Though her voice was kept to a whisper, her tone was slightly sharp, reprimanding him for his punch, although he had defended her honor. The action could have been enough to get him removed from the palace. Her slight irritation quickly disappeared and was replaced by relief. Had he not been there she wasn't sure what would have happened, with or without her consent.

"I told them that I would be staying with you for a few hours," Badrick explained as he finally let his gaze fall on her. She turned and walked back into her room, unable to face him. "What was it you needed to talk to me about?"

"You expect me to act like *that* didn't just happen?" he growled as he kicked the door shut.

She whirled around to face him. "I'd honestly like to forget that it happened. So if you wouldn't remind me, that would be great," she snapped. She couldn't remember what Chao had just done. No, she didn't want to remember. That kiss was the last thing she needed. It jolted everything out of place. It made her bones rattle and her hands shake. It frightened her. Her tone grew sharp. "Why does it bother you anyway?"

"Do I have to spell it out for you?"

"Perhaps so. I'm not as smart as all those tavern women and maids who gawk at you."

"You're plenty smart enough." He stepped closer to her. "Why else would I have kissed you before?"

She lowered her voice, hoping he would do the same. There were too many listening ears here in the palace. "You were drunk, Badrick."

She couldn't let her feelings show through. Not if she wanted to keep him safe. If Silas found out how deeply she cared for Badrick, he'd use him against her. He'd kill him without a second thought. And now that Chaol had walked off with a split lip, she could only imagine what consequences were yet to come.

"That doesn't mean the feelings I expressed that night were any different than the ones I have now."

"If you love me, let me protect you."

"I can protect myself, Kira." His hand cupped her cheek. "Stop running from me. Please, let me show you. Let me prove to you how much I care about you."

Kira took a shaky breath, tears building in her eyes. Oh how tempting his words were. "I ... I can't. He'll use you to get what he wants. I can't bear to put you in that kind of danger. I'd never forgive myself."

His other hand came up and he wiped a tear away. Badrick dared to take a step closer. Kira felt like a young hare poised for escape. One wrong step, one wrong word, and it would be over.

"Stop trying to be the hero and let someone rescue you for once."

She peered up at him through blurred vision. When she spoke, her voice faltered. "It's not that simple. They have our plans. They took the key while I was knocked out. They know everything, Badrick. They will kill you; they will kill everyone without hesitation."

He shook his head. "It's all right. Sapphire guessed that would happen. So she and Felix thought of another plan together."

A bit of hope beamed through her. "So that's where she's been going all these nights. I knew she wouldn't be able to last long around him without giving in."

Kira straightened. Sapphire hadn't turned against her like the others had first feared. She …

Badrick's patience was up. He brought his lips down to hers for a brief kiss, wiping away any trace Chaol had left behind. "I won't be able to last much longer around you either. Be mine for tonight. Though I have full faith in their plan, I can make no promises about what is going to happen tomorrow. I am not a man who lives with regrets, but not following through with what is about to happen would be the greatest regret of my life. So please Kira, please allow me to make you feel like the treasure you are."

His voice shivered through her, goose bumps rising on her skin. Though she did not want to admit it, he was right. There were no promises.

Slowly, she nodded. Was it truly all right to allow herself to feel as though she was someone's treasure? Or was that a selfish desire?

Without missing a beat, Badrick crushed his lips to hers. Her hands tangled into his hair and she twirled a lock around her fingers. She let out a gasp as he pulled her close against him. Warmth suffused her cheeks as his palms followed her body down before settling at her waist. This dress exposed every curve normally hidden beneath her armor. Most women would be thankful, but she felt nothing but self-conscious.

It was wrong. So beautifully wrong. Every touch, every breath they shared was like poison. It raced through her blood, spreading faster with every heartbeat. Only for this poison, there was no antidote. And she did not seek one.

Badrick bent down and lifted her into his arms. He carried her to the bed and laid her down gently on the silk sheets.

Never before had Kira felt such passion. At one time she would have never believed that Badrick would share such feelings with her. She would have thought that they were false. Yet, from the way he kissed her, the way he touched her, she knew he wasn't feeling only lust. He loved her. He loved her so much that it hurt.

Kira had never felt as beautiful as she did in that moment. Before tonight she had been nothing more than a thief, an orphan. She was no different than the women around her. She did nothing extraordinary. She wasn't blessed with the talents of music, art, or seduction. She wasn't a proper lady like those in the palace. She was just a rock in the dirt.

But Badrick loved her. Kira's heart fluttered as he gently pulled down the collar of her dress, exposing her shoulders. The feeling of him speaking against her skin made her stomach flip.

"You have no idea how many years I've been waiting for this."

Kira sank further into her embarrassment, surrendering to her shyness. She still found it hard to believe that this was real, that he was real.

"Do you know how hard it is not to kiss you, not to hold you, when you're right there in front of me?"

In response, Kira pulled him down to her. "Then do it."

Badrick obliged. Everything melted away. The room became a blur as her mind focused solely on him. For tonight, there would be no more restraint, no more jokes, no more worries. The outside world would become nonexistent.

Kira's heart pounded as his fingers danced down the curve of her hip. She slid her hand under his tunic to his bare chest, running her fingers along the scars he had earned from fights. There she could feel his beat of his heart. His was pounding too. He was just as nervous, just as excited and relieved as she was.

Her dress slipped off the bed and onto the floor. There it lay and, like everything else, was long forgotten.

Chapter 49

THE NEXT MORNING KIRA'S EYES fluttered open. Badrick peered down at her, his hands brushing back her bangs from her face. He gave her an apologetic smile. "I'm sorry if I woke you."

Kira couldn't stop herself from returning his smile. "No, it's fine. I want to be able to enjoy this while we can."

The warmth of his bare chest branded her cheek while he rested his chin atop her head. Time passed and neither moved, neither daring to break this moment. Kira absent-mindedly traced his scars while he drew circles in the crook of her back. Perhaps for once she'd be selfish. She'd allow herself to take the time to enjoy what she had been longing after for so long. She pushed back the thought that this could be the last time she'd be able to enjoy something as precious as this. Still, in the back of her mind she knew that reality was just around the corner, waiting to snatch her up in its merciless claws.

~ * ~

Kira watched Sapphire shift awkwardly as the brush stroked her lips. Isabella frowned and pulled back, placing her hands on her hips. "If you keep squirming, I won't be able to finish!"

Kira hid her chuckle as Sapphire frowned like a young daughter being reprimanded by her mother.

Sapphire finally sat still, and Isabella dipped her brush again and resumed her work. When Badrick left that morning, Kira had spotted her dress on the floor, reminding her of the reason she was there. She and Sapphire both needed to be unrecognizable. They couldn't rely on the safety of the dark nor their cloaks. Not tonight. So, late that afternoon, she had made a trip into town to the one girl she knew could help them.

Kira had barely even finished her question before Isabella ran off to get everything she needed. A few moments later she had appeared at the door with her hands full of the cosmetics she would need to get the job done.

As Isabella worked, Kira realized just how beautiful the young girl was. She was several years younger than Kira, yet as she focused on painting Sapphire's lips she seemed to mature. She bit her lip in concentration, strands of her hair falling from her bun and her eyes sparkling with determination.

When she was finished, Sapphire turned and stared at herself in the mirror. Kira got up and walked over to stand behind her. She couldn't stop herself from grinning as shock swept across Sapphire's face. "You look stunning."

"I can't believe this is me." Sapphire turned from side to side, causing the skirt of her emerald dress to sway along with her movements.

Kira's eyes met hers in the mirror. "I'm sure Felix won't either."

Sapphire's lips pressed into a thin line. "I could say the same about Badrick. He won't know what to do with himself once he sees you."

Kira's cheeks heated as memories from the previous night flooded through her mind. She took a moment to study her reflection. Isabella had painted her lips a bold red to match her dress, making them look fuller than usual. She blinked, taking notice of the coal that lined her eyes. Kira reached up tentatively to touch one of the perfect curls that Isabella had somehow managed to get her hair to form. "You've outdone yourself, Isabella."

Isabella smiled. "I only accentuate the beauty that is already there."

Kira's heart warmed. Love poured out from her as she planted a kiss on the younger girl's cheek, leaving behind an imprint of her lips.

"Look what you've done; now I have to paint over them again." Though Isabella tried to act angry, her happiness still shone through.

"I'm sorry." Kira sat back down in front of the mirror.

Isabella gave a playful roll of her eyes. "No more kissing, me or anyone else."

In the glass, Kira's cheeks reddened. Did she know, somehow? She swallowed. "Of course not. I'll be more careful, I promise."

A soft knock sounded on the door. When Kira turned, Felix stood in the doorway, dressed in his clothes for the festival. Beside her, Sapphire fumbled with her skirts, acting as if she hadn't noticed he was there.

"Are you ladies ready?"

Kira strolled up to him and he scowled down at her.

"What's wrong?"

He looked at her for a moment longer. "I don't like that dress on you."

As the disappointment swept across her face, he quickly finished his sentence. "You're too beautiful in it."

Kira's glossed lips turned up. She straightened his collar as he stood there like a statue. With every day that passed, he reminded her more and more of a guard. The guard that he had once been. The guard that he kept locked on the inside. "You're not too bad yourself, Felix."

Felix matched her smile with a small smirk.

"You don't plan to stay locked up in this room all night, do you?" Badrick grinned as he emerged from behind Felix. "That would be rather unfair to us men."

"Badrick, this is not a night to enjoy. Remember why you're here," Felix snapped.

Badrick sighed, running a hand through his hair. "Aye, aye. Perhaps one day we can cherish a night like this, giving these fine ladies our full attention, rather than needing to focus on our enemies."

As he said this, his eyes slid to Kira and he winked. Her stomach danced and she turned, both angry and happy that he could make her feel the way she did.

As if sensing she needed her aid, Sapphire walked over and handed Kira her weapons. Piece by piece, the women strapped them onto their limbs. They had hidden blades under the sleeves of their dresses, wire bracelets they could easily unwind to choke a man, pearls that would inject poison into the blood of a victim when pricked by the pin used to decorate their hair. Sapphire strapped several knives and daggers to her thighs, but Kira stuck to one. She gave a flick of her wrist. With ease her blade popped out. Smooth, deadly, and precise.

"Looks like we've found ourselves some killer women."

Kira shot Badrick a glare, to which he responded with a sheepish grin. Though it was clear that Felix and Sapphire had been spending time with one another, no one had dared to make a comment. Leave it to Badrick to have the guts to.

"Yes ... I suppose we have."

Sapphire faltered as she finished strapping the last knife onto her body. But she quickly recovered and let her skirt fall over it, hiding any evidence it was there. She cleared her throat as she straightened up. "I suppose we should be heading down to town then."

Felix held his arm out, waiting patiently. Sapphire eyed it cautiously. Kira gave her a soft push to urge her on. There were no promises of tomorrow. The last thing she wanted to happen was for someone to die with regrets.

Sapphire was someone Kira had looked down upon for many years. But once she had learned the truth, her heart began to cave, until she finally saw eye to eye with the beautiful redhead. Badrick stepped forward. "If it's all right, I'd like to talk to Kira alone for a moment."

Felix eyed him then his shoulders fell in defeat. "All right, but not too long."

Badrick nodded, waiting until Felix and Sapphire disappeared down the hall before he turned to her. Isabella curtsied. Kira returned her curtsy. *Please stay safe.* Isabella slipped out into the hallway, closing the door behind her.

When she was gone, Badrick studied Kira. *Can he sense all the emotions pooling within me?* Hope that they'd survive, fear that they wouldn't, doubts that she would be strong enough to defeat Silas, determination to at least try. He calmly walked over to her. Kira tilted her head back so she could meet his gaze. She inhaled then exhaled a shaky breath, not even attempting to hide her nerves. She couldn't hide anything from him. Not anymore.

He reached for her hand. "We will make it out. All of us."

Kira enjoyed the warmth of his hands against her skin as his fingers tangled with hers. "Sapphire's plan is too risky. The king and queen did not approve of it."

He gave her hand a small squeeze. "We don't have any other choice, Kit."

Her gaze fell to the floor. For the past week she had been preparing herself for this night. No, ever since the first murder. She assumed it would feel as if she could finally breathe. But once it was here, she felt more suffocated than ever.

Suddenly Badrick gave her a spin, stopping her once her back was to him. She opened her mouth to question him, but he shushed her quietly, his breath warm against her ear. His hands slipped over her eyes. "Don't look."

Kira swallowed and did as she was told. Something cold bounced against her chest a moment later. It took her a few breaths to realize what it was. When she did, she reached around and lifted her hair off her neck.

Badrick finished clasping the necklace. "You may look."

Kira opened her eyes and walked to the mirror. A small silver fox rested just above her breasts. It stood mid-step, ears on alert, as if hunting its prey. Its body was sleek and flawless, capturing the true beauty of the ones she had seen in the wild. But it was the eyes that made her gasp. Two beautiful emeralds sparkled wildly as the setting sunlight caught them at the perfect angle. Other than her nightgown, it was the most precious thing she had ever owned.

Badrick wrapped his arms around her from behind, pressing his lips into the crook of her neck. "I wanted to give it to you before tonight." Kira's eyes fluttered shut as she gave in to his warmth. His lips trailed his way up, then down her neck again.

She spun around and pressed her lips to his. Though it threw him off guard, Badrick didn't hesitate to return her kiss. His arms felt strong at her waist, a barrier against danger. A barrier she wished she could hide in forever.

Kira grazed his cheek with the back of her hand. "Thank you."

"There is no need to thank me." He kissed her forehead.

Kira wanted to smile. To enjoy his presence. But her stomach twisted in such a way that she was sure she would be sick. She held her composure as well as she could. When another knock sounded on the door, Badrick released her and went to answer it.

A young boy stood in the hallway. "Mister Felix sent me to fetch you, sir."

"Thank you." Badrick turned back to her.

Kira waved a hand through the air. "Go, before Felix sends up the cavalry. I'll be right behind you."

His eyes narrowed as he studied her a moment then gave a curt nod. "Don't be long, or I'll send the cavalry myself."

She managed a small smile before he left the room. Kira made her way to the window, desperate for fresh air. Once she had opened the panes, the wind caressed her nose, cheeks, and lips. She looked over the town. Ribbons of red and orange streaked across the evening sky. People were already filling the streets and the air thrummed with excitement. Kira pressed her palms to the window ledge. She prayed Sapphire's plan would work. If it didn't, the excitement of the townspeople would, very soon, turn to terror.

~ * ~

Badrick walked down the hall, listening to his own footsteps. Thoughts whirled through his mind. Would the new plan work? He reached the corner of the hallway and pushed back his shoulders. It had to. There was no other choice.

He was only half way through his turn when a rag smothered his face. Badrick's hand flew to the fingers that pressed the cloth over his nose and mouth, desperately trying to rip the rag away.

"It's about time. We thought you would never leave that room."

Badrick's eyes narrowed as he recognized Pierceton's voice. He tried to gather his wits about him, to do what he had been trained to do, but everything began to turn into a big blur. His nose burned with the scent of Nightlock and his throat went dry.

Kira flashed into his mind. He had to save her, to warn her. Yet the memory of who she was began to drift away like sand in the wind. Piece by piece his recognition of her was carried off. Then she was nothing.

Chapter 50

KIRA PEERED THROUGH THE SECOND story window of the shop. The doors were locked, all light gone out other than the one lantern beside her on the desk. There were two doors, the front and back, both with locks that no one would be able to pick easily. The only ones who could get in would be the two people who had a key, she and Badrick. She watched as crowds of people gathered, waiting for the king and queen to show themselves.

Her fingers tingled.

She turned and looked at the empty corner Badrick was supposed to be in. Sapphire had explained the plan to her. Silas had made her job clear. Kill the royalty, leave the throne empty. So that's what they planned to do. Or at least pretend to do.

The feathers of her arrow were soft against her fingertips. Sapphire had explained to her that they had been laced with a sleeping poison. One scratch and the poison would settle into the bloodstream almost immediately, leaving the victim in a deep sleep. All she had to do was graze the arm of the king and his wife. Kingsman and Chaol would jump to the thrones, looking for who had done it. In only a few moments both their royal highnesses would fall, giving the illusion of a deadly poison. It should be enough to lure both Pierceton and Silas out into the open, which was why Badrick was to hide and wait for them to arrive.

She turned and stared at the empty corner again. It had nearly been two hours. Where was he?

Kira peered down at street below, where Sapphire waited patiently among the crowds. The redhead peered up and gave a shake of her head. Still no sign of him.

The fox charm burned against Kira's skin. He had to be all right. Silas hadn't found him, Badrick would be too careful to let that happen. Unless Silas had caught him unaware, planning to use him as bait to make sure she didn't fail at her job. Silas was not dumb. It wouldn't be long before he realized that it was sleeping poison on her arrows and not a poison to kill. Her heart pounded. He could easily threaten her. And harming Badrick would be the best way.

Kira turned to run down the stairs to tell Sapphire to send word to look for Badrick. That they couldn't start without him. But she knew the truth before she even took her first step. They'd have to follow through without him. Still … she had to try.

As her hand reached for the door, it flew open. Relief washed over her at the sight of him. "Oh, thank goodness you're okay." She wrapped her arms around him, "I was starting to worry something had happened to you."

Badrick didn't hug her back. He just stood there. There was no sign of passion, no attempt to give comfort. Nothing. Kira's heart fell slightly, but she pushed the feeling away. *He's just nervous, that's all.* Like she was.

She moved to the window and gave Sapphire the signal that it was clear to follow through with their plan. Sapphire nodded as the crowds hushed to a whisper. Kira watched as the king and queen made their way to the stage, standing as proud as ever. Though she tried to ignore the eyes burning into her back, the hairs on her neck stood up. She had to calm herself, she needed to relax.

As the introductions were made, Kira reached back for an arrow. Taking a deep breath, she notched it into place. Then she waited. The king gave a wave to his people, followed by his wife. Both looked stunning, decorated in gems and silk. Neither showed any worry. As if they weren't putting their lives into her hands.

Once they sat, she pulled back the string. Her uneasiness towards Badrick had not faltered. Not for a second. If she had done something to irritate him, though, she'd discuss it with him later. Right now she needed him to deal with it and wait until her job was done.

Kira peered down her arrow with a steady eye. She had one shot at this. She couldn't mess up. Otherwise there would be blood on her hands.

While the crowd was cheering she let her arrow fly. It barely even left her bow before she had another loaded. Quickly she moved the bow to the left. The queen grabbed her shoulder, pain showcased on her face. As her body started to go slack, Kira readied herself for the second shot. There wasn't a moment to lose.

As she let the string loose, a hand slipped to her shoulder, causing her to jerk her bow. She watched in fear as the arrow slipped into the king's arm. His beautiful clothing ripped, blood seeping heavily through his fingers as he clutched his arm. Kira cursed and jerked Badrick's hand away.

"Look what you made me do! You know better than to do something so stupid. Now he's in more pain than I wanted."

Badrick looked down at her, his face blank. His eyes seemed dull, empty even. As if he had no soul or guilt. Kira pushed back the urge to slap him. Instead she returned her attention to the royal couple.

Kingsman leapt onto the stage, dressed in a guard's uniform. The queen's skin had grown pale, her body lifeless. The king had gone into a matching state, both of them taking such shallow breaths that they were unnoticeable. Kira hoped that, in the eyes of the members of the audience, it looked as if the arrows had been laced with poison. Kingsman checked the pulses of the king and queen, who had both slumped down in their seats as though dead, before ordering the other guards to convey them to the palace. His eyes scanned the crowd as if he were looking for something, someone. Kira gritted her teeth. *Chaol.* Then they settled on her. Kira clenched her teeth. Where was the head guard?

"He won't be there."

Kira whipped around. In one swift movement, Badrick drew his knife and held it to her throat. The frame of the window pushed into her lower back as she leaned away from the weapon. Her stomach dropped as she caught a glimpse over her shoulder and saw how high she was. The fall wouldn't be enough to kill her, but it wouldn't be painless.

When she took a step to the side, Badrick pushed the blade harder against her skin. Slowly blood began to trickle its way down her throat, the color matching her dress. Kira searched his eyes for a reason. Had they not spent the night together? Had he not laid beside her only that morning? Or had it all been an act?

A second later she pushed those thoughts from her mind completely. Badrick wasn't that type of man. There had to be another reason. She kept her voice calm. "Badrick, give me the knife."

He cocked his head to the side as if amused. "Why would I do that?"

The light from the lanterns that hung in the street below shot up against him. His hair was messy, the way he liked it. His eyes sparkled with curiosity, making him the beautiful man he was.

~ * ~

Sapphire scowled. Kira was only supposed to graze the king's arm, not give him a wound that would need stitching. It wasn't like her to make such a mistake. She turned her head and tilted it back, ready to question. Then her breath stopped.

The crowd around her had turned hectic with whispers and cries. None of the people noticed the man holding a blade to a woman's neck above them. She shook her head. She knew that look in Badrick's eyes all too well.

Sapphire ripped around the corner, shoving into shoulders as she went. Her fingers flew to the handles of the door and she yanked then cursed under her breath. The door wasn't budging. She patted herself in search of a lock pick. The one thing she hadn't thought of bringing. She needed to think and fast. Otherwise Kira's throat would be slit and by the time anyone got to her she would lying on the floor, dead.

~ * ~

Kira maintained her composure as well as she could. Badrick kept the blade poised to slit her throat at any movement. Her heart hammered against her chest, her throat dry. She should have known Silas would do something like this.

She licked her lips. "So he decided to reenact the night of Sapphire's betrayal, huh?"

Badrick's brows furrowed together in annoyed confusion. "I don't know what you're talking about. But I suggest you keep your mouth shut."

She had to keep him talking. He was somewhere in there; she just had to find him.

"Such a shame, to think that you would be so weak as to fall for it."

He pushed the blade farther against her neck, causing her to bend back even more. Kira's stomach dropped as her head hung over the edge.

"I said shut your damn mouth!"

Kira winced as the wood dug into her back. Her palms became sweaty, throbbing in pain as she gripped the sill to keep herself from toppling over.

"You don't even have the strength to kill me." She pushed him. "There's a part of you that struggles to follow through. Have you considered why?"

"I could kill you with a flick of my wrist."

Kira felt herself grow bold. "Then do it."

She watched him tense in thought. Now was her chance. In one swift movement, she shoved away his arm and lashed out with her hidden blade. Badrick withdrew, her blade skimming past his chest. Once he retreated to a safe distance, he looked down to where her blade had caught his fabric. He brought his hand to it and scrunched his face, as if disgusted that his once flawless costume was now ruined.

Kira slammed the shutters of the window closed and retreated into the dark. Often shopkeepers used the first floor for their merchandise, leaving the upstairs for living quarters. Although not many could afford to buy such grand furniture like the dresser she now hid behind. Never before had she been so thankful for such extravagant things.

Kira squatted as close to the ground as possible. Her shaking hand reached for her neck. When she pulled back she was relieved to see very little blood. She'd be fine. For now.

She knew Badrick would search for her through the dark. They had fought plenty of times before, both of them coming out with an even numbers of victories. However, they usually restrained themselves from doing too much damage on one another. Now he wanted to kill her. Which meant no restrictions and all drive.

Kira's breath hitched as she spotted him walking up to the window and locking it. The only way out now was the door and it was on the other side of the room. Even if she did manage to get out of the room, it wouldn't change anything. Better to fight him alone than risk everyone else's safety. All she had to do was act the way she normally did. Use the dark to her advantage.

Badrick's steps were slow and taunting. He knew that her places to hide were limited.

He began to close in on the dresser. It was all or nothing. She couldn't hold back or there would be no chance to save him. She rolled her wrist and took a deep breath. The dresser she crouched behind began to scrape along the floor.

Kira's chest clenched. She had considered many things that could happen during this night, but being killed by the one she loved wasn't one of them.

Chapter 51

Sapphire gave the door another kick. There were two entrances, the front and the back. Badrick must have managed to sneak past her and go through the back. Fear swept through her at the sight of Kira hanging over the windowsill. Then she had disappeared and slammed the shutters closed. Sapphire could only hope that Kira would manage to hold Badrick off until she could break in.

She looked at the people surrounding her and spotted Felix. He easily cut his way through the crowd, taking wide steps. Kira's arrow had done a number on the king's arm. They'd have to take him away and stitch him up while he was asleep. If she'd been fighting Badrick off, however, it made sense she couldn't have gotten a clear shot. The thought of Silas planning such a thing fueled Sapphire to kick the door again.

"Open, you goddamn door!"

It was only a matter of seconds before Felix was by her side. He too had noticed that something had gone wrong.

"Sapphire, what's happening?"

Her hands were balled into fists, her chest heaving.

"It's Badrick."

She lifted her leg and slammed the heel of her foot into the door with so much forced that it knocked her back. Felix quickly stepped behind her and caught her before she fell to the ground. "What do you mean it's

Badrick? Is he hurt?"

Sapphire hiked up her dress in frustration. She blew the few pieces of hair that had fallen from their design out of her face. She took a moment to gain her sense of balance, then was back on her feet kicking at the door again. And again and again.

"Sapphire!"

She didn't answer. She had to get to Kira before it was too late. The Badrick they knew was gone. All memories or emotions he had towards Kira were also gone. Silas would have given Badrick one task, and he wouldn't stop until it was done.

"Sapphire!" Felix spun her around. His hands squeezed her shoulders, obviously desperate to get her to focus on him. Even just for a second. "What's wrong with Badrick?" His voice was no longer soft. Yet it was exactly what she needed to hear to knock some sense into her.

"Nightlock," she blurted out. "Silas and Pierceton used Nightlock on him."

She didn't have to say any more. "Ah." Understanding flashed across his face. "And Kira wouldn't be able to do what she had to do to stop him, would she?" Felix strode to the door. He threw all his body weight into his kick, the door rattling from the impact. But it still wasn't enough. "It's not going to budge."

"Isn't there another way to get in?"

"The back door is as sturdy as the front. No matter how hard we try, we won't be able to enter, not without a key. That's why I picked this shop."

Sapphire shook her head in frustration. She didn't believe it. She couldn't let Kira fall victim to Silas. She wouldn't. Not after everything Kira had done. Kira wasn't afraid to voice her opinion. She wasn't afraid to point out Sapphire's mistakes. Kira said exactly what she needed to hear.

Sapphire blinked back tears. Even after every mistake she had made,

Kira still took a chance on her. It was because of her that Sapphire was able to be accepted back into the guild, even if it was temporary. She turned on her heel and began to walk.

"Where are you going?"

Sapphire paused and looked back at Felix. For the first time in years she allowed herself to take a good look at him.

The worry was strong in his eyes. Those beautiful emerald eyes. She knew that he loved Kira as much as she did. It was because of Kira she was able to have another chance at love. To have the chance to explain herself.

"I'm tired of running. I'm going to find a way to save her."

Felix straightened to his full height. When he spoke, his tone of voice had changed. It was more powerful, like a general leading his men into war. "You thought you would get away without my help?"

~ * ~

Kira managed to push Badrick off of her, giving her a few precious seconds to regain her strength. Her chest ached and her shoulder burned where his blade had struck. The blood now trickled down her breast, just above her heart. A reminder of who he was now and where he planned to bury his blade.

Badrick rushed at her again, barely giving her enough time to regenerate. She ducked and dodged his blow before retracting her blade, coming up with a fist to his gut. Which she quickly followed with a punch to the jaw. He hissed in pain. Yet instead of damaging him, it only fueled him more. His hand came down, striking her on the side of the temple. Hard.

A cry escaped her lips as she slammed into the floor. It took all she had not to give in and pass out.

"You'll have to use more than just your fists to kill me."

Kira slowly pushed herself up onto her forearms. He was right. She couldn't go on using just her fists. But she didn't dare use her blade on him any more either. She had already used it once and that was one too many times for her liking.

His boot collided with her stomach. Tears welled in her eyes as she doubled over. He squatted in front of her, taking her chin harshly in his hands. "I was expecting a better fight from you. Silas spoke so highly of your abilities."

His hand snaked up her bare leg, pushing up the skirt of her dress along with it. Kira felt him pause from the contact before continuing on. With one swift movement, he removed her blade and threw it across the room. The sound of the metal skidding against the wood made her cringe. One less blade she had.

"At least put up some sort of fight before I kill—"

His words were cut off. Kira ripped his hand away from her face before latching her arms around his neck. She kissed him as passionately as her heart would allow her to. She had seen the recognition in his eyes as he touched her bare skin. She could only pray that her touch would be more effective than her blade.

Badrick tensed and for a brief moment she felt him kiss her back. Kira's hands dug into his hair, begging, pleading for him to return to her as she pushed herself against him. Then he shoved her as far away as possible.

"You can't seduce me into letting you live." The disgust was heavy in his voice. As if she was a wench begging at his feet for his love. Then again, at the moment, she supposed she was.

The door opened. Badrick's shoulders tensed as he readied to fight any intruder who interrupted them.

"Relax. It's me." Pierceton tossed Badrick the key. "We've already made a copy of it. No need to keep it."

Badrick's eyes narrowed. "I've got it under control."

"Is that so? Then why is she not *dead*?"

The way *dead* slithered through his teeth made Kira shiver. She could take Pierceton one on one. But Badrick would sacrifice himself to make sure Pierceton walked out alive.

"I'm taking my time. It'll be nice to see her suffer."

As silently as she could, Kira crawled her way to Badrick, keeping his feet in sight. Her body screamed at her with every movement. Judging from the pain that inflamed her side, she guessed his kick had cracked a rib. If not two. She could only pray that the two men were too wrapped up in their argument to notice her.

Pierceton spat. "I should have done it myself after the trouble she's caused me. It's because of her that Russell got killed." Pierceton's eyes flickered down to her as she reached out. "But, unlike him, I won't let her get away alive."

Kira didn't have time to whisper her apologies. With regret heavy in her heart, she unsheathed her hidden blade and ran it down Badrick's shin. He let out a howl as blood began to stain the precious fabric of his trousers. Pierceton already had her by her hair, barely leaving her enough time to strike the back of Badrick's legs with her hand. He fell backwards, hitting his head against the wall.

Kira cried out as she was forced to her feet. Pierceton threw her against the wall and came at her with his sword. Their blades hummed from the collision. His sword against her small blade. She was overpowered. She had to think fast.

Kira kicked him in the groin as hard as she could. But her strength was quickly dwindling. She didn't have much time before she would be as weak as a babe. She tossed her blade to the floor and untwined the wire bracelet from her wrist, twirling it around his throat as she stepped behind him.

He stumbled backwards until Kira was crushed between him and the shutters. The pressure against her ribs made her knees go weak. As her legs buckled, the wire pulled tighter against his throat, creating a clean cut against his skin. He squirmed, panicking.

The shutters creaked behind her, threatening to break. She pulled down harder. If she was going to fall, she was taking him with her.

Pierceton's sword clattered as it hit the ground. His hands shot up to the wire, desperate to free himself so he could get air. Kira braced herself as the shutters snapped. The cold night breeze seeped through the crack and slithered its way around her.

His arm came around, reaching for her. Kira dodged it with ease. But she could not stop him as his hand knocked the lantern off the desk. The glass shattered, fire leapt up the wall, and smoke began to stain the air.

Chapter 52

Pierceton took advantage of her shock and smashed his elbow into her damaged ribs. Her grip slackened just enough for him to slither his hands under the wire and rip it away.

Kira's eyes shifted from him to the fire, which was now consuming the desk. It wouldn't be long before the whole building was on fire. Her eyes darted over to Badrick, who had slumped to the floor, unconscious. If she could get him to Sapphire, perhaps they could find him an antidote. Otherwise they would have to wait until the Nightlock wore off. Which she preferred not to do, given what he could accomplish in the meantime.

"You know, part of me is relieved that Badrick didn't kill you."

She turned, clutching her side. The sight of Pierceton in that moment would forever be burned into her mind. His face contorted with rage and pain, a crimson line wrapping around his throat that would always scar his skin.

"Now I'll be able to kill you myself. If I'm nice, maybe I'll leave you to burn beside your sorry excuse of a lover."

If that was nice, then she didn't dare to think of what he would do if he wanted to show no mercy.

"That's funny, I'm just as excited to feel my blade go through your heart as you are to kill me."

Pierceton let out a laugh that approached hysterical, as if he had lost his sanity. His sword had disappeared into the flames, leaving him with no weapon. But Kira was in no shape to take advantage of that fact. If he got a hold of her knife, she'd be dead.

She lashed out at him. When he lifted his arm to block the blow, she ducked underneath. Her fingers grazed her knife as she dove for it, attempting to latch onto its handle.

Pierceton caught onto her plan and reached out blindly. His fingers had just begun to tangle into her locks when she spun. The pearls Sapphire had worked into her hair scattered across the floor as strands of hair were ripped out of their perfect form. Pierceton cursed as she grasped the knife and aimed her blade right at his heart. He whirled and managed to kick the blade out of her hand before his foot collided with her cheek.

One of the pins attached to the pearls had scratched his hand. Her heart leaped at the sight of the small trickle of blood that slipped down his wrist. The poison would soon enter his bloodstream and delay his reactions, giving them at least a small hope of escape.

Kira's mind buzzed. Heat swelled around her, the fire nipping at her fingers, forcing her back. Pierceton snatched up her knife. Sweat dripped down her face as she looked around frantically. The flames were closing in on them quickly. If she didn't kill Pierceton soon, she'd have no chance of saving Badrick.

Pierceton's gaze stayed on her as she backed up, the heels of her shoes catching her dress. It didn't take much to overpower her. With a simple kick to her chest, he sent her flying backwards; she landed on the floor so hard the air was knocked from her. He wasted no time. He threw himself on her, his body weighing heavy on her abdomen, as if rocks had been stacked on top of one another. His eyes were wicked as he held the knife to her throat. His patience was gone.

Those few seconds were the longest of her life. She closed her eyes and mumbled her apologies to everyone she loved. The guild, Sapphire, even the king and queen. She had let them down. She couldn't help them after all.

Suddenly the weight pressing down on her was lifted. Kira opened her eyes. Hope shot through her chest. Sapphire had sent for help. They had managed to break in. She wasn't dead after all.

But her savior wasn't Sapphire. Neither was it Felix or Kingsman or Maddox.

Chaol. Her rescuer threw Pierceton to the ground before looking back at her. The flame flickered in his eyes and for a moment no words were exchanged. Regret was heavy in his face. For what?

"I knew you had grown too soft for her." Pierceton made his way to his feet. "But I never expected you to choose her over everything we have worked for, Silas. Or should I call you Chaol now?"

Kira's eyes widened. Chaol was Silas? How was that possible? He couldn't betray her in such a way, could he?

Chaol's jaw tightened as he turned. "You're wasting time. The entire building is going up in flames."

"I'm not leaving until the thief is dead. If you can't stand to watch, then I suggest you turn the other way."

Chaol looked back at her. Kira struggled to push herself upright. Her eyes searched his. He loved her, didn't he? He wouldn't let her die. He couldn't. She knew that there was a part of his soul that was still good. Regardless of how small a part it was.

He stood as Pierceton walked closer to her, his eyes darting back and forth. Chaol raised a hand. "I'll do it."

Pierceton scowled at him.

Chaol ripped the knife from Pierceton's hand. "You're taking too long. I sent two men in, and both failed. I'll finish this myself." The head guard didn't look at Kira as he walked towards her. But he couldn't avoid her gaze forever. He knelt close to her and grabbed hold of her shoulder, pulling her close to him. His mouth next to her ear, he whispered, "You can still run away."

She took a deep breath, the heat of the fire overbearing. "I'm tired of running, Chaol."

He winced. Had her words gotten through to him? Had they clawed at his heart?

"If you're going to kill me, then do it."

He met her gaze, finally. His grip tightened as he glared at her. "You know I can't do that."

Her breathing slowed as smoke filled her lungs. He'd never be able to carry her out of the room. Not with Pierceton standing between them and the door. Even if they did manage to get out somehow, she would never leave Badrick there to burn alone. Her choice was simple. The fire or his hands.

"I love you more than you will ever know." His fingers slipped to the nape of her neck. She didn't doubt him an ounce. He had given her a chance to run, to save herself, which likely would have cost him his own life. He pressed his forehead to hers and murmured how sorry he was. Her breath hitched as she waited for her world to end. Instead of Chaol raising his hand, she saw, over his shoulder, Pierceton snatch a knife from Badrick and lift it, ready to kill.

Kira could only watch in helpless horror.

Chapter 53

Pain. Fiery, burning pain as hot as the flames licking his skin slashed through Chaol as the knife dug into his shoulder. Tears swelled in his eyes, but the smoke made them hardly noticeable. He had expected as much from Pierceton. He had since the day Pierceton asked for a job. And Chaol deserved it. He had failed in his mission of destroying the guild in every possible way.

Kira cried out as he faltered. Pierceton leapt forward, leaving Kira barely enough time to roll out of his range. A piece of her heart shattered as she turned her back to the two men. She had to let Chaol go so she could get Badrick out before it was too late. And she had to do it while Pierceton was distracted.

Pushing the pain back, she scrambled over to Badrick, just as the flames started to bite at him. She tossed his arm around her neck and tried to stand. But she shook, making her stance weak. So she resorted to kicking her blasted heels off and tossing them into the flames. At least she was more stable.

Step by step. Breath by breath. That's what she had to do. She couldn't focus on the two men who had turned against each other on the other side of the room, or how her bare feet burned from the heat, or the hem of her dress had begun to smoke. She couldn't think about the pain, no matter how overwhelming it was. She had to focus on the door in front of her and the freedom it would lead to.

She reached it and flung it open. By the time she managed to drag Badrick down to the stairs, her strength was gone. Desperation drove her forward. She didn't have time to wait. The step underneath her creaked then gave out beneath her weight, sending the two tumbling down the last few stairs. Badrick spiraled out of her grasp, leaving her alone on the barren floor.

Though the flames hadn't managed to snake down to the first story, smoke still choked her. Tears flowed down her cheeks as she dragged herself across the floor. It was as if she were in hell. Her feet were blistered, blood caked her skin, her head throbbed, and the sharp ache in her side made it almost unbearable to draw in a breath. But she wouldn't give in.

A loud thump shook the ceiling over her head and her chest clenched. Had Chaol fallen? Was he dead? Shoving back the thought, she continued to crawl toward Badrick. Somehow she reached him, and caressed his cheek with a trembling palm. Bending down, she closed her eyes as she brushed her lips over his. Her eyes, swollen with tears and smoke, fluttered open again as she choked back a sob. Someone lifted her from behind and started for the exit. *Pierceton.* Kira summoned the last bit of strength in her body and lashed out with her hands and feet. Though her attempts were pitiful, it was better than being killed without a fight.

"Kira stop! I'm not going to hurt you." Chaol tightened his hold on her as he strode for the door.

"I'm not leaving him behind!" She beat her fist against his arm and chest. Chaol stopped. His eyes, dark with sorrow, found hers.

Guilt pricked her. He was hurt that she was choosing Badrick yet again. That she was risking her life for him. But Chaol knew how she felt. She'd made it clear that she loved Badrick, that she couldn't be with Chaol. Why did he keep hanging on? Would he still help them? Or would he leave them both to perish in the flames?

He hesitated, as if warring with himself over that very decision. Then, with a heavy sigh, he lowered her to her feet. "Stay here I'll be back as soon as I can."

Once the strength of his arms left her, Kira reached for the nearby counter to hold herself up. Anything to lessen the pain.

She watched Chaol struggle as he attempted to haul Badrick up. When he turned back, Kira caught a glimpse of the blood pouring from his shoulder where Pierceton had struck him. For a brief moment her heart skipped a beat and her gaze darted to the stairs. Was Pierceton still alive? Would he come for her, determined to finish the job he'd started? Or had that thud signaled the death of the man who had made every one of the guild member's lives miserable for so long? Although she kept her eyes glued to the top of the stairs, he didn't appear.

The sound of the door swinging open caught her attention, and she stumbled toward the opening. Ahead of her, Chaol, still supporting Badrick, stepped out into the street, the smoke swirling into the air as it escaped from its confinement. Sapphire stood a few feet outside the door. Her eyes grew large at the sight of him. She pointed now, at Chaol. "There he is. That's Silas, the man who has tried to kill us all."

A guard shook his head. "That's not possible. Chaol would never do such a thing."

Chaol stopped in his tracks. Carefully, he lowered Badrick to the ground. He looked back and, for a few seconds, his gaze locked on Kira's. She struggled to her feet, using all her strength to keep herself upright. It seemed as if time froze within those few short seconds. Then his shoulders fell in defeat.

"She speaks the truth. I'm responsible for everything that's happened the last few months."

Kira longed to look away as guards surrounded him, ripping his hands behind him and tying his wrists together, but she forced herself to hold his gaze until he was hauled away.

"Where is she?"

Kira moved into the doorway. Astien's bright red hair bobbed through the crowd. He stopped in front of Chaol and fisted the collar of his tunic. "Astien." Kira's voice was weak and raspy, but he turned toward her as she fell against the doorframe and slid to her knees. Astien let out a shout, alerting the others that he had found her.

Kira fell forward, nearly hitting the ground before hands caught her. They were small, delicate, shaking with fear. They pushed her to look up at their owner, whose eyes were glossy with tears.

"Thank god you're alive." Sapphire sank to the ground and tugged Kira toward her. "Lie down before you pass out."

Sapphire adjusted her so Kira's head rested comfortably in her lap. Above her, Felix kept her talking, squeezing her hand whenever Kira's eyes started to drift closed. She turned her head as a familiar voice rose above the commotion. Kingsman stood, demanding to know where she was. A nearby guard pointed in the general direction before turning his attention back to the fire.

Kingsman rushed to her, dropping to his knees at her side. His hands cradled her face. His voice was tender as he assured her that all was well.

It took everything she had in her to lift her head and draw in a shaky breath. "Badrick?"

Kingsman nodded. "He is being taken care of."

She slumped back onto Sapphire's lap, the last of her energy gone.

As darkness crept over her, she smiled.

~ * ~

Kira grew more and more fidgety with each day that past. Every hour dragged on terribly slowly and nothing changed. She was confined to her bed, barely able to sit up straight. She had a sprained ankle, which was almost healed, and her bruises had all but disappeared as well. She'd suffered three fractured ribs, two on the right, and one on the left. But cracked was better than broken. They would heal in time as well.

"Sapphire, get me out of this damned bed before I kill the next person who walks through that door."

Sapphire shook her head with a sigh. Kira had been patient. She had listened. But now that a month had passed she would do anything to get up on her feet.

"All right, but Kingsman will be at my throat if he catches you."

"And I'll be at his if he makes me stay in this bed any longer."

To her surprise, the pain was barely noticeable as she stood. She'd have to treat Sapphire for finding such strong medicines that helped speed up the healing process.

Kira happily stripped off her nightgown, replacing it with a gown from her limited wardrobe. The sleek, plum-colored dress was simple but elegant, making her look more beautiful than she felt she was.

"Where are we going?" Sapphire asked as Kira studied herself in the mirror. Her hand trailed the low cut of the dress, stopping where her collarbone was exposed. A scar was embedded into her skin. The one thing that would never heal.

"*We* aren't going anywhere. I'm taking a walk."

Sapphire crossed her arms and frowned.

"It's bad enough that I'm letting you leave the room. I won't allow you to go wandering off alone, not until I know you can support yourself."

Kira turned around and flashed her a smile. "So you get pregnant and suddenly you're my mother?"

Sapphire's cheeks reddened to a deep crimson as she averted her gaze. Kira couldn't help but feel her heart flutter. She was the only one

Sapphire had confided in when she had found out. Her friend had told her of the morning sickness, how she often found herself fatigued or craving roasted duck. Every night when she visited, the two of them sat on the bed, their hands on her stomach, wondering what her child would be like. The swelling of her belly was barely noticeable, but Kira had begun to see the difference in the way her dress hugged her. Sapphire wouldn't be able to hide it for much longer.

"I hope he has Felix's eyes," Sapphire mumbled as her hand rested on the slight bump of her stomach.

"I'm sure he will have much of his mother in him."

Kira turned her head and spotted Felix standing in the doorway, donning his new uniform. A golden emblem on his left shoulder showed his title as one of the head guard's most trusted soldiers. A title only he and Maddox had the ability to bare.

"I knocked twice and no one answered." He lifted a brow as he took in Kira's new dress. "Going somewhere?"

Kira straightened out her skirts, preparing to argue with him. "I'll go insane if I don't get out of this room."

"I wasn't going to stop you. In fact, it might be what you need." She blinked as he walked over and wrapping his arm around Sapphire's waist.

"Besides, I'm sure Sapphire might just go insane herself once she's further along, and you'll need to help her with that." He slid a finger under Sapphire's chin and tilted back her head until she was looking at him. "No jobs, no fighting, nothing." His voice was gentle but firm.

Sapphire stuck out her lower lip. "I don't need you to remind me," she snapped.

Kira couldn't help but laugh to herself. The sparkle in Felix's eyes was back after so many years. At first Sapphire had been hesitant to accept Kingsman's offer to join the guild. But all it took to convince her was one glance at Felix and her heart was sold.

Kira turned and headed for the door, leaving the couple alone in the room. As much as she enjoyed talking with them, she was ready to explore. To feel the sun on her cheeks, to let the breeze sweep her away.

"Oh Kira," Felix called out. "He's in the gardens. I suggest you hurry before he leaves."

She didn't waste any time.

Chapter 54

Kira walked as fast she could without running. It had been a month since she had seen Badrick face to face. Astein had told her that guilt weighed heavy on his heart. That Badrick didn't have the strength to speak to her in person. When he visited her, he made sure to come when she was asleep. But nothing would stop her from seeing him today. Not a damn thing.

The palace walls whistled by as her walk turned to a run. As she passed by the practice fields where the soldiers gathered, running through their drills, she noticed Maddox and Kingsman, both sporting the same uniform she had seen on Felix, the golden emblem sparkling when the sun hit it. She slowed for a moment to sneak a glance.

Kingsman's voice roared loud and clear as he ran his men through drills. The corner of his lips turned up in approval as his men ran through the maneuvers flawlessly. He started to turn toward her, and Kira darted off, giggling like a child, before he caught sight of her.

It was hard to believe that their lives had changed so dramatically. When she first faced the king and queen, she had been prepared to be banished from their presence forever. To resign herself to having to live on the streets and resort to stealing to survive. Instead she had been rewarded with a coveted position. She was now the palace's head spy, with Badrick, Astien, and Sapphire—when she was able to resume her duties—under her. Kingsman had been named the head guard in place of Chaol, with Felix and Maddox as his right hand men.

Her steps faltered.

And Chaol, well, Chaol had been confined to prison since he'd been arrested; his trial was to take place within the week. Kira had no idea what his punishment would be, or even what she felt he deserved. Part of her hoped he might yet be redeemed, that the good she had seen in him would one day expel the evil that had driven him.

But now wasn't the time to think about that. Instead she focused on which way to turn and which pathway to take. Then she saw him.

Badrick must have heard her steps as she left the stone walkway, her slippers swooshing through the grass. He turned, hands in his pockets. From the look that flashed across his face, he was contemplating running, but his feet remained cemented to the ground.

Kira hesitated, unsure what to do now that she had found him. Then she shook all second guesses from her mind.

"Kira, I'm so—"

He didn't have time to finish before she darted across the garden. Her momentum as she threw herself at him caught Badrick off guard, sending them both tumbling to the ground.

For a moment, he didn't move. Kira waited. Would he run? Or would he reach for her, giving in to the hunger she saw in his eyes? She held her breath. After what seemed like an eternity, he lifted his hands and clasped the sides of her face. Not a word had to be exchanged. She could feel him begging for forgiveness as his lips worked at hers. She felt him smile daringly when he caught her lower lip between his teeth, earning a gasp of pleasure. However he felt about it, what had happened in that room above the store was in the past.

Kira rose up on her knees, responding to his kisses with the same fierceness she'd called on to drag him to safety, once from the hideout, and once down the stairs of the burning shop. Her dominance in their battle didn't last for long. Whatever hesitation Badrick had battled when he'd first seen her was gone. He pushed himself up until he hovered above her then crushed his lips to hers.

She prayed he could feel the forgiveness on her lips, the acceptance. The truth that, no matter what he had done when he was not himself, she loved him no less.

When she tried to pull away, gasping for breath, he refused to allow her to do such a thing. He granted her a few brief moments of respite while he trailed kisses from her jaw down to her neck, brushing his mouth over her newborn scar. Kira bit her lip. Did the sight of it fill him with sorrow? She hoped it would remind him, as it did her, of how strong she had been, how she had refused to give up. Of how she had brought about justice for the guild and given them all a new life, a new chance.

His lips met hers once again. Sparks flew across her skin as his hands roamed over her arms, across her back. Finally he withdrew and held her tightly. He repeated her name over and over, the same way he had when he was relieved to find her well and alive.

Minutes turned to an hour, which melted into two and then three. As the sun began to set Kira found herself lying with her head settled comfortably on his chest. Their legs were tangled together, his arms wrapped around her. Beneath her his heartbeat pounded, matching her own.

That's how they stayed for the night. Badrick's love and protection drowned her, but she didn't complain once. Instead she closed her eyes and enjoyed the security he brought as his hand softly played with her hair. For the first time in a long time she was able to breathe in deeply, and breathe out. Time stilled and all that mattered was the man by her side.

~ * ~

The door creaked as Kira slowly swung it open. There in the center of her chambers Sapphire stood, her arms crossed and her face twisted in anger. Kira gave her a smile as she stepped in and closed the door behind her.

"Hello mother," she teased.

Sapphire rolled her eyes. "Do you know how stressful it is to make something up about you and try to get Kingsman to believe it? I'm lucky he didn't wrap his hands around my throat when he came to the door and I told him you had a headache and didn't want to be disturbed."

"I'll treat you to plenty of roast duck," Kira promised as she sat on the bed. Sapphire stiffened, but didn't argue any more. Kira knew it had been weeks since she had been able to have any, and she wouldn't pass up the chance to get her hands on some.

Kira ran her hand through her hair, letting it fall gracefully down her back. Happiness fluttered through her heart. As Kingsman had promised, everything was well. Scars were healing and they had made it past all their troubles.

The new ring she had donned was heavy on her left finger. Its band was a daring silver and the gem in its center held a starburst of green green, much like the emeralds in her necklace. She had barely managed to convince Badrick that she needed to return to her room. She knew that he had wanted to be with her, but it was still out of character for him to constantly find so many excuses to extend their time together. It all clicked in her head once she saw ring he held between his fingers.

She couldn't stop herself from smiling. And she couldn't hide it from Sapphire any longer.

"Here, this came for you. I don't know who it's from." Sapphire passed her a note before Kira had a chance to say anything. Kira broke the seal and scanned the hastily-scrawled words inside. Her smile faded as she crumpled the letter in her fist. Kira rose from the bed and strode toward the door. Behind her, Sapphire called out, asking her what was wrong.

Kira didn't answer as she flung open the door and stalked into the hall.

~ * ~

Kira squinted as her eyes adjusted to the dark. Her feet needed no light as they trod the familiar hallway. She had been down here before and the memories were not pleasant.

"Well, I'm here. What is it you wanted to say?" she asked, her voice cold.

From his seat on the ground, arms chained above his head, Chaol gazed at her. Very little damage had been done to him as far as she could see, although his brown locks were disheveled, and dirt stained his face and tunic. Sadness was thick in his gaze. It was begging, pleading for her forgiveness. But she couldn't bring herself to offer it.

"I wanted to apologize." His voice was hoarse.

"In my experience it is easy to say the words and much harder to mean them." She spun on her heel.

"Kira no. I'm begging you, please don't leave."

She stopped in her tracks and peered back at him. Her shoulders fell slightly and she let out a sigh. Chaol stayed silent as she ordered a tankard of water from the guard standing inside the door she'd just come through. As they waited, she kept her back to Chaol. Not saying a single word. Did he honestly deserve anything better?

"Leave me with him," she demanded when the guard returned and handed her the tankard from the guard.

"But my lady—"

She silenced him with a look. "Leave the keys as well."

Kira felt Chaol's eyes on her as she walked, chin high, over to his cell.

With a click, the door opened and she stepped forward and turned around to lock herself inside with him. She slipped the key into his shackles and turned the lock, letting them fall into his lap. Chaol rubbed his wrists.

"Here, drink it."

He took the tankard from her hands. His eyes grazed over the ring on her left index finger then back up to her face as she leaned against the bars across from him. He lifted the jug to his lips and gulped greedily. When he lowered it, he wiped a few drops of water from his chin with the back of his hand.

Kira crossed her arms. "I'm here. Why did you want me to stay?"

His title had been stripped from him, the emblem on his shoulder gone. He was nothing now and Kira knew she was likely the only one willing to offer him such a precious necessity.

"I want to explain everything. To tell you why I've done what I have."

Their eyes locked and Kira took a deep breath, her entire body tingling from his words. She slowly nodded, preparing herself for what she was about to hear.

Chapter 55

"I was young when I first saw Kingsman. Just a kid who didn't know any better. I looked up to him more than I had any other soldier. He risked his life freely; he would give up everything to keep others safe. During that time there had been a man out killing the innocent. All in hopes of trying to spook the palace. Soon his plan drove everyone to chaos and the riot happened."

Kira kept quiet, her arms crossed and her jaw locked.

"I remember seeing Kingsman carrying down boxes of food and supplies every day. He was always the first one to volunteer to rebuild the houses and stores. I suppose you could say I had grown to love him in a way. But then he just vanished. It was too much for him and he just … abandoned everyone.

"Surely you could understand why I grew to hate him. I wanted to make him regret everything he had ever done. I wanted to make him regret running. So I planned to recreate his weaknesses.

"Of course no one would go out and kill a person on demand. Not unless the one demanding it was someone they respected and feared. So I started becoming Silas. For all my efforts, though, I didn't appear to be getting to Kingsman. I tried using Sapphire to get to Felix, since I had seen how close those two were. But she couldn't do it. So I took aim at the one thing he treasured most. The little orphan girl he'd carried home on that rainy night."

He looked up at her through the dark. Though Kira had yet to show any emotion on the outside, she was becoming anxious. He had aimed to destroy her?

"Then I met Pierceton and Russell. It wasn't long before we realized that we had something in common. So I waited for the right time. When I followed you to the brothel, I knew it was my one and only chance. I had planned to kill you. I expected nothing more than a spoiled brat, so I assumed it wouldn't be hard to earn your trust and carry out my plans." He let out a small chuckle under his breath. "How stupid I was to think such a thing. You hated me. You despised me. I saw it in your eyes. All the more reason to kill you, right? It wasn't until it was too late that I realized I had fallen in love with you. The way you couldn't trust me as far as you could throw me, the way you wouldn't give in, everything about you. You captivated me with just a simple flicker of your eyes.

"I wanted to go back on my plans. I knew that there had to be another way. I just couldn't bring myself to kill you. I loved you too much, and even now I still do. But Pierceton was persistent. He was watching me to make sure I'd follow through; otherwise he'd kill you himself. I thought that if I could manage to convince you to run away, we would both be free of him."

Silence fell over the cell. Kira moved her foot in closer to herself, not wanting any part of her to be near him. If she got too close, maybe he would be able to trap her in his web of pity. That was one thing she refused to fall victim to. She would not, could not pity him.

"When you took that job, I didn't realize it was you until you returned to the palace and I was able to piece it together. You had taken the bait. All I had to do was follow through with the kill." He took another swig of water then set the tankard down on the floor beside him.

"Pierceton used the Nightlock on Badrick without my knowledge. When

I saw how badly your second arrow wounded the king, I knew what Pierceton had done and that I had to get to Badrick before it was too late. I already had a copy of the key, all I had to do was get to you in time. You broke my heart when I saw you lying on him the way you were. And when you kissed him, I felt as if I had lost a piece of myself. I'd die for you, Kira. But I know that you deserve better. I've seen the terrible pain in your eyes, and to think I'm the one who caused it is the most regretful thing I will ever live with. I've done you more harm than good. And I've done more harm to myself than Kingsman. It was a fool's errand I set out on, and I've shown that by ending up the fool." He lifted up the shackles as though to prove his point.

As he finished speaking, Kira uncrossed her arms and pushed away from the bars. Calmly, she brushed off the front of her skirt and started for the entrance.

"Where are you—?"

"I've listened to your story, Chaol." Kira threw one last glance at him then quickly averted her gaze, her knuckles turning white as she gripped the iron bars. "There isn't anything else I can do for you. I'm sorry we couldn't have met under other circumstances. Perhaps things could have been different." She went out of the cell. The door clanged shut behind her as she headed for the exit.

"I will never forget you, Kira," he called out to her.

Kira stopped and pressed a hand to the wall as she peered back at him. Determination shone brightly in his eyes despite the lack of light. She didn't doubt for a moment that he loved her. She had seen it multiple times. Every time he looked at her it was as if his heart was chained up and only she had the key. Yes, she knew just how much he loved her. Almost as much as she loved another man.

She parted her lips, her throat suddenly dry. "And I will never forget you, Chaol."

Then she turned and left, this time not looking behind her.